JACOB'S GRACE

Praise for C.P. Rowlands

Jacob's War

"C.P. Rowlands has another winner on her hands. An excellent and realistic police procedural about drug dealers and killers. She is an excellent storyteller."—*Library Thing*

Lake Effect Snow

"This is my kind of political thriller—methodical, dangerous, and complicated. It challenges the reader without frustrating her, and there is just enough realism thrown in to make it relevant to today's international political scene as the story features the war in Iraq. The politics are easy to digest, though, adding to the context and setting, but not preaching. The romance is genuine and thoughtfully done, but it does not distract us from the main plot. The non-stop action and impressive storytelling make this a must read for those who like thrillers in the tradition of Frederick Forsyth, quite a feat for first-time novelist Rowlands."—*Curve Magazine*

"Anyone looking for a book that comes straight off of the front pages of the newspaper or headline news doesn't need to go any further. *Lake Effect Snow* is set in the middle of today's war on terrorism and its far-reaching consequences. It tells a story that's chilling in its reality and starts with a scene that will keep the reader hooked until the final pages...*Lake Effect Snow* is a page turner, one of those books the reader hates to put down. This reviewer highly recommends you give it a try."—*Just About Write*

Hardwired

Hardwired "pulled at my heart with both sorrow and joy. The plot is a huge eye opener that needs to be more publicized...you will learn something from this book. Rowlands did a magnificent job developing the main characters Clary and Leefe. This book helps in understanding the truth for the children displaced due to homelessness."—*Library Thing*

By the Author

Lake Effect Snow

Collision Course

Hardwired

Jacob's War

Jacob's Grace

Visit us at www.boldstrokesbooks.com

JACOB'S GRACE

by

C.P. Rowlands

2018

JACOB'S GRACE
© 2018 By C.P. Rowlands. All Rights Reserved.

ISBN 13: 978-1-63555-187-7

This Trade Paperback Original Is Published By
Bold Strokes Books, Inc.
P.O. Box 249
Valley Falls, NY 12185

First Edition: September 2018

Credits
Editor: Cindy Cresap
Production Design: Stacia Seaman
Cover photo by Kathie Solie
Cover Design by Sheri (hindsightgraphics@gmail.com)

Acknowledgments

Thanks to Bold Strokes for publishing this book, the sequel to *Jacob's War*, and for all the hours and work that go into a single book. It is an astonishing process, from author to printer and everything that comes after that.

Thanks also to all the local law enforcement and volunteers. They give everything, each and every day.

In memory of "Agent Jack" of the Bureau of Alcohol, Tobacco, Firearms, and Explosives. He made a difference.

Chapter One

Brutal August heat held them like a fist. Allison Jacob turned her back to the hot wind that peppered her with dirt and debris and ducked behind her vehicle with two of her agents.

"What's taking them so long?" Grace grumbled beside her while they waited for the Milwaukee Police to enter the house across the street. Bonnie stood at the back of the SUV, adjusting her vest and swiping at her face.

Allison squinted down the elegant street with its manicured yards, flowers, and century-old trees. How had they ended up here? It had mostly been back streets, condemned houses, and alleys with Chief William Whiteaker's Special Forces during their temporary summer assignment. Worse, if this wasn't the headquarters of the trafficking network they'd been chasing, they'd be out of the loop after today. Her new ATF task force began tomorrow.

Finally, the police went through the front door, and it was quiet for a few minutes. Then there were shouts, and two people ran from the back, across the yard. It looked like an adult woman holding a kid's hand as they ducked into the alley. Skidding on loose stones, Allison and her two agents moved right, guns drawn. Grace led the charge as they rounded the corner.

"He was falling before he hit the garbage cans...like he was fainting," Grace said, hands braced on her knees as she caught her breath. "The woman ahead of him just disappeared."

Heart racing, Allison went to her knees by the young boy and checked for breath and a pulse, but there was nothing. She shook her head at Grace.

"Bonnie, get the medics. Look at his skin. It's yellow." She shoved the hair off his forehead. "He's just a kid." An ambulance squeezed down the alley toward them.

"What the hell, AJ?" Chief Whiteaker called out, walking around the EMTs working on the young boy. "Did you shoot?"

"No shots fired." AJ watched them work on the kid, still hoping. "Is the house under control?"

"Yes, but the freakin' place is like a furnace. Only four kids in there, but they look well fed and healthy. I saw a woman's touch to the place."

"There was a woman leading this one, but she disappeared at the end of the alley. Was it the right house?" AJ pulled in a breath when he nodded. "Good."

The medical team shook their heads and stepped back from the body.

"Wait for the ME. I'll get him identified," the chief said as they walked back up the alley.

"Poor kid." Grace tossed her sweat-soaked vest into the back of AJ's vehicle and pointed at the clock tower. "Look at that." The LED thermometer sizzled at ninety-five degrees.

"God." AJ threw her light body armor on top of Grace's and Bonnie's. Black clouds were building up to the north. "Go help Bill process that house and make sure they call CPS for the kids. Catch a ride back with his cops, and I'll wait for the medical examiner. I want to know what happened to this boy."

❖

At home, AJ braced herself against Katie's car in the garage as she tried to get her wet boots off. The storm had broken while she and the ME stood over the body in the alley, and she was soaking wet.

The boot finally came off, and she hurled it against the kitchen door. The noise was sudden and loud, followed by complete silence. She looked around the garage. A few months ago, she'd known exactly what her job was, but now she was out of the drug world, chasing sex trafficking. Worse, she couldn't get the young dead boy out of her head.

She picked up the boot just as the back door flew open. Katie stood there, wrapped only in a towel with a stunned expression. Her wet, black curls hung across her face. "What was that?" she said.

AJ held up the soaked boot. "It wouldn't come off. When it finally did I—"

"Threw it?"

"Um…yes. You were in the shower?"

"What do you think? Drop everything in the garage and go to the shower."

AJ looked down at her sopping, dirty clothes. The pants and shirt were salvageable. Maybe. "I have to go out again." She dropped the boot and began to pull off her clothes. "Is this how you open our door?" she snapped.

"Hey." Katie looked hurt.

AJ strode past Katie toward the shower wearing only a frown. She turned the water on and stepped inside. Katie followed, slipping an arm around her.

"Here, stand still. Let me wash your hair. I assume you got caught in the rain?"

"The storm broke while I was outside."

Katie's warm, strong fingers calmed AJ, but when she closed her eyes, the dead boy was still there. She grabbed Katie's shoulders to steady herself.

"I'm sorry for what I said," AJ murmured against Katie's ear, starting to explain why she didn't know how the boy had died and neither did the ME. Katie kissed her, long and slow. She said something else, but AJ was beyond listening. The world was manageable in Katie's arms.

Later, lightning painted the sky over Lake Michigan as AJ sped north through dark city streets, water licking at her tires. They'd eaten dinner, both wrapped in big robes, and afterward, she'd fallen asleep in Katie's lap. The temperature had dropped into the low sixties, and she now wore dry boots, a clean black hoodie, and jeans.

She stopped at a red light. Milwaukee had been a battlefield since May, including two full-blown weeklong riots. The city was struggling with drugs, guns, and car thefts. The house they'd taken down today might solve the murder they'd chased all summer, but they were just beginning on the human trafficking operation they'd stumbled into. In all of her years of law enforcement, she'd never seen anything like it. It was huge. She'd fought to continue working with Chief Whiteaker's group, but her bureau chief, Lawrence Kelly, was dead-set on his new task force in northern Wisconsin. He'd hardly paid any attention to any of her requests.

She pulled over to the curb in the quiet, dark neighborhood and checked her time. Right on schedule.

A full August moon hung in the sky behind the retreating storm but began to fade behind thick patches of Lake Michigan fog that turned the ancient brick church ahead of her gray and silver. Her boots scraped on the old stone steps, and she settled into the dark doorway. The wood vibrated against her shoulder as the church revved up for its single night song, the stroke of midnight bell. One deep note rolled out through the air, trembling across the city.

She jammed her hands into her black hoodie and waited for her confidential informant. Last fall, she'd found Frog, homeless and selling drugs on the streets, the orange jacket with the frog on it catching her attention. For a couple of months, Frog was invaluable for the drug task force until AJ had found her almost dead from meth after a winter blizzard and gotten her into rehab. Frog had gotten a job and gone back to school. Then everything had gone to hell.

They'd met right here three weeks ago when Frog had told her about human trafficking at the group house. AJ had immediately taken it to the Department of Justice as part of the FBI's ongoing national investigation. The next day her bureau chief had surprised her with an order to take a week's vacation. Katie had been thrilled with their first-time-ever time away but AJ had been puzzled at the timing. Then, when they returned, she'd found she had a task force on her hands and Frog was going north, right in the thick of the trafficking. She hadn't intended on Frog going anywhere and was still angry.

Steps sounded to her left, and a young voice said, "AJ?"

"Here, Frog."

"Damned fog. Can't see more than two feet in front of me. Hurry, they're leaving soon."

AJ pulled the girl into the doorway. "How many are going with you? Be careful. This is dangerous."

"Eleven girls and two women, brought in this afternoon in a big box truck. We'll ride in that on the trip up north." Frog impatiently shuffled her feet, looking every bit of her nineteen years, her spiked hair weaving shadows in the fog.

"Here's the phone. Leave it on but toss it after you settle." AJ shoved it into Frog's light jacket. "Greg and Jeff will be about twenty minutes behind you. Any idea where you're going?"

"No, but here's the bank card for the money they gave me." Frog handed her a debit card. "You know…just in case."

Her heart lurched and she grabbed Frog's arm. "Someone gave you money?"

"The two cops that hired me to go with the girls."

"How do you know they were police?"

"What the hell, AJ? I've known cops for years. They had IDs and badges." She backed up. "I gotta go," she said, fading into the fog.

AJ gripped the bank card and moved back into the dark doorway. She didn't know anything about someone paying Frog to do this.

An owl hooted in the trees behind the church. The fog lifted for a moment, and she stopped. She thought she heard footsteps. Suddenly, there was a sharp gunshot. A bullet lodged right above her shoulder with a jarring thud. She went down, ears ringing, and crawled forward, trying to get to her weapon.

The second shot hit the wood just above her head, and she sprawled on the wet stones. Heavy footsteps moved away into the fog. She took a breath so deep it hurt and dialed her team.

❖

Chief Whiteaker sank down on the church steps beside her. His police and her ATF group were still going through the side streets.

"We've got the brass," he said over a tired breath.

"This is crap. My task force's not even official until the meeting tomorrow, but look." She held out Frog's bank card. "She said two policemen gave her cash to go undercover. She put it in the bank."

He gave her a stunned look. "I don't know of any police that have contacted her."

"She's dealt with police for years and believed them, right or wrong."

"I have Frog marked everywhere as ours. There isn't a cop in this city that would have touched her. That money's off, damn it." He stood and started toward his car. "My team's waking people up, and I'm going to finish the neighborhood. Go home. Get some sleep. We'll talk tomorrow."

AJ pointed her agency SUV toward home on back streets, sliding carefully through patchy fog. She'd argued when Frog told her about the undercover scheme, but the kid never said a word about money. *The kid.* She thought about the young boy this afternoon.

"Damn this day." She hit the steering wheel with her hand. For the first time in her career, she wanted to fight an assignment but she was busy. There was the meeting in the morning to pull Chief Whiteaker's group into her new task force, the press conference to announce the new Milwaukee human trafficking task force, separate from hers, and then pick up the surprising new member of their group at the airport tomorrow afternoon.

CHAPTER TWO

Crashing glass jolted Tag Beckett out of an exhausted sleep, and she groaned at the noise. A man swept up the spilled tray beside her. Her head felt like a bowl of Jell-O as she lifted it off the bar. The bartender placed a glass of ice water and a bottle of aspirin in front of her. "They said you'd probably need these," he said kindly.

"They?" Embarrassed, Tag read *Mitchell Int'l Airport, Milwaukee* on his shirt. "Do I owe you anything?"

He pointed at three women at a nearby table. "They paid."

Tag rubbed her bleary eyes, following his hand. *Hell.* She was about to meet her new team. The two women in dark suits probably were agents, but the third, smaller with dark loose curls, was too relaxed...and damned adorable. The pale green summer dress was mostly business but a little risky. She straightened for a better view.

"Aren't they amazing?" A female voice came from behind her left ear. An attractive blonde with amused brown eyes was looking at the same table that Tag was. She turned to Tag with a smile. "Your bag's ID says Captain Tag Beckett, US Army, IIC. If that's you, I'm Allison Jacob, but call me AJ." She held out her hand and Tag automatically shook it. "I'd take that aspirin if I were you."

"Yes, ma'am." Tag washed two pills down with the water. Trying to stand, she knocked her bag off the stool, but AJ caught it before it hit the floor.

A hand on her shoulder steadied her. "How long since you've eaten?"

"Early this morning when I got on the plane." Tag tugged at her clothes. Her khaki cargo pants looked as if she'd slept in them. She had but remembered changing her shirt in a restroom somewhere. "What time is it?" she said.

"Time to get you some food. Come with me."

She followed AJ's easy path through the crowd watching people automatically move out of her way. Of course they did. Taller than average, her new boss was lightly muscled with sun-streaked blond hair and tan skin. *And all that authority shining around her.* Her almost gold, elegantly tailored suit matched her bright hair. Tag went over things she'd heard about. Allison Jacob had earned a lot of respect, but she was also the woman who'd killed one of her own ATF agents.

The two women in dark suits stood as they arrived at the table. The third stayed seated with a friendly smile. AJ placed Tag's bag under a chair. "Ladies, meet our new team member, Tag Beckett."

Both women shook Tag's hand, strong grips followed by nice grins, and she relaxed a space.

"Bonnie Logan," the more muscled of the two said, moving her long brown-gold braid over her shoulder.

"Grace Fields," the other woman said.

"They were supposed to watch for you and get you to the table," AJ said to Tag. "Are you certain you want to work with them? They're supposed to have your back."

Bonnie rolled her eyes. "C'mon, AJ. She was out like a rock."

"She didn't even drool." Grace shot a mischievous glance at Tag.

AJ placed her arm over the back of the chair next to her. "And this," she said with something else in her voice, "is Katie Blackburn."

"Hi, Tag, and welcome home." Katie extended a hand. "Thank God I don't work for the ATF. These women are relentless."

Tag held Katie's hand, feeling about sixteen. Katie was vibrant and yes, adorable.

"How about a steak or would you rather see a menu? The chef is a friend," AJ said, a smile playing at the corner of her mouth. "You can let go of Katie's hand."

"Yes, ma'am." Tag sat abruptly and felt her face warm.

"The chef has a restaurant downtown, but his wife runs this little business." AJ sat next to her. "We're a team, not a platoon, so the 'ma-am' isn't necessary. You've done your time and darned well. Here's the cook."

A short Asian man in a green T-shirt and white jeans stopped beside AJ. She leaned back, shook his hand, and pointed at Tag.

"Uh, steak, medium rare, baked potato, and house dressing on the salad."

"Make that two, Jimmy. I'm starving. How're the kids?" AJ said.

Jimmy held up his hands in mock despair. "The worst kids on the block." He turned to Grace. "How was the food, Miss Grace?"

"The best Thai in town." Grace pointed at her empty plate.

Jimmy repeated the orders and left.

AJ shook her head. "He's still crushed on you, Grace, but watch your back around his wife. She's dangerous."

"That's one of the better chefs in town. You're in for a treat," Katie said.

"She's right." Grace stood. "I'll get the drinks."

"I'll have what Katie has," AJ said.

"I'm sticking with water. My final run is tomorrow," Bonnie called after Grace.

Tag's numbed brain cleared a bit, and she checked her pocket for her thumb drive, a large part of the reason she was home. Risky business. It wouldn't involve this group, but AJ would have to know at some point.

"Sorry to be late." AJ took her drink from Grace. "The meeting ran over, but our task force is a go, and better yet, we're officially separated from the DEA. The press conference to announce the other task force, the new Milwaukee human trafficking task force, also ran late."

"Awesomeness." Bonnie saluted her with a water bottle, rummaged in her suit pocket, and laid a paper in front of AJ. "Bill said you need the report on the bullets from last night."

There was a loaded silence, and Tag felt the energy around her change into anticipation.

"What?" Katie swiveled to AJ.

"I'll explain at home."

"No," Katie said. "Explain now."

"I'm okay, I swear." AJ bent to look into Katie's face, her hand over her heart. "You were asleep when I got home and gone early so I didn't get to tell you."

Tag watched the group's interaction and wondered how long

they'd worked together. Her last deployment in the field had that same close feeling, but the last two years in the office on base hadn't. She caught Grace's curious gaze and her heart gave a quick bump. Never in her life had she seen eyes that shade of blue.

A trace of surprise ran across Grace's face followed by honest interest. "Is it true you've done four tours in Afghanistan?"

"First three tours were hard duty, but the last was intel. I rarely left base."

Grace studied her. "The information said you led the cyber division."

Tag perked up and smiled. "Is that your gig here?"

"Sometimes."

"No, Tag, she's definitely our geek and worked in Cyber Crime for a while. She's my right-hand woman," AJ said. "Tomorrow, after you've had a good night's sleep at Grace's, we'll go across all of this at the office. We share space with the Milwaukee Police Special Investigations group. And before I forget, are you going to be okay with Grace chauffeuring you around or are you going to whine if you don't get your own vehicle?"

"Whatever it takes." Tag tipped the beer back for a long drink.

Grace reached for the necklace that Tag never removed. "What is this?" Grace held the tiny silver pendant in her fingers.

"A dragon from the unit I commanded. We all wore them."

"It's beautiful, and thank you for your service," Grace said. "I never served. I went directly from college into the Bureau."

"And I was a Milwaukee cop last week," Bonnie said, moving closer to Grace, her arm possessively over the back of her chair.

"And I'm in public relations and advertising," Katie deadpanned. "Don't I get something for battling the boardrooms of Milwaukee?"

"Me." AJ held up her hands, laughing as everyone threw napkins at her.

Tag felt a little dizzy when the food arrived. The first bite told her they were right. It was out-of-this-world delicious.

After the meal, they walked to the parking garage through lengthening shadows of the late August afternoon. Tag looked up at the seagulls running on the airport's glass roof and the creamy blue sky above them. Despite her exhaustion, something tight inside her began to uncoil. She could hardly believe she was here. Home.

"Let me get those bags," Tag said.

"No." Bonnie switched the luggage away and tossed it into the agency SUV. "You still look like the walking dead."

Tag watched AJ and Katie get into a beat-up dark blue sedan and looked over her shoulder at Grace and Bonnie. She might look like the walking dead, but everyone except Katie appeared exhausted and they all displayed the same hyper-vigilance.

"The hell...what's she driving?" Tag said as AJ backed out of the parking space. The big motor growled and then echoed in the parking structure.

"An unmarked police car she picked up down south." Grace laughed and snapped her seat belt. "You don't want to mess with that. It's got a Dodge Charger cop engine, six on the floor, with a 340 hp Hemi V8, heavy-duty brakes, and zero to sixty in seconds. It looks like crap, but it's all about speed."

"You should see her motorcycle," Bonnie said from the front seat. "That car's like AJ. Appearances are deceiving and you'll never see it coming."

Tag leaned forward for another look at AJ's car, her mind at cross-purposes trying to imagine that striking woman on a Harley.

CHAPTER THREE

"God almighty." AJ slammed her office phone down the next morning after another heated discussion with her bureau chief, Lawrence Kelly. He'd overridden all of her ideas, adamant about the full-blown task force in northern Wisconsin. Cursing under her breath, she swiveled her chair to the window, staring at the familiar Copper Penny bar across the street. Her life had done a one-eighty in the eleven months she'd been in Milwaukee.

They'd promoted her to special agent in charge last spring and turned this extra conference room into an office. While she'd been stuck in bed and then on those damned crutches recovering from her leg injury, Grace and Katie had decorated here, and she really liked it. It beat the old closet she'd had when she arrived last September. She'd moved into Katie's house and she more than liked that. She loved it.

She saw no new updates on the takedown of the house two days ago. "Well, damn," she muttered and pulled the worn manila envelope out of her desk drawer that held the details of the murder that had started the whole summer.

Last spring, sweating in post-surgical physical therapy for her leg, she had watched breaking news on the hospital television. A teenage girl had been found in an abandoned warehouse, nailed to the wall in an exaggerated X pose, dead and mutilated, hands cut off and acid on her face. The medical examiner had declared it a homicide, but privately he'd said the girl was raped to death. The ME identified five sperm donors. AJ had called Chief Whiteaker immediately, a conversation she'd never forget.

When AJ's doctor released her a week later, her ATF team was temporarily assigned to Chief Whiteaker's group, chasing the young girl's murder. The victim became known as the "X-Girl," and every law enforcement person in the city wanted this solved. The FBI's Human Trafficking task force had taken charge and, in a rare moment of cooperation, had allowed AJ into the morgue to view the devastation. She still had no words for that moment. Their investigation over the summer had led them to the house they'd just taken down as the beginning of the young girl's dark journey. Or so they thought. There was still a lot of work to be done to prove it.

AJ scanned photos and papers she knew by heart. Dr. Bergs, the therapist she had to see every other week, was convinced that her murder of their young ATF agent, Ariel, had intersected with this girl and she was obsessed. She closed the folder. The doctor might be right. It had even nagged its way into her dreams, hadn't it?

"Are you okay?" Chief Whiteaker stood in the doorway.

She held up the folder and he gave her a grim look.

"Have a minute?" he said. She nodded and he walked into her office. "Nice job on my department at the meeting yesterday."

"Just theater, Chief. I had to come up with something to get you involved and basically shuffled my bureau chief's words around. I just spoke to him and still have nothing. He still isn't clear why we're going up north or why as a task force."

"He's probably waiting for more information." The chief's uniform was an immaculate dark blue against a white shirt and a silver tie matching his hair. "You impressed my chief at yesterday's press conference. Did you see the photo in this morning's newspaper?"

"No, I got up late." She gestured at her denim shirt and faded jeans. "I wasn't happy. Your chief only talked about local prostitution regarding that house we took. What about the human trafficking we uncovered? And he never even mentioned X-Girl. He should have."

The chief held up a placating hand as they walked into his office next to hers. "Just politics. He tried to keep it simple to introduce our new human trafficking task force."

"I wouldn't call it simple. We start out with murder and stumble into human trafficking. It's huge and organized and we've only seen a small part of it. And yes, I know it's the world's oldest business, but I've known madams, working girls…not to mention Frog, and I've never seen anything like this."

"I agree, but I certainly am not going to tell my chief that." He handed her a photo. "Here's our young victim, Kevin Owens, with his older brother, John, our prime suspect from that house. The kid was fifteen and John's thirty. Their grandfather owned that house and sold it to John. Did you see the autopsy on the boy?"

"No, and why are there no updates on that house?" AJ studied the photo as they walked to Bill's office. "Can we help?"

"I know you're off the case, but we need your group's skills on the confiscated computers. The new Milwaukee Human Trafficking will take the lead, but I'll begin the arrest process. Today I'll show them the surveillance video of you and Grace contacting John Owens. Here, let me show you." He ran the video on his big plasma screen.

"You know I want to stay here and work with you. If you hadn't asked when the doc released me, the ATF would have assigned us to the tsunami of guns in town or the heroin and opioid epidemic. Again, what about X-Girl? You'd think the FBI would have the DNA nailed down by now."

"Who knows what they have? I'm hoping they'll work with the new task force." He backed the video up. "We wouldn't have had this without your group, especially you and Grace."

"That was Grace following social media and why we hung out where they meet at the gym on Forest Avenue. John Owens fumbled over the money." She held up the photo. "Look at the clothes he wears. Those have to be thousand-dollar suits. He wants to be noticed, and he's calculating. It's all money. Power."

"I know." He pointed at the screen. "I need to mark our people and your group inside the room with some kind of little mark so they can see how you set it up. See? You've got people posted on each wall and on the machines beside you. I don't know how you two did it, but you looked like a seller, and Grace appeared so innocent."

"But she is, Chief. That kind of innocent." AJ sat at his desk and backed the video up to the beginning. "I can put a little mark on all of our people." She inserted a little "zero" on each person. "Will that do it?"

"Perfect." He stood off to the side of his desk, scanning the video. "What do you mean? Grace is *that kind of innocent*."

AJ looked up at him. "That's what she is…actually, more *immune* than innocent."

"You're kidding. The way men…and women…hit on her?"

"She doesn't even see it, as in *unaware*. She's the real deal."

"I thought she was just ignoring them." The chief frowned.

"Nope." AJ took a closer look at the video. "Wait. This is different from what I have. Let me show you." She retrieved her laptop and placed it on the chief's desk. "See? You've got the security from the north door. Mine is from the front." They both watched the scene unfold. "Look." AJ stopped the video and pointed at a table. "There's the victim, Kevin, with three older men." She zoomed in a bit, frowning. "Did the new task force identify those men? They have to do that as soon as possible." She stopped the video. "Let's go back to my office. We picked up Tag Beckett at the airport yesterday afternoon, and she and Grace will be here any minute. I want to show you something else."

Back at her desk, AJ swiveled her computer monitor so he could see it. "I sent you this yesterday. Tag's résumé and service history."

"I didn't see it. I had to meet with the new trafficking group after the press conference and it lasted past dinnertime. Then I was on time for Bonnie's run at the training facility this morning so she can transition into your group." The chief sat and scooted closer to her desk. "How'd she do?"

"Aced it, of course," he said absently, reading the information on her computer. "Tag Beckett, Wisconsin's most decorated female soldier. And Menominee Indian."

"*Part* Menominee. Her father's English. That's where Beckett comes from."

"I remember when she played basketball at UW-Madison. All-American. Look at her education and all those decorations. Plus…" He pointed at a line. "She led the Dragons, the first all-female special operations unit, and got a medal for those two years." He adjusted his glasses to see the screen better. "And I thought *you* were something, graduating from West Point with honors and a Presidential Commendation."

AJ took a drink of her now-cold coffee and tapped the screen. "Something's off here. Tag asked for Wisconsin and, even more interesting, asked for the ATF."

"This is her home state. Maybe she just wants to be here."

"She's qualified for much more. Computers, for example. One of her degrees is in that field. She was in charge of an entire section of intel during the last tour, so it wouldn't be much to switch to cyber crime, so why is she a *rookie* agent out in the field and why the ATF? She could have gone anywhere." She tapped the screen again. "She was up for a promotion too. I've never read recommendations like this."

He looked up from the monitor. "Where's the psych evaluation?"

"When I spoke to the Bureau this morning they said they'd send it. Tag's only been stateside two months and they've rushed her through everything. That's concerning."

He looked at his watch and stood. "Yeah, it is. I've got to get this information downtown. Are you staying here?"

"I want Tag up and running before my last appointment with the doctor this afternoon, and don't forget the barbecue at our house tonight. Bring your wife. Katie's cooking the chicken you love. Around six is fine."

"Katie called the wife about a recipe. Tell her we're bringing the nut salad, the one with cashews and spinach." He started to leave but turned back. "Which doctor?"

"Dr. Bergs. My therapist over Ariel's shooting. It helped, but I'm glad it's over."

"That doctor's been a great help to the task force. Bonnie said she gave you the ballistics report from the shooting at the church. My group did a full day search in that neighborhood but found nothing. You didn't hear a vehicle?"

"As I said, only footsteps running away, but they sounded big and heavy."

"I don't like this. It's weird, like Frog's money."

AJ wondered again about her own new task force and the connection between the money and the police. "Frog is pretty savvy, but is there any possibility it could have been Milwaukee Police?"

"Why would you even think that? I would have known since I have Frog marked throughout our entire system."

"I'm wondering what's behind my new task force, not to mention that unexpected vacation Lawrence Kelly *ordered* me to take. Did you talk to him?"

The chief shook his head and moved toward the door. "I'd have told you."

"I'm sorry. Of course you would have. Don't forget the meeting with the two men from Niagara tomorrow morning."

He flashed a smile and was gone. If there was anyone she valued in this office, it was Chief William Whiteaker. He'd hung in there with her throughout that whole screw-up last winter and spring. She looked at Katie's photo, thinking about yesterday. She had been exhausted, but the night had been great...after the two-hour argument over the new assignment and the damned shooting with Frog. Katie had loved the shakiness out of her, and she'd slept long and deep. Katie had been gone when she woke but had left a note, and AJ placed it on her desk now, rereading it. *You need rest. I'm going to feed you lots of food tonight and put you to bed early. OXOX.* She dialed Katie's number.

"Morning, sweetie," Katie said, her voice dropping to intimate.

AJ closed her eyes. "I love you and missed waking up with you this morning. How'd the meeting at the bank go?"

"The next month is going to be insane, and I'm bracing myself for long hours. I can see why David Markam is the senior vice president at Bennings Bank. He reeled them in. Zack's already working on graphics." Katie's voice picked up as she added details, and AJ let her ramble until she ran down. Katie had said *long hours.* Had she already forgotten that she'd be out of town, or was she saying it was okay to go because she was going to be really busy*?*

"I just called to say hello. I reminded the chief about the meal tonight, and he said they'd bring the nut salad you like."

"Not just nuts. That's a Chesapeake salad." Katie laughed. "I'll be home this afternoon. Mom's helping, so don't worry if you have more people at the dinner than we talked about. Don't forget to tell Dr. Bergs about the shooting. Wait...nice photo in this morning's paper."

"Haven't seen it yet." AJ heard voices nearing her office. "Gotta go. See you soon." She hung up as Grace peeked inside with Tag behind her. Both of them had cups in their hands and looked rested.

"Did you get breakfast?" AJ said, seeing their smiles.

"Grace could run a B and B with no problem," Tag said, folding her tall body into the chair.

AJ handed Grace some papers. "Tag's office is ready, but will you complete these? Send her the Michael's Angels file and then what little we have on the new assignment. Oh, and include the summer's work with Bill. If I had my way, we'd still be working with them."

"Will we still report to Justice?"

"Yes, and list Peter Adams as our liaison over there. I want Tag to read everything as a timeline of where we've been, what we've done." AJ watched Grace's reaction. "I have a five o'clock doctor's appointment this afternoon, and then I'll see both of you at our place around six o'clock. Today we'll have lunch across the street and talk over what you've read, Tag." She held up the worn manila envelope. "If there's time, we'll look at this together." Grace nodded and left for Tag's office, leaving AJ alone with her new agent.

CHAPTER FOUR

Tag gestured at the door. "Want me to close the door?"
AJ nodded at her. Tag wore confidence like her clothes, easy and naturally. The jeans, boots, and white collarless shirt stressed comfort before fashion. Straight black hair fell just below her ears, and warm, dark eyes matched the hair. A silver necklace was half hidden by the top open button.

AJ blinked. Tag looked exactly like Katie's favorite fiction character, Bren Black. "Great boots. I'm fond of boots myself," she said, bending to look at the footwear to hide her grin.

"Big feet," Tag said, sitting and crossing her long legs, a boot resting on her knee. She smiled with practiced ease, and AJ saw that Tag had done a zillion interviews. "Nice office," Tag continued. "I like it. Not overwhelmingly professional."

"Katie and Grace did it while I was recovering from an injury last spring."

"Grace said as much. I was surprised you weren't downtown."

"Don't like the politics down there...or anywhere. This building houses municipal police, Chief Whiteaker's Special Forces, and our ATF group. It's quiet out here," AJ said. "Since you went to college in Madison, I assume you're familiar with Milwaukee?"

"I spent a lot of time here. Some of it academic, working with a mentor at Marquette, and some with my parents when they taught Native American Culture at UW-Milwaukee."

AJ turned her monitor so Tag could see it. "I see your parents are involved with the College of Menominee Nation."

"They love it. Will there be time to get up to Keshena?"

"Is that where they live?"

"Actually, north and east, out in the country where I grew up. I haven't been there in a long time and I'd really like to see them."

"We'll be in that area with the new task force but not sure exactly where."

Tag's dark eyes widened. "Something's wrong up there?"

"The bureau chief, Lawrence Kelly, believes trafficking, but let's do the personal stuff first." She pointed at the computer. "You ran government backgrounds, so you know I have everything from your shoe size to your fingerprints. Any questions?"

"No, but Charles Ryan said to mention his name."

"I'll bet he did." AJ laughed. "We've worked together since I left the army, and you'll see him all over our last assignment, the Michael's Angels task force. He was in charge of three states. I ran this end in Milwaukee, a combined DEA-ATF task force working with Chief Whiteaker."

"Charles is your number one fan."

"He was my mentor, and I taught at that facility before I came into the field. Then he had me undercover for a while, which I really liked—still do—but the last assignment in California was an experience I'll never repeat. After that he talked me into the ATF and it's been a fit, so fire away with anything you want to know. We won't get much time once this begins."

"Well, the obvious. How did you happen to kill your own agent?"

AJ's gut tightened. It sucker-punched her every time. "That agent, Ariel, was rogue and none of us knew. She reported to Charles and blindsided him too. She put a gun to my head. Believe me, I had no choice. It was that simple."

"And that complicated." Tag frowned at the floor. "I'm sorry."

"Me too. She had no living family, so Charles and I took her home and buried her beside her parents. Today's my last doctor's appointment over that." The ghost of Ariel's last breath as she died beside her swept through her mind, and she paused. "That brings me to this question. With all of your experience, skills, and education, why are you here as a rookie? And why the ATF? You could have gone anywhere. And it appears you were up for promotion."

Tag's eyes flashed. The confident smile slid away and she straightened in her chair. "It's complicated, but some of it is my family.

Menominee County is the poorest in Wisconsin and one of the most poverty-stricken in the United States. The annual per capita income is less than eleven thousand dollars, and they tell me the whole area is drowning in drugs." She pulled in a breath. "Maybe I'll teach there someday like my parents. I'd love that."

"You came home for your family? I wasn't aware of the poverty, but of course know about the drugs. It's a pretty good dream, Tag."

Tag turned to the window. "I'm grateful to the military for what they taught me, plus it gave me the best friends of my life. I believe in protecting our country." She was quiet for a moment. "If I'm going to fight for my country, I'll do it right here. In America."

AJ took a mental step backward and waited.

"How's the mood here? In the city? The state?" Tag turned back to AJ.

"Restless with this election. People are divided and polarized. Bad vibes everywhere, not to mention all the crime or drugs. You name it, we've got it, and I don't like politics."

Tag looked down at her hands. "Do you know where I've spent the last six weeks?"

"I thought you were on base, training for my group, here."

"No. I was hauled all over Washington DC doing PR or something like it. As you just said, I don't like politics either. Lots of photo shoots, and I hardly ever got out of my dress greens. Congressional committees or individual politicians, all wanting to talk to the big hero…blah, blah, blah. The one good thing was a meal and night out with what remaining Dragons I could find." Tag scowled at the desk. "As to *why* the ATF, Mom's mother, my grandmother, married an American-Swede after WWII, and he worked for the ATF in northern Wisconsin during the last mob years. I loved that man."

AJ looked back at her computer. Had she seen that information? "Your grandfather was an ATF agent? So you're…?"

"About half-Indian and I'm sure you know my father's English. His mother was Irish so by the time you get to me, it's a real stew. I got the black hair, eyes, and darker skin from my grandmother and the Nordic bones from my grandfather."

AJ studied her. "Nordic bones" was a spot-on description of her stunning high cheekbones, straight nose, and wide, expressive mouth.

"What about your family?" Tag gestured at the photos on the desk.

AJ picked up a group picture and handed it to Tag. "I was adopted as an infant along with four other girls and raised on a farm in Maine. That farm is home to me. This is us, my four sisters, Mom and Dad. These two are married, supplying all of us with nieces and nephews. This one's in post-grad work on the West Coast, and the youngest is an army medic, just transferred to Afghanistan two weeks ago." She frowned at the picture. "I worry about her."

"Let me know where she ends up. I'll track her for you."

"I'd appreciate that." AJ set the picture back on the desk. "Anyone special in your life?" AJ said casually. The rumor mill loved Tag Beckett.

"My stupid reputation." Tag laughed with a shrug. "Truth? Lots of women that ended in friendship but nothing close to anything more, and not for trying. I can't seem to find the right fit and I've about given up."

"Oh, I know. I was in the same spot when I met Katie here, last winter."

"Oh God. Katie." Tag rubbed her face. "I apologize for that moment with her at the airport yesterday. Can I plead exhaustion, and the appreciation of an adorable woman?"

"She is adorable with the best mind plus a wicked sense of humor, and you might have noticed her quick temper." AJ held up a hand. "Fair warning? Katie's father was city police for decades, and she spent a lot of time inside police stations." She glanced at the photo of Katie on her desk. "Like Charles Ryan, you'll see a lot of her in what you read today."

"Speaking of beautiful women, Grace—"

"My second in command and quiet." AJ glanced at Tag's hopeful face. She obviously hadn't given up, no matter what she said. "Like Katie, men and women flock to her. Bonnie has drooled for months, but Grace is firm on friendship only. I have no idea what she prefers except horses. She loves horses." AJ handed the remaining papers to Tag. "You'll meet most of our ATF group at our house tonight including the chief's police that work with us. Greg and Jeff are already up north, so you'll meet them up there. Our task force doesn't have a name yet and we'll be undercover. You'll be a huge help because you know the area, plus you have experience with small ops. We have a meeting with two people from up there tomorrow morning. You'll be here for that."

"What about this group's last assignment? That was kind of a big deal."

"The Michael's Angels task force was covert, ferreting out high-end meth dealers and manufacturers in this area, not street-level commerce or gangs. We tracked boardrooms, doctors, banks, that kind of thing. Charles Ryan still has a DEA group here, but they work the streets. I'd rather you'd read it first and then we'll talk."

"One last thing. Someone shot at you?"

"Ballistics says forty caliber pistol." Anxiety slid inside AJ again just as a light knock sounded on the door. "We'll break for lunch when you're hungry."

Grace took Tag to her office, leaving AJ with all the things she hadn't said. That shooting could be a lot of things. Something still lurking from Michael's people to the group that Frog was a part of up north or something they'd run into this summer. A random robbery gone bad? Her worst fear was that it was connected to the new assignment. She glanced at her computer. At least she now knew some of the reasons Tag had come home and not taken the promotion, but there was more, something sliding around in the background. Something Tag hadn't said.

"She likes the setup," Grace said, back in AJ's office.

"And I like her. She listens hard, and leadership oozes off her. And listen to this. They rushed her through the last six weeks with almost no training, and coming home is a big adjustment. Seriously, Grace, keep an eye on her for me. I doubt she's even had time to breathe, and there's no psych evaluation yet."

"I noticed the psych eval was missing, and that's a first." Grace leaned back. "One thing I can tell you after less than twenty-four hours. She spent a lot of time on the phone and computer last night and appears highly organized. Also, she did some work with human trafficking over there."

"She'll need the organization for undercover. How'd you know about the trafficking?"

"She told me this morning when we ate. Did you see her necklace, that nice thin silver chain with the little dragon that I asked her about yesterday? I thought that whole thing was really cool, that all-woman group."

"I do too," AJ said. She had noticed the necklace and knew about the Dragons but hadn't checked all of Tag's ops. She would now. "What about Frog?"

"The GPS is working fine, and I talked to Greg this morning. The girls are west of Niagara in a motel by Crooked Lake, the resort where you and Katie vacationed. There are two adult women, one man, and twelve girls including Frog."

AJ opened her desk and handed Grace the bank card. "This is creepy. When I met Frog at the church she gave me this. Said two cops paid her to go undercover."

Grace studied the card. "That's not possible. Our police? The chief has her marked." She shook her head, frowning. "Does the chief know?"

"Yes, and he agrees all of this is weird. As to the task force, we might get something useful from the two men from Niagara tomorrow." AJ brought the file up on her computer. "What do you think of Pete Adams's suggestion if we end up in Niagara?"

"I like his idea but I didn't know he grew up in that area. Being undercover at his uncle's delivery business would get us into the community," Grace said. "Did you see this morning's Milwaukee paper, the press conference yesterday?"

"No. I haven't looked at today's paper."

"I filed the link to it under our missing people too." Grace tapped her pen on the desk. "The chief kept us connected with the new task force so we'll be alert to the locals."

AJ shoved the photo the chief had given her across the desk. "The chief needs help, so while you're working with Tag, I'll search the group they arrested at that house. The victim, Kevin, had relatives involved. His older brother, John, owns the house. That was the man you and I met with at the gym when I tried to sell you."

Grace snorted a little laugh and tossed a newspaper onto the desk. "Tag found this on the plane."

AJ read the British *Guardian* headline. "Milwaukee's a Human Trafficking Hub? You've read it?"

Grace nodded.

AJ laid the paper on her desk to read later. "I argued with the bureau chief on the phone again this morning about this assignment. What if we run into the FBI-DHS operation up there? I tried to tell him we'd be a lot more effective here, working the source, but he didn't buy it. We're going up there with nothing, no actual suspects. It's like we'll just be there to protect Frog and the eleven girls, and that's okay…but a whole task force doesn't make sense."

"I see it too. I agree with you."

"Our tax dollars at work."

Grace leaned back in her chair and changed the subject. "Tag said you are *striking*," she said with a grin.

"It was probably the suit Katie's mother made for me, but I don't think so." She laughed. "Oh hell, there goes my badass reputation."

"What badass reputation? Get serious."

"One can only hope," AJ said, still grinning.

CHAPTER FIVE

AJ left the doctor's office that afternoon with time to get home for the cookout to introduce Tag. The doctor had signed her release today, which was good news, but she'd miss their conversations. She had come to admire Dr. Bergs, a part of the reason Milwaukee now had a new trafficking task force. She'd pounded the city all summer and worked with the FBI to show that they needed to act soon on the problem.

Today, the last appointment, they'd talked about the young victim, Kevin Owens, and anxiety and panic…and her obsession with X-Girl. Always that.

Thick summer sunlight flooded the quiet parking lot and surrounding trees, and she paused at an abandoned bird's nest in the ivy on the wall. Her skin prickled, and she turned, glancing at the car where she'd left her weapon. *Too quiet.*

The first shot hit the ivy, ripping the wood to splinters, showering her face and hair. She went down. The next bullet tore through her shirt and skin, nicking her left forearm. Her vehicle took several hits and shook with a metallic scream with rust falling underneath. Then silence with only her ragged breath and ringing ears. Out of sight, a motorcycle roared to life with that distinctive Harley sound.

She blanked into pure panic for a moment before shoving into a sitting position. It hurt, and blood always made her vomit. She gulped for breath. The door above her flew open, and Dr. Bergs ran down the steps.

"Were those gunshots? Are you hit?"

AJ held out her arm, looking away from the blood. "They shot my car too," she said and dialed the chief at her house. "The police are on their way. Everyone okay inside?"

"Yes. Let me see your arm." The doctor moved the torn sleeve carefully. "Listen to me. I know you want to throw up, but you won't." AJ stared at her doctor and swallowed the nausea.

"Let's clean that." The doctor helped her stand.

❖

AJ made it all the way to their bedroom before Katie caught her.

"Honey, you're late, and the chief and Grace disappeared—" She stopped. "Your shirt. Were you in an accident?" She reached for the torn, bloody material.

AJ leaned past her for a clean shirt and tugged her into the bathroom. "Sit beside me on the tub," she said, unbuttoning her shirt. "Someone shot at me again. I'm sure it was a pistol, but I never saw the shooter. Shot the car too, but that thing's a miracle. It started right up. Grace brought me home in the chief's car. He took my car to the station to look at it further and someone will drop him off here."

"Damn it." Katie held the damaged shirt like it was a sharp knife.

"A motorcycle followed me all the way from the office, and I heard one leave after the shooting. I was coming out of the doctor's."

"Let me see."

"The doctor used that liquid skin and butterfly bandages." She showed Katie. "By the time she was done, the chief and Grace were there with the police. It's just a graze."

Katie went to her knees, buttoning AJ's shirt and wiping her face with a washcloth. "Enough. No more getting shot at. That's twice and you're leaving soon and—" Eyes glistening, she wrapped AJ against her. The late afternoon light poured through the bathroom's glass skylight, turning the room soft gold. AJ sighed. The world settled again in Katie's arms.

There was a knock on the door. "AJ? Jock's here, looking for you or the chief," Grace said. "He's in the living room with Bonnie. Something about Home Base."

Home Base was an enormous house where the girls lived, the ones that had worked the streets for Michael. They'd been his "Angels," distributing meth, and were damned effective. When Frog had been released from rehab, AJ had hidden her there to keep an eye on the girls, and things had been fine until Frog discovered the girls and women funneling into northern Wisconsin. Now, instead of drugs, they had the trafficking assignment.

"Grace, stay with me and Frat Boy so I don't miss anything. Tell him I'll be there in a minute. Katie, take Bonnie back to the party."

"Frat Boy? Jock?" Katie said.

"He leads Charles's group here like I used to." She'd worked with Jock for years and trusted him but didn't like him. The feeling was mutual.

Jock waited by the window. His well-muscled shoulders strained his black T-shirt and he'd cut his hair. The ponytail was gone.

"We have a problem, AJ. Home Base burned to the ground today," he said.

She tucked in her shirt and checked her jeans for blood. "Was anyone hurt?"

"They have two bodies, but there's gotta be more."

"About twenty girls and women were there, plus the children." Her mind raced, trying to remember what Frog had told her about the house.

"I'm going over there with Milwaukee Arson tomorrow morning. Want to go?"

"Can't. I have a meeting involving my new task force, not the Milwaukee trafficking task force." She baited him with silence.

"Charles notified me that you and the chief are officially separated from the DEA, but I thought you might want to see what pops from this." He shot her his familiar arrogant look. "My guys regularly check that house, but nothing happens there anymore. I still had the Michael's Angels list and gave them a body count."

Seeing he didn't know about Frog at Home Base, she simply nodded. "Take Bonnie. She knows that neighborhood better than any of us." AJ gripped the back of the chair, steadying herself.

"I heard she's part of your team now." Again, there was his *boss* expression, part of the reason she didn't like him. "What's going on here? Food smells good."

"Stay and eat with us. The old group's here and the chief's on his way. Talk to Bonnie while you're out there."

"Thanks. I'm hungry." He swaggered through the kitchen to the deck.

AJ raised her eyebrows at Grace. She'd left Jock feeling comfortably in charge.

"Mr. Ego, but I'm shocked about Home Base. Thank God Frog's up north," Grace said. "And I found nothing on Frog's money. It was a cash transaction."

"So where did the surviving Home Base girls and women go? Or the kids? Frog said the girls she's with up north are new, brought in from the outside. I'll call the chief about Home Base before he gets here. Oh, and follow Jock's tracks on the computer when you get home tonight. You're still plugged into that surveillance. Have Tag help you. Let's see how she likes our setup."

❖

After talking with the chief twice, AJ walked outside to the deck. Old Bob Marley music drifted through the almost-dusk air mingling with the aroma of barbecued chicken. Katie was watching Tag in the crowd, and she'd lay odds Katie was thinking exactly what she had this morning. Tag resembled Katie's favorite fiction superwoman, Agent Bren Black.

Grace was at the food table also watching Tag, and AJ paused at the look on her face. *Interest? Attention?* She picked up a plate as Grace muttered, "Killer smile."

"The chief called Charles and then called me back." AJ chose a fork. "Who has a killer smile?"

"What?" Still distracted, Grace scooped potato salad on her plate.

"I talked to the chief. Twice," AJ repeated. "As usual, Jock had not called him, and Charles had some kind of breakdown on the phone. Said to spank him good for not calling, but I'm not dealing with him today."

"How's your arm? And in case you're not counting, that's twice you've been shot at."

"I was fine until Katie found me. She said that too, in spades." AJ forked a piece of chicken.

Grace eased past her and sat beside Katie. She'd stayed here with

Katie when AJ was out of town last winter and it'd been safe, like circling the wagons. AJ glanced at them with a chilling thought. If the shooter knew where she worked, did it involve this house or Katie? "No," she said under her breath. They weren't going through this again.

She scanned the vegetables, thinking about Katie's family's wonderful garden this summer. She loved to grow them, but Katie's creative cooking with herbs and seasonings made them special. AJ spotted the bread and cucumbers. It was only melba rounds with fresh dill, homemade mayo sauce, and cream cheese on top of sliced cucumbers, but it made her mouth water.

"Oh, man." She chewed slowly. She could eat a thousand of these. Jock moved toward Bonnie. For some reason, Jock's arrogance just rolled off Bonnie's back, and this would be a good experience for her. For that matter, if she needed someone to stay here again, Bonnie would do it, but Katie would raise hell and she didn't look forward to any of that.

Katie held a book in her hand, and Grace motioned at Tag to meet them. Tag went around the back of the group just as Jock took a step back, knocked Tag sideways, and her beer fell to the grass. Tag looked stunned, and in a blur, Jock was suddenly on the ground. Tag's hand was fisted, but it froze, hanging in the air. She straightened, helped Jock stand, and apologized.

It was over before AJ could move, but she'd seen the dangerous part of Tag. *There's the warrior.* Tag didn't move an inch, right in Jock's face, her expression blank. The two were the same height. Jock said something, gave her a murderous look, and strode away. The side gate slammed, leaving a heavy quiet behind him.

"Show's over," AJ said. "Let's get you another beer." She picked up the bottle, nudged Tag toward Grace and Katie, and the noise resumed. *That was worrisome.* AJ wondered again about Tag's missing psych evaluation from Lawrence Kelly's office.

Obviously embarrassed, Tag said, "Sorry. Guess I'm not civilized yet. What was his name? I have to apologize again."

"His name's Jock, and not many women have knocked him down." AJ handed her a fresh beer. "He's in charge of Charles Ryan's DEA group here and a hothead, but he's good." She didn't say that Jock would never forgive Tag, no matter how much she apologized.

"She's right. He's a hothead." Grace grinned at AJ. "You say not many women have knocked him down, but you pounded him in training."

"Yeah, and he's hated me ever since," AJ said as Katie held out the book.

"What's this?" Tag took it with a stressed smile.

"The first book in a mystery series that I read. I was showing Grace how much you resemble the main character. Look at the cover." She tilted her head at AJ. "Can you believe it?"

"I thought so too this morning. I was curious when you'd come to same conclusion."

"I'm a long way from this woman." Tag tried to hand the book back.

"Keep it and read it as a favor to me. AJ laughs at it," Katie said with a smile.

"All right, as a favor. I could use a good laugh. Where's your bathroom, girls?"

"I'll show you. I lived here too, once upon a time," Grace said and they moved inside.

AJ put her arm around Katie's waist and tugged her closer, catching her scent that she loved. "I was over there in a food coma. You should work with Jimmy at his restaurant."

"Sweet talker." Katie grinned.

"You look nice. I like the shirt." AJ ran her hands under the white collar with lace trim, studying the gray patterned shirt. "Did your mother do this?"

"Who else? It was one of Dad's shirts. She took the collar off, put on a new one, and refit the shirt. She couldn't stand for it to hang in the closet."

AJ dropped her hands to Katie's slender hips, holding on tight. The first time she'd ever touched her like this she'd thought she was delicate. She'd been dead wrong.

"Mom helped set up the party, and…what's that look on your face?"

"Only a memory but a good one."

Katie wrapped her in a quick hug. "Do you want some ibuprofen?"

"No, but that denim shirt was a favorite. Could your mother save it?"

"Are you kidding? She'd love the challenge."

"Good. I'll call her. I'm going for more of that nut salad. I ate all of the cucumber thingies."

"Nut salad and cucumber thingies? You're my gourmet." Katie pointed at the chair. "Sit. I'll get your food. There's something I want you to taste."

"Wait. I need to talk to Tag about X-Girl tonight. Do you mind cleaning up with Grace?"

"I'd rather scrub floors any day than hear about that." Katie took her plate, and AJ watched her choose something that looked like squash. She resented Lawrence Kelly's new task force one more time, already missing Katie. Sweating, her hands shaking, she felt her heart pick up. The doctor had warned her of this, panic and anxiety left over from Ariel and the new shootings. Her legs were so weak she almost fell into the chair.

"Damn it," she said under her breath, seeing Katie watching her. She straightened, fighting to keep it together.

"Here, and yes, you need ibuprofen." Katie handed her the plate and left.

Tag slid into the seat next to AJ. "Grace told me what happened at the doctor's."

"I didn't even get a glimpse of the shooter, and damn, it's got to be personal although I don't have a clue why. Anyway, before you leave tonight, I need a couple of minutes with you. Katie and Grace will clean up."

AJ stepped into her home office that night with a fresh beer for Tag and saw her going over the shelves of music and books.

"I love your house. Grace gave me the tour," Tag said.

"I love it too."

"It's *home*. I can feel it." Tag held up the glass-framed Presidential Commendation of AJ in formal military attire that Katie kept on her desk. "This is something too."

"No, it's not. Just publicity for the job we did in Ecuador years ago. A lot of other people were there with me. I just happened to be nearby and they grabbed me, or as you said this morning, 'blah, blah, blah.' The real story isn't nearly so commendable, but Katie's proud of it. Otherwise it'd be in a drawer somewhere." AJ placed it back on Katie's desk and handed Tag the X-Girl envelope. "In addition to our new task force, I need your take on this. This victim is the reason we took that house down with the chief and his police and hope to God we have the people who got her murdered. It happened last spring, before we knew about the human trafficking."

They were silent as Tag went over each gruesome photo slowly, pausing now and then, taking her time over the paperwork and autopsy.

The late summer air still smelled of barbecue, and AJ watched a moth beat at the screen of the open window trying for the lamp. She understood its frustration. Finally, Tag placed the papers on the desk with a sigh.

"They cut her hands off? And what did they do to her face?"

"No hands, no fingerprints, and the acid on the face made identification impossible. We still don't have a name. The FBI has her here at the morgue and is still working on the DNA."

"Christ." Tag pulled in a breath. "Here's another part of the answer about why I left the military. Our final Dragon assignment was brutal. They sent us down to investigate a nest of imprisoned women and children. I think the thought was that we'd do better because we were women, but it was a trap and we lost eleven out of twenty-five." She stopped and pulled in a deep breath. "This is cultural over there. A lot of the women are owned by the men. That's not the case in the United States even though sometimes it feels that way." She held up some of the photos. "Is there anything that ties that house you took down to this? Have they caught any of the perpetrators?"

AJ nodded. "There were five different sperm samples. The FBI found two of the men in Utah, but both were killed in a robbery. Then one in Michigan that they're holding on trafficking charges, but we have no further information from the FBI at this time. So that leaves two, and I'd like you right beside Grace, looking at the information."

"Any chance they're local?"

"If they are, we haven't found them, and now that we're officially off the case, the new Milwaukee task force will take over the search."

"And what's this?" Tag held up a spreadsheet.

"Those are the business locations we've found that manage the kids and adults involved in the trafficking. Look." AJ pointed at the sheet. "A doctor's office, a hair stylist and beauty consultant, a used clothing store, a photographer's studio…you name it, they run it in Milwaukee and its suburbs. Once the new task force charges John Owens, the man who ran that house, they'll go after each business." AJ stopped when she realized she was up and pacing. "My doctor says I'm obsessed with this case."

Tag only shook her head and leaned back in her chair, studying the ceiling. Finally, she turned, face composed.

"Are you okay? Getting shot isn't an everyday thing."

"You're combat tested. Shooting has to be familiar."

"You never get used to it," Tag said softly. "I've shot people and been shot. It changes a person for the rest of their life." Her feet hit the floor as she straightened and tossed the folder on the desk. "And I can relate to your obsession. I've seen worse than this, AJ."

AJ heard what she'd sensed about Tag this morning, the *something more*, and pushed her chair closer. "Tell me."

"I'm tight with the remaining Dragons, and we all agree. Our country's beginning to feel a lot like *over there*."

When Tag added nothing more, AJ wondered what the hell Tag was holding back. Finally, she said, "I've read about human trafficking until my eyes bled, not to mention what I've already seen. I thought the drugs I chased were the worst, but this has changed me and I'm not the same person I was four months ago."

Tag stood, took the file, and stacked everything neatly back into the folder. "Sometimes it sucks to be us, and how could you be the same? Grace says your entire group trusts you with their lives, and that's a burden. I think it's the heaviest thing we carry." She handed the paperwork to AJ. "I'll work with Grace on this, count on it."

Chapter Six

The next morning, Tag worked at her desk while Grace made coffee in the chief's office. The men from Niagara would be there soon for the meeting.

She downloaded a thumb drive onto a personal tablet and leaned back in her chair, absently rubbing the dragon necklace. Outside, a group of noisy sparrows shook the pine tree limbs. No one bird stood out. That was safety in numbers, exactly how she was tucked away in this ATF group while working with two other federal agencies. Keeping secrets was not new, but AJ's honesty last night had made her stare into the darkness for a long time when she'd gone to bed.

What they'd stumbled onto during her last year in Intelligence on base meant there was going to be an uproar in this country now that the Feds had everything. In the meantime, this job with the ATF came first. So far, it was pretty much whistling in the dark.

No wonder AJ looked so stressed. Well, that and getting shot. If this was Afghanistan, she'd have someone riding shotgun with her, but apparently they did things differently here. She'd talk to Grace tonight and see what she had to say.

A sound made her turn. Grace leaned against the doorway, gray skirt wrapping her like smoke, her arms crossed. Tag swallowed hard.

"Your clothes." Grace gestured at Tag's black boots and pants, lilac shirt, and purple blazer. "Nice colors on you."

Tag locked her tablet in her desk and sent her a thank-you smile. Grace blushed, so flustered and beautiful that Tag's heart leapt. They stared at each other for a moment.

"The chief's here and coffee's ready," Grace almost whispered, cleared her throat, and left.

Tag scrambled to follow the gorgeous long legs and white lacy top that exposed toned tan arms. Grace was the perfect name for her.

Chief Whiteaker paced behind his desk and covered the phone's receiver with his hand. "I'm trying to see what they found about the shooting yesterday. Have some coffee while—" He broke off, speaking into the phone. "Look at the surveillance video, for Christ's sake. She heard a motorcycle, and I gotta believe her. Have you seen her Harley?"

Tag savored the coffee's aroma and took a careful sip. They'd gotten up late and talked about their favorite coffees all the way down Howell Avenue. She watched Grace arrange coffee cups and made herself turn away, checking out Chief Whiteaker's office to calm her heart. There were almost as many plants here as in AJ's office. She smelled spearmint. Come to think of it, AJ smelled like spearmint too.

The chief slammed the phone down. "Nitwits," he said, holding his cup out to Tag. "Give me coffee. Please? AJ's going to be a bit late, but the men should be here any minute."

"Sir." A young female cop stood at the door. "You have guests."

"Bring them up," he said. "Tag, brace yourself. Grace is used to this. I know one of these days AJ will show up dressed as a clown."

Grace laughed. "Just play along. It won't be too bad no matter what it is."

The cop ushered two men inside. Tag had never seen the first man, but the second surprised her and they smothered each other in a hug.

"I saw your parents yesterday," he said. "They mentioned you were back."

"And I miss them," Tag said, her hand on his shoulder. "Everyone, this is my cousin, Jay Yardly."

"And this is my client, Clint Weeks," Jay said, turning to the second man.

"Sit down and have some coffee." The chief shook their hands and finished the introductions. "I received your email, gentlemen. You have a nice trip down?"

"We did," Clint Weeks said and reached for a cup. Grace unleashed her smile on him, and Tag watched him pause for a closer look.

The chief moved to his desk. "How did you get our name, Mr. Weeks?"

"It's Clint, Chief. Earlier this summer, I finished the financing for my Niagara project at Bennings Bank and then dropped by the Federal Building. I met with Peter Adams in the Justice Department. He referred me to you."

Tag took another look at Jay. He was more than their lead Reservation lawyer who happened to be family. He was her personal lawyer. He looked up at that moment and they both smiled. Once again, she settled deeper into *home.*

"As I explained in the email," Weeks continued, "I've rebuilt the old Niagara Inn in northern Wisconsin and will open it soon. Last year I needed a local lawyer and met Jay."

"Justice emailed me but they weren't forthcoming with details and we've worked with Pete Adams," the chief said. "The SAC, Allison Jacob, will be leading anything the ATF does in Niagara but she's a little late this morning. I'll be running things down here as a combined unit. While we're waiting for her, let me give you my personal contact information."

Tag measured Clint Weeks while the chief rummaged in his desk. Average height, he definitely took care of his body. His tanned skin set off pale blue eyes and thick, blond hair threaded with gray. The gray suit was expensive, as was his haircut, and the well-manicured hands. Everything about him shouted money. Entitlement.

"Hello, everyone." AJ flew into the room, fast and hurried. She thumped a briefcase onto the chief's desk, grabbed a mug, and poured herself a cup of coffee. "I am sooooo sorry to be late. Let's see, which one of you is Jay Yardly?" Jay stood and AJ shook his hand. "So, that leaves you, sir. Clint Weeks." She reached across the table and shook his hand vigorously.

"SAC Allison Jacob." Her brassy voice shattered the relaxed atmosphere in the room. Both men looked startled and Tag blinked. AJ's bright yellow dress left very little to the imagination. Her hair was styled big and sort of sloppy, and she wore enormous gold earrings and vivid red lipstick.

Just about a hooker was the first thing that entered Tag's stunned mind. Had she put on twenty pounds last night? And bigger hair? AJ sucked up every shred of air in the office and seemed taller. Grace was staring at the table and the chief found some papers interesting.

"All right." AJ rubbed her hands together. "Where are we?"

"I was about to ask if they were hungry," the chief said and cleared his throat.

AJ tossed a suggestive look at Weeks. "Hungry?"

"Uhhh," he stammered. "No, we ate earlier."

"Sorry, but I haven't. Late night. I'll be right back." She turned and left the room with a saucy wiggle, her high heels clicking down the hallway.

"She has a standing order for pastry," the chief said to the quiet group and laid a map of northern Wisconsin on the table. "Help me out here, Mr. Weeks...Clint. Where is Niagara?"

Weeks drew a circle around the town, adding a little information about the area. Tag concentrated on the map, identifying the back roads to the south where she'd grown up. Jay grinned at her.

Suddenly, AJ was in the office again with a large crystal plate, stacked with pastries. Her lipstick was a full shade lighter and her hair was styled more conservatively. Her suit was a more subdued yellow that showed less skin. Tag was sure the earrings were smaller...or had she just imagined it? Both Weeks and Jay were staring.

Tag took two large pastries. Grace refilled everyone's mugs, and Tag tracked her slender body and discreet curves around the table, enjoying every move.

"What's this all about, Mr. Weeks?" AJ said, munching on the food. Even her voice was less brassy but still a little loud. "I know the Inn was a mob hangout, built back in the twenties."

He swallowed before he spoke. "The Floritinos from Chicago were the original builders and owners. Their mob ties were enormous. The last one, a great-grandson, sold it in the eighties. A local family took it afterward but couldn't make it go."

AJ wiped her hands briskly with a cloth napkin. "Is there still a mob presence up there?"

"No. The Inn was empty for over several years before I bought it. We had to rebuild and bring it up to code."

"I found some history and old photos. Would you be interested?" She raised her eyebrows at him and stood when he nodded.

Tag watched her leave the room. AJ's shoes were the same color, but certainly a lower heel.

"Nice August day, isn't it?" the chief said and took another pastry off the plate. "How's the weather up there?"

"Outstanding," Jay said, turning to Tag. "Your dad and I nailed some bass at Crooked Lake earlier this week. You'd have drooled."

"I haven't fished in years," Tag said as AJ entered the office for the third time with a folder and some magazines. Sure enough. AJ wore no makeup and there were gold studs in her ears. Her hair was the familiar bright, sun-streaked hair and style that Tag was used to. The curves were diminished, replaced by her true athletic body shape in a high-end linen suit, the color of island beaches. Tag grinned. She'd never seen anything like it. Jay began to laugh.

"Good show, Agent Jacob," Weeks said.

"Thank you," AJ said in her normal voice with an easy grin. "I'm sorry to take your valuable time, gentlemen, but I wanted to give you a quick visual of what can be done with very little time and effort. If we go up there, don't even look for us." She poured another cup of coffee. "Peter Adams from Justice mentioned your banker at Bennings, Michael Cray." AJ had Clint Weeks's complete attention.

"Yes, Michael. I liked him. He came up to the building site, early March, after the bank secured the project."

"And Mr. Cray is still your contact?"

"No. The bank said he'd transferred to California, and it's a shame because he had some very creative ideas, including design. I liked working with him. A nice young man from Kansas, I believe. Am I right?"

"We knew Mr. Cray regarding another matter that was successfully resolved." AJ leaned forward. "Also a group of children living there when you began the tear down and remodeling, and—" She shuffled papers. "There was something else in the basement that you were concerned about?" she said to Weeks.

"There were children in the basement. That's why I spoke to Peter Adams at Justice. I've also known Lawrence Kelly, your bureau chief, for a long time. We each have a ranch in Wyoming in the same area and see each other frequently."

Tag felt the sudden alertness in the room at the mention of Michael and Lawrence Kelly. She also recognized the bank. It was Katie's current project. However, AJ calmly continued to explore Weeks's background, the subtext of his interaction with Michael Cray, and the remote possibility that he was involved with Michael's meth operations. Tag stretched her legs under the table with a quick look at

Jay. He looked tense. Clint Weeks's political affiliations in the western part of the United States were well known. A staunch conservative, Weeks bankrolled a huge super PAC and was influential in Congress.

"The children you found," AJ said. "How old were they? And were they girls…boys?"

"Mostly girls, but some boys, early teens or younger, and there were adults with them. They were actually living in the basement of the Inn, not just hiding out. My builder called me and I flew in to view the problem myself. My family lives at our home in Vermont."

"That wasn't mentioned in the article on you and your company in *Biz* magazine last month. A nice write-up." AJ held up a magazine.

"Thank you." Weeks beamed. "Business is off a bit because of the slowdown in Afghanistan. I'd hoped for further involvement, but the current president is too weak. As you know, I manufacture military vehicles. I not only keep us safe in the US, but my company provides a lot of employment over there."

Tag's stomach tightened as a trace of arrogance leaked into Weeks's voice. Here was one of the men she so disliked. She thought of Islamabad where she'd been injured and the private American industry her group had to work with.

"They're familiar with your trucks and other products, Clint," Jay said, obviously uncomfortable. "Both SAC Jacob and Agent Beckett are decorated veterans."

Weeks looked embarrassed for a split second but covered it quickly. "I didn't mean to imply that I'm profiting off your service, ladies."

AJ's eyes never changed nor did she acknowledge his words. "The children in the Inn. Are they still there?"

"No, they've disappeared." He looked at Jay for confirmation.

"He's right," Jay said. "The police looked into it but couldn't find them. When we began to investigate, the locals reported various groups of children and teenagers. The way that town talks, someone should have said something. However, the Inn has always had a reputation, that old mob threat, and people avoid the place." Jay laid some papers and a thumb drive on the table. "This is what the police found. The meth lab in the basement had been there a while." He pushed everything across the table to AJ. "We also took some video of the area and Clint's construction."

AJ plugged the flash drive into the tablet in front of her and studied it. "This *was* functioning recently." She handed the tablet to Grace and turned to Weeks. "You want us to investigate the meth lab?"

Weeks shook his head. "No, the local police took care of that. It's the children I want to pursue. Also, I saw a group of young girls and boys in tents by the Menominee River and took some video for the local police on my phone. When we went back the next day they were gone."

AJ's expression was innocent but interested. "Do you think it was trafficking?"

"I don't know. I have children that age. I'm sure some of those kids weren't more than ten or eleven." Weeks held up his hands. "You tell me. I'm just a citizen, asking for advice and assistance from the government."

"There's a Homeland Security and FBI national task force currently in northern Wisconsin. I wonder why Peter Adams didn't mention that to you. They've made quite a few well-publicized arrests."

Weeks nodded. "He did bring it to my attention, but with the Inn opening this month, I wanted something soon, and he recommended your group."

Tag thought he wanted to sweep all of this under the rug so the public would never know.

More interesting was the information he hadn't mentioned. Grace had discovered that Clint Weeks had a daughter who had gone missing four years ago and was still missing.

Tag was sure, regardless of his politics or money, he was thinking of that girl now, but why hadn't he mentioned her?

Chapter Seven

The chief walked Yardly and Weeks out of the office and down the steps to the main floor of the police station. AJ waited until the voices faded, and then firmly closed the door.

"*Ladies,*" she mimicked Weeks. "*I'm just a citizen.* Don't you wish you'd met him in Afghanistan, Tag? He'd have wet his pants." She opened the tablet again. "Grace, look at this. Anything familiar with the setup?"

Tag stood behind them. "Tell me what I'm seeing."

AJ pointed out tubing, jars, and faucet couplings. "It's a meth lab like Michael's setup we found last spring. Those sink couplings were his trademark. He must have bought loads of them. See all that ephedrine stacked against the wall? Where is it now?" She touched the screen. "I'll notify Charles."

"Where is the video Weeks claims to have given to the local police? Or is there more?" Tag shuffled the papers Jay had left for them. "This is off Weeks's computer. Has anyone talked to the police up there? Jay's normally precise about details."

"The chief will contact the local police." AJ rubbed her throbbing temples. "I'm still hungry. Give me time to change clothes again and I'll buy lunch at the Copper Penny."

Later, AJ leaned against the Copper Penny bar and studied her worn boots. She'd changed into comfortable jeans and a soft, long-sleeved light green cotton shirt to hide her wounded arm. She hadn't liked Weeks, and it wasn't just politics. Like Jock, his arrogance was obvious.

The usual old swing music was playing, and she took a steadying breath. Her first Milwaukee meal had been here almost a year ago, and she still liked the old, dark polished oak with the smell of burgers and beer. This bar held much of her history in this city. And Katie. Their first kiss had been by the exit sign at the back entrance.

The chief hung his coat over a chair at a table at the back and loosened his tie. Tag's skin looked darker than usual in the subdued bar light. She was certainly attractive. AJ's gaze skidded to a stop. Grace was laughing at Tag with an expression AJ had seen before, but never on Grace's face. Some of it was interest, like the party last night, but this was *happiness* or *anticipation*, something brand new. "Huh," she said under a breath and turned to order.

"I'd give anything for a picture of their faces when you flew into the room the first time," Tag said when AJ joined them.

"That whole act was for Clint Weeks. What did you think, Tag?"

"She's too polite to say you did a good imitation of a hooker," Grace said. Everyone laughed, including AJ.

"Yeah, what she said." Tag stretched her long legs.

"Good. I was trying for rough and hard on that first shot. Katie helped. Did it work?"

"Are you kidding?" The chief gave a little snort.

"He looked like he wanted to take a bite out of Grace." Tag grinned.

"That happens a lot." AJ lifted an eyebrow at Grace. "Still, think how he'll look at people every time he's in Niagara. Or anywhere. His eyes will be sore, but I still couldn't get him to talk about his missing daughter."

The barkeep brought a big tray of burgers and fries. AJ slathered mustard on her burger, and added onions. The door opened just as she took the first bite. Jock was suddenly in front of her, covered in soot and grime from the burned-out building. Bonnie stood behind him, equally dirty.

"What the hell, AJ?" he said. "Why didn't you tell me you had someone at Home Base?" He gripped the table and leaned toward her.

She swallowed her food. "You didn't ask."

He bent over her. "And someone's taking shots at you? You could have mentioned that. We should share," Jock said.

"Okay, get some food and eat with us. I'm buying. Tell me about the fire."

"Bonnie can fill you in." He gave Tag a cool look and left. The door slammed behind him.

"Bonnie, go order and put it on my bill," AJ said and got back to her burger before it was cold. Someone had plugged in the jukebox and Ella Fitzgerald began to sing. A shot of déjà vu ran through her as she thought about last winter and Jock. Or Michael, Elena, and Ariel in this room, all dead now. She fussed with the straw in her glass.

"I would have done the formal apology," Tag said, "but he was so angry."

"He's always angry, but you won't see much of him." She glanced at Tag. "He's very good at some things but hard to deal with personally."

"This business in Niagara is connected with Michael and the meth?"

"I don't know. This is the first we've heard about that, and I'm glad Clint Weeks doesn't know Michael's dead. If I were the bank I wouldn't say anything either. Michael's operation here wasn't anything compared to some places in this country, but his contacts were huge. They're still finding traces of him. Niagara might have been simply someone he was trying to develop." She drank the remainder of her iced tea.

Three Milwaukee cops were at the bar, noisy and laughing, giving Bonnie a hard time about her dirty clothes. She gave it right back to them.

The chief was watching Bonnie, and AJ said, "How's she doing?"

"She's ready, but I hate to lose her."

"She's a natural," Grace said. "AJ, you'll swear her in tomorrow."

"Oh darn. I forgot. What time?"

"One o'clock at the Federal Building." Grace checked her phone. "I sent you the information this morning, but you were busy being all those women and didn't catch it. Tomorrow's a combination of departments, including the police. You'll be up first so don't be late. Want to go, Tag?"

"I'd rather spend time at the office, catch up with my folks, and is it okay if I call Jay Yardly? I can do a little fact-finding about the area. By the way, you should know he's my personal lawyer."

AJ grabbed some fries before Grace got them all. "Will he help us?"

"He's family and a great lawyer. He'll help."

"Check anything you think will be useful. Skip tomorrow's formalities. You've already been through it." AJ stared out into the room. "You were right, Tag. Why was that information on Weeks's computer, not from the local police, and where is the video of the kids by the river that he said he gave to them? Chief, did the—"

The chief's phone beeped and he held up a finger, asking her to wait.

"I'm starving," Bonnie said as she sat at the table.

AJ made room for her. Bonnie was Katie's best friend since high school. They'd worked together at Katie's father's security business while they finished college.

Staring at her empty glass, AJ remembered last March. She and Bonnie had been injured when the Michael's Angels assignment went bad. Bonnie was a good person to have beside you in dangerous situations, as was Grace. She flicked a glance at Tag. Who knew until you were there, the moments that made your heart stop.

"Damned Jock. What an ass," Bonnie said, wiping her mouth with a napkin.

The chief put his phone away. "What'd he do this time?"

"Walked in all the wrong places, shot his mouth off, and irritated the entire arson squad." Bonnie munched on the fries. "Arson is like our CSIs, looking for clues. Jock threw things all over the place, moving the crime scene around. The man I know said he was sure it's arson, but they need lab work to prove it."

"No more bodies, I hope," AJ said.

"Not yet, but it really did go to the ground, so it's possible. It'll take them a while to get it cleared. They wouldn't tell us anything because Jock got in the way, demanding this and that. Charles should hear this from us."

"He will," AJ said. "After you eat, stop at the office and I'll get you prepped for the swearing-in tomorrow. Then you can go home, clean up, and get a good night's rest."

"AJ, they just sent me the security video from your doctor's office. Let's go look at it." Bill stood and tossed some money on the table for a tip.

"Girls, finish your food. Come over when you're done."

❖

The chief put the surveillance video on the big plasma screen in his office but didn't run it. Instead he put a hand on AJ's shoulder.

"I want a word. We can't have you out there with people taking shots at you. You wouldn't stand for it if it was someone in your group."

"I'm staying alert—" she began, but he shook his head.

"This is twice. Start taking someone with you. You can use one of my cops."

"Okay, I'll think about it. Maybe Bonnie after she's been sworn in tomorrow." She took a shaky breath, and they both were quiet for a moment. "Let's run the video." At first glance, AJ thought it was a biker guy but then saw it was only a young man. The video was grainy and blurred. All they could see of the bike was the top of the handlebars.

"Stop the video," she said. "That guy looks familiar."

"I agree, but damned if I can pin it down."

"Yeah." AJ heard the girls' voices. "Grace, come in here. Actually, all of you. Does this guy look familiar?"

"Maybe, but I don't know why." Grace moved closer. "Bad video."

"Ballistics says it's the same gun and forty caliber," the chief said.

"And he was a terrible shot or I wouldn't be here," AJ said. "Plus, where was the shooter? I didn't see anything in that parking lot." AJ shoved herself up from the chair, and pain ran up her arm. It was time for ibuprofen.

"Let's go, Bonnie. We'll review the ceremony for tomorrow. You two," she said to Tag and Grace, "give the chief a hand on the computers from that house we took down. The new Milwaukee task force is going to take the lead tomorrow or the next day, but he has to get them started." She started for the door but turned back. "All of you should know that I'm going to contact the FBI-DHS group and bring Peter Adams in as well. We need to integrate information, and I don't want to involve Lawrence Kelly." She and the chief shared a look.

AJ's office still smelled like burned wood from Bonnie's clothes, so she opened a window. She checked Greg's and Jeff's vehicles parked at the back while they were up north. Two men in T-shirts, jeans, and baseball caps walked across the parking lot toward the back entrance below her and she spotted a Confederate flag tattooed on the forearm of one of them. She stepped back so as not to be seen. *A Confederate flag?*

She checked her email for Tag's psych eval, but found nothing except an addendum to the ME's autopsy on the young victim, Kevin

Owens. His skin had been yellow because he'd died from an untreated liver infection. The lack of treatment had just hurried the process along. She sent an email to the chief to see if the older brother, John, had commented on this.

AJ looked at the task force file. When she'd returned from vacation and discovered her bureau chief had initiated a task force, she'd called Lawrence Kelly immediately. He'd explained it was a continuation of Michael's Angels because the information had come from Frog, but she'd felt it was a pissing contest between the FBI-DHS and the ATF.

Pete Adams at Justice confirmed the task force and seemed to think they'd be in Niagara up by the Michigan border, close to Crooked Lake where she and Katie had stayed. He proposed hiding her group in his uncle's delivery service up there, the area where he'd grown up. Also, he mentioned that the DHS had come in with the FBI because Canada had contacted them. They'd seen activity at the border north of Wisconsin and Michigan.

AJ went over that in her mind. Now that she knew Lawrence Kelly and Clint Weeks were friends, she understood why she had another task force on her hands and that Clint Weeks was trying to keep this out of the public eye. Well, that and Frog's money from the "cops"… or whatever they were. "Just plain politics," she muttered under her breath.

Her phone rang with a text from Katie and she smiled. Dinner tonight at Jimmy's downtown Asian restaurant felt perfect for a little downtime with her favorite person. She sent a confirming text to Katie just as she heard footsteps running in the hallway and people yelling about a fire.

"I don't believe this," Grace said as AJ stood beside her in the parking lot. Tag and two cops were working on Greg's and Jeff's SUVs with fire extinguishers. Sirens sounded in the distance.

"There were two guys walking toward the back door when I opened the windows. Get the surveillance, Grace. I'll call the dealership. They have three of our vehicles in storage."

Back in her office, AJ called for new vehicles and waded through the replacement form on her computer to justify everything. When she finished, she got up for the ibuprofen she'd forgotten.

"Crap," she said, holding the water. She had to call Charles about the meth lab in Niagara and Jock's behavior. Charles answered immediately. After, she stood and watched the tow trucks in the parking lot for a moment, then slid down the wall and sat on the floor.

"You okay?" Tag said from the doorway. She held out a plastic bag and folded down to the floor beside her.

"Just stretching my leg. We've never had anything like this fire." Tag held up the bag and AJ frowned. It looked like a dead snake.

"Check this out. It's a C-Strip, burn wires wrapped in a kind of cloth, and the only place I've seen it is Afghanistan. You push it down into tire treads, light the end for a slow burn, and in about fifteen minutes, the vehicle is engulfed in fire from the bottom up. Everyone uses them over there. Our side, their side, and the fire department said the same. I'm thinking whoever did this is ex-military. I found two of them in the rear tires of one of the SUVs and gave one to the fire department."

AJ examined the strip. "Could you use this on a house?"

"Never saw it used that way, but that doesn't mean it wouldn't work. Huh. You're thinking about that house that just burned, right?" Tag said, changing positions to sit cross-legged. "What are the chances these fires and your shootings are connected?"

AJ shrugged. "Who knows, but it feels a lot like a warning, doesn't it? Call Bonnie and have her contact her person at Arson about those things you found."

"Watch your six, AJ. Seriously," Tag said as Grace walked into the office.

"We've got the surveillance video. Why are you two on the floor?"

"Looking at something Tag found." AJ pointed at the bag. "She's going to call Bonnie, have her update Milwaukee Arson, and then let's work together on the computers from the house we took down." She shoved herself up from the floor. "Tag, I just had a thought. Work on the history of the house itself. When it was built and who built it. I see John Owens's grandfather owned it, but it doesn't look like the task force searched any further. If they did, it's not on the information link we're all using."

Grace and AJ watched the surveillance video in the chief's office but couldn't get a look at the faces, just approximate heights and body shapes.

"Hard way to learn that we need better cameras." The chief slapped his desk. "Look, only two angles and none of their faces."

Tag stepped into the office. "You have to see what I found. That house, the Owens house, has quite a history. John Owens's grandfather bought it after he came back from Vietnam and started the motorcycle business. Your local police pulled him in multiple times for suspected prostitution, gambling, and money laundering, but it appears nothing stuck. Looks like he retired, moved, and deeded everything to John, the grandson. John's father runs the La Crosse business. I sent it to you, Chief."

The chief brought it up on his computer and they all read over his shoulder.

"Is it possible—" Grace began.

"They've been in business a long time." The chief finished for her.

"Tag, good job. Send this to all of us. I'll take the grandfather and family," AJ said, starting to the door. "Grace, search the La Crosse Police and the business there, and, Tag, do the land and licenses, and all of that in both cities."

Hours later, AJ rubbed her eyes. The Owens grandfather had "retired" years ago, moved to La Crosse, and turned this house over to John Owens. She counted eleven attempts to arrest the older man, but nothing had stuck. She wondered what Grace would find in La Crosse and how his new business was doing.

Her phone rang and a cranky tech informed her that her shot-up personal car was ready at the crime lab. They needed the room and wanted her to pick it up today.

"Sure," she mumbled and hung up before he could go on. She stood and stretched, every muscle complaining. Even her leg was sore, and then she noticed the time.

"Oh hell." She had dinner plans with Katie and needed a ride with Tag and Grace.

CHAPTER EIGHT

AJ drove her personal car home from the crime lab with Grace and Tag following so they could drop her off at Jimmy's restaurant. There was more to be found on the Owens family, but what they'd seen had made their eyes pop, and they'd talked about it all the way down the road. They might have found a break for the task force on the X-Girl investigation.

AJ stood off to the side, searching the waiting restaurant crowd for Katie. She had a pretty good idea why they were having this dinner. The week had been crazy, almost as bad as when they'd met six months ago. She'd long ago stopped sleeping with a gun under her pillow, but the shootings had triggered nightmares and probably woken Katie.

Thank God Katie would be focused on her job at the bank, but the thought of her in their empty house was creepy, and—her breath hitched. The crowd parted and she saw her. Katie's daring wine-colored dress made her mouth go dry. She slid through the crowd until she was behind her and placed her hands on Katie's bare shoulders.

"Hi, love."

Katie put her hand over her heart but looked up with a smile. "I didn't see you."

AJ moved her chair close. "Can't keep my hands off you. Nice dress. Is it new?"

"For you."

"I like it a lot, and thanks for this. Have you ordered?"

"Just the tea. I waited for you to make a decision about the wine."

"I'm done for the day." AJ picked up the wine list. "The usual?"

"That'd be fine. How's the arm?"

"I took ibuprofen a few hours ago." AJ caressed her with another glance, heart speeding up. "Is tonight something special?"

"I only wanted to share a meal and celebrate the best summer of my life." Katie linked their fingers. "Our first summer."

"Thanks, but I know I haven't made it very easy." AJ fiddled with a spoon, touched by Katie's words. "Sorry I'm late. I had to drive my personal car home from the police lab. Grace and Tag gave me a ride here."

"Do I smell smoke?" Katie wrinkled her nose.

"Someone burned up two SUVs at the station today."

"Are you kidding me? Do you know—"

"We caught them on surveillance video but haven't identified them." AJ scooted closer. "You are so beautiful. You make my heart... eager." It always shocked her how much she loved her.

Katie gave her a warm look through her long lashes. "How did this morning go with the outfits and makeup?"

"Clumsy. I almost lost that first wig." AJ shook her head. "You'd have laughed."

"How did Bren Black take the whole thing?"

"Tag? She was stunned when I flew into that room. The chief and Grace tried not to laugh out loud." They both grinned as the waiter came to take their order.

For dessert, they shared fried apples in sweet sauce, and Katie mentioned Charles had called. "He wanted to know how you were, how we were, and if you saw the doctor like you were supposed to. He mentioned the shootings too."

"I talked to him today about the new assignment up north. He didn't say any of that to me. It was all business." AJ took another bite of the dessert and scanned the room. "Maybe he's worried about the shootings. The chief wants me to start taking someone with me so I'm not riding alone. I think I'll take Bonnie."

"He's right and you've been having nightmares again." She leveled a hard, straight look at AJ with a deep breath. "Remember the day you threw your boot in the garage and I was in the shower? I rushed to the door in a towel because I thought it was a gunshot."

"What? God, I never even thought—"

"Whatever this is, it's picking up speed and you know it."

"Okay, that cuts it. Unless we catch this person or persons before we go up north, Bonnie will stay at our house while I'm gone." One look at Katie's face and AJ knew she'd said the wrong thing.

"No. And don't give me an order. I won't even be home except to sleep."

They stared at each other.

"Katie, don't do this to me because I'll—"

"You'll what? It's not always about you."

AJ took a deep breath, placed her fork deliberately on the plate, and stood. "I should have waited to bring that up." She picked up the bill and left to pay.

"Wait," Katie said.

AJ heard her but kept walking, determined to discuss this in a less public place. After she paid, she saw Katie leaving through the side entry for her car and scanned the parking lot through the glass doors. Two men in baseball caps, white T-shirts, and jeans leaned against a pickup and turned to look at Katie, saying something to each other. A warning brushed through AJ, and she moved toward the exit.

A twentysomething guy with a square jaw and shaggy blond hair held the door open. He looked surprised to see her, but he walked away as Katie drove up and stopped. She was watching him too.

"Do you know that blond kid?" Katie said when AJ got into the car.

"Go around. Let's look at him. I thought he looked high...or maybe drunk."

Katie took the circular drive behind the restaurant and pointed at the kid about to get on a motorcycle. "Does he look familiar?" she said.

"Yeah, there's something familiar about him, but look at that gorgeous, customized Harley."

"He handed one of his takeout bags to the two men with the pickup parked next to his bike before they left," Katie said and drove onto the busy city street.

AJ heard the motorcycle right behind them, and a sudden noise like fingernails on a blackboard. He gunned the bike, flipping them off as he passed.

"Damn," Katie yelled. "He just keyed my car."

"Katie, no," AJ said. She was thrown against the door as the SUV shot forward, but Katie was focused on the bike. A city cop cut the motorcycle off with full sirens and lights. She screeched to a stop.

"Ha," she said triumphantly, unsnapping her seat belt.

AJ leaned across her and held the door closed. "Uh-huh. Nice job, Speed Racer, but stay right here." She was out of the car before Katie could argue. Apparently, the police had seen it all, and they were gathered in a little knot around the bike. The blond kid argued, pushed one of the cops, and there was a quick scuffle. He ended up in the back of the squad car. A cop and AJ walked back to look at Katie's damage.

"I'm driving the bike to the cop shop. Follow us and fill out a report there." AJ kept her voice firm, holding Katie's gaze through the open window.

"I know how it's done," Katie snapped, starting the engine.

They didn't talk all the way home from the police station. AJ wiped her sweaty hands on her jeans and felt her headache trying to return. God. Katie could have been hurt. If the cops hadn't been there she would have confronted that little smart-ass without a second thought. As they turned into their driveway, AJ started to ask if she had the papers on the biker guy but saw tears glittering in Katie's eyes and swallowed her words.

"If you hadn't been there, I'd have done the same thing." Katie parked, and turned to her.

"I know and that scares me. I'm going to be gone and—"

"And what? You can't be with me every minute."

Sudden headlights behind them reflected across Katie's hurt face. Grace and Tag got out of their vehicle, both in T-shirts and shorts.

"Got something from Jimmy's for you," Grace called out.

"How'd you know about what happened tonight?"

"They notified the chief when Katie pressed charges. He called us and added resisting arrest to keep the kid overnight. We went to the restaurant, and Jimmy gave me their security videos." She handed her a flash drive.

"Jimmy would probably give you the whole restaurant. Come in. I'll make some coffee."

Tag had walked in with Katie and stood in the living room, pointing down the hallway. "She said she needed to change clothes. That dress was impressive."

AJ nodded and put the coffee together. She'd loved the dress too and had wanted to come home and take it off her.

Katie emerged barefoot, wearing white cotton drawstring pants and a pink tank top. She took AJ's hand as she went by, adding a light squeeze. Relieved, AJ sat next to her at the big kitchen table while Tag and Grace argued good-naturedly how to run the video on AJ's laptop. Katie studied the screen. Suddenly, she pointed at the monitor. "There. See? I thought he was going to talk to you, AJ."

Tag backed up the video and enhanced the figure. "It's that guy again."

"I agree," Grace echoed.

"What guy?" Katie said.

"We saw him on the crap security video from the doctor's office. Or at least someone who resembles him," AJ said. "Did you get paperwork on him at the police station? A name or address?"

Katie handed the papers to AJ.

"You won't believe this," AJ said, reading the information. "He's Robert Owens. Look at this address. It's the house we took down." She shoved the papers to Grace and Tag. "Worse, I thought he was high." Her phone rang just as she reached for it. It was the chief. He had just seen the name and address and was getting a warrant to go back into the house. In all of their research today none of them had encountered another man named Owens.

"Do you want us to work on that first thing in the morning or do it now?" Grace stood. "Also, the chief gave all our information to the Milwaukee task force and they'll start proceedings tomorrow against John Owens."

AJ shook her head. "No, don't do it tonight. Robert Owens will spend the night in lockup. Do what you can in the morning." She closed the door behind Tag and Grace, set the home security, and reran the video. Katie put cups in the dishwasher and readied the coffeepot for morning.

"If this is the shooter, we don't have to worry about Bonnie staying here."

Katie kissed the top of AJ's hair. "Let's call it a night," she said and tugged her toward the bedroom. AJ tossed her jeans in the hamper while Katie was in the bathroom and sank down on the side of the bed. Katie came in and stood at the closet, studying her business clothes.

"Aren't you going to bed?" Katie said. Their eyes met in the mirror.

"Not until I apologize for tonight." AJ began unbuttoning her shirt. Katie finished the buttons. "I thought it was this." She traced the bandage on AJ's arm.

"You scared me tonight. I never want to see you hurt, and—"

Suddenly, Katie was on top of her, holding her down on the bed, her mouth a kiss away. "Do you have any idea how much I love you? I never want to see *you* hurt either." She sat up. "I'd planned another ending to this evening." She pulled the covers down and got in bed.

AJ scrambled up to the pillows beside Katie and claimed the kiss she'd missed. She'd wanted more too and inhaled Katie's familiar fresh scent.

"You're tired. I'm tired. Let's talk in the morning." Katie snuggled against her.

AJ held her until Katie drifted off, and then she stared at the ceiling, unable to sleep. She remembered Katie mentioning the men and the pickup next to Robert Owens's motorcycle. Was there a chance in hell they were the same two men she'd seen in the police station parking lot this afternoon? She couldn't remember much about them other than the Confederate flag tattoo on the one guy and what she'd seen on the surveillance video.

She eased out of bed and went to their office, searching the computer for tonight's charges. Nothing yet. She searched the information and photos from the summer case. The biker kid certainly resembled John and Kevin Owens. The Milwaukee group had enough to nail John Owens, but who the hell was *Robert* Owens? Or had she missed it when she looked at the family?

She shut the computer down and walked out onto the deck. None of this would have gotten past her last spring. Where the hell was her normal alertness? Something had dulled her normally sharp edges. And what was all this *snapping* at Katie about?

She looked at the moon's silky shadows on the yard and turned back, scanning the house with a new thought. This had become *home*, just what Tag had said last night. For the first time since she'd left her parents' farm, she'd settled. It was everything from throwing her keys on the counter when she came home to knowing where the towels were. She ran on automatic here. AJ looked back at the yard again, the flowers and shrubs she'd planted. Katie was right. This had been a very special summer.

And as much as she loved working undercover and as worried as she was about Frog, she didn't want to leave the house or Katie.

When she slipped back into bed, Katie woke up, her gray eyes sleepy and smoky in the moonlight. "Can't sleep?"

AJ pulled her close, thankful to hold her. "Let's have breakfast here in the morning."

"You're cooking?" Katie murmured with a smile in her voice. "That'll be fun."

AJ buried her face in Katie's hair and bit back a tease. Not fair. She'd worked on her breakfast skills all summer long. She now knew her way around an egg.

Chapter Nine

Tag drove them home from Katie and AJ's while Grace entered notes on her tablet. She glanced at the dim lights shining on Grace next to her but looked away, concentrating on the road. She had to stop this glancing stuff.

"AJ's right," Tag said. "Jimmy's eyes actually dilate when you're close."

Grace rolled her eyes and shook her head.

"Does that happen often?" Tag asked.

"What?"

"Men's eyes dilating around you?"

"Who has time for that? And why are you driving so slow?" Frowning, Grace stared out at the highway.

"Because it's been years since I've driven in traffic like this, not to mention this vehicle. I mean, look at all the stuff you've got." She pointed at the electronics on the dash.

"Never even thought of that. AJ says it's a huge adjustment to come back to the States, especially when you've been gone as long as you have."

"She's not kidding. I feel like everything's new. I was in Afghanistan four years and came home. When I got back they formed the Dragons, so it's been six years since I've been here." She changed the conversation. "AJ said that scene at the restaurant was dicey and she came down hard on Katie."

"Those two have to be true love. It was a battle from the beginning last winter. Neither of them gave an inch, and I teased AJ every chance I got. Still, I've never witnessed what they have. It's truly special." Grace stared at the road again. "Finding a new Owens guy is weird." She shook her head. "The new task force is off, too. Everything has that odd little shimmer like last winter and spring. Were you ever in a situation that began to *feel* bad, then things happened and it really *was* bad?"

"Yeah. That happened to me in the field."

"Exactly, and we have to be up north soon." Grace closed the tablet, and Tag could feel her eyes on her. "I've never seen combat and it looks like you did, a lot."

"Yes, and I have some scars, but I'm okay." She could still feel Grace watching her. "I'm fine," she said defensively. "You've seen my psych evaluation."

"No, I haven't because we don't have it."

"That's wrong. It's usually automatic."

"It'll be here eventually." Grace shrugged. "But why *did* you leave? It looked as if you were about to be promoted. You were a captain?"

"My tour was up in June and I was up for a promotion, but something happened." Tag parked the car, but Grace didn't move and just looked at her expectantly.

"My best friends on base were doctors, a man and woman. They'd done time with Doctors Without Borders before they joined the army, and a lot of us helped them save abandoned women and children." Tag shifted to face Grace. "We had a building off base where we'd bring victims for clothes, water and food, medical stuff, that kind of thing. Last May, we got a truckload and brought them back to the doctors in the middle of the night. Everything was fine when I left, but the next morning someone had killed them all, including my friends. Cut them all up. The place reeked of blood…and other things."

"Did you ever find out who did it?"

"Oh sure. The usual terrorists. The children were the worst, but my friends…" Her voice trailed away. "That was the day I was done with Afghanistan."

"God," Grace said over a deep breath and got out of the car.

Tag followed and heard the dishwasher begin. They had been cleaning up from dinner when the chief called. They had dropped everything and left.

She went on to her bedroom and dropped her bag on the desk. Where was her psych eval? And of all the things she could have said, why in the hell had she told Grace that story? Shadows of that moment always lurked inside her. She'd walked outside and thrown up. The doctors had said it would go away. It hadn't. And why had she told Grace?

She stood for a moment, searching her mind. Well, it was the truth, and something about Grace demanded that piece of her. Actually, *something about Grace* made her want to talk, period. If they'd sat in the car any longer who knows what else she'd have said? AJ was right. Grace was quiet and a straight shooter and smart, all of those things, but that *quiet* somehow rewired her. For the first time in a long time, she *wanted* a conversation, but she'd have to be careful, considering what she was carrying around. AJ would have to hear that first.

With a calming breath, she looked at the room, examining it for the first time. The light on the desk was soft and inviting against the warm rose color of the walls. All the furniture was wood, even the desk, with lots of old gold and burgundy accents. It was comfortable and she'd slept deeply here. She caught the light scent of furniture polish and bent over the small desk, tracing the scrollwork at the edges.

There was a wall of books. She took time to see what Grace read. There was some pretty good fiction and poetry but also psychology, behavioral science, and what? *Survival?* She scanned those books further. A book at the end of the row caught her. *The Last Unicorn.* She pulled it off the shelf and took it with her to the kitchen.

Grace was standing in front of the refrigerator with the door open.

"Hungry?" Tag said.

"Nope. Are you up for watching the end of the movie we started last night? It's either that or I go to bed, stare at the ceiling, and worry about that kid in jail or who burned up the cars today." They'd watched the first part of Spielberg's *Lincoln* last night but had been too tired to finish it. "Want a beer?"

"That'd be great." Tag did want to finish the video. She loved history. "I've been meaning to mention that bedroom back there. It's the most comfortable room I've slept in for a long time. On base or in the military, everything's metal...well, except for the mattress, and sometimes it felt that way too."

Grace smiled and handed her the beer. "I hit estate sales when we found out we were assigned to Milwaukee for another year. Katie and I were redoing AJ's office so I grabbed some things and redid that room. Glad you like it."

"And how did you happen to have this book?" Tag held up *The Last Unicorn* so Grace could see it. "I used to carry it with me to relax my mind."

Grace froze, staring at the book. "Where did you find that?" she said.

"Behind a row of books." Tag handed it to her. Something, a piece of paper, fell out, and she picked it up. It was a photo of a young Grace. The person taking the photo had caught her looking kind of afraid, as if she hadn't expected someone to take a picture. Tag handed it to Grace.

"I'm sorry." Tag fumbled her words and felt like she had somehow pried into a place she shouldn't have been. "You were young. Twelve... thirteen?"

Grace held the picture as if she were searching the years. "Probably." She tucked the photo back into the book. "I thought I'd lost this. You've read it?"

"My mother gave it to me and I read it to pieces. Loved it. She loves magic and hope, and so do I." She settled back into the couch. "Are you from Wisconsin?"

"No. Arizona, but I spent a lot of time on my grandparents' farm and horse ranch in southern Illinois." She sat beside Tag, still staring at the book in her hands. "I wouldn't mind living on a ranch after I retire or whatever happens to me. I work with horses every chance I can. There's a ranch here where I go when I have time. I bought a horse this summer, and I love being out there with her."

"I can ride but don't know much about horses. I agree, when all of this is over, I'd like to teach history and live in the country somewhere. AJ said she'd always wanted to open a law office and live on a farm." Tag took a long drink. "And we talked about her Presidential Commendation last night."

"That's odd." Grace looked up. "She never talks about that. It's been a strange last few months for her. I'm glad you're here with your experience. It's good for her. Actually, she didn't want the lead here and told Lawrence Kelly as much." Grace rested her gorgeous long legs on the coffee table in front of them. "Maybe we should all buy farms and ranches up north, together. Why didn't you do that when you left the military? Come back here and teach?"

Tag swallowed and looked away. "I guess I just wasn't ready to stop trying to make a difference." Her mind swirled as she tried to figure out where to go next. "How did you meet AJ? I mean, were you assigned to her unit or…?"

Grace shook her head with a little laugh. "The second year I was in Cyber Crime we screwed up an assignment for the task force Charles Ryan was running. They sent some of us down there to see what we could do to fix it. AJ and Charles were regrouping after the misinformation we'd given them. It was a mess."

"So was it bad?" Tag grinned.

"Oh yeah. Luckily, no one died, but it cost a lot, and I mean a lot, of time and they weren't very happy with us. Some of the people they were after had gotten away over the border, not to mention lost informants, all the kind of things you rely on in the drug trade. They started over in northern New Mexico. The rest of my group went home, but I stayed because of AJ. She wanted to know more about computers and asked if I could go with them, showing her how to access certain things along the way. So much of this is out there if you know how to find it."

"I've never chased drugs, Grace."

Grace studied her. "I've seen you work. I'll show you the nuances, especially social media, but I think you already know."

"I'd like that, but back to AJ. What's the rest of the story?"

"She was so alive. Your first day here, you said she was *striking*, and I think I felt that too, as well as smart and tough. And you should see her train a group. Not just shooting or other skill sets but how to follow someone without them knowing you were there, and I'd never seen anyone use martial arts. She'd see me hanging around, watching them. Finally, she included me, and I was, um, honored I guess. She always told me that it was my sense of humor." Grace frowned. "I wasn't aware that I had one. I don't know. Maybe she just showed me how to be…me. Anyway, that was years ago. It's been a learning curve for me. Still is." With the book still clutched against her stomach, she gave Tag a tired smile, picked up the remote, and began the movie.

Tag stole another glance at Grace's incredible body. She certainly liked that, but there were other things that intrigued her as well. Grace was totally unaware of herself. She had a sort of odd innocence that fascinated her. She wondered about the book Grace still gripped. It certainly had upset her, or maybe it was the photo?

She'd grown used to checking everything in Afghanistan, mind and eyes constantly reviewing. It wore her out. She'd hoped to leave that behind when she came home, but it hadn't happened yet.

The night breeze moved the curtains, and she took a deep breath. The air was fresh and light, unlike the dusty, heavy smell of the base in Afghanistan. She watched the actor playing Lincoln and began to get involved in the story. Lincoln must have felt the weight of constant vigilance too.

Chapter Ten

The next morning, AJ realized that she had to swear Bonnie in today and she'd forgotten to tell Katie. At that moment, the back doorbell rang and she went to answer. Katie yelled from the deck, "Who is it?"

"It's your wonderful, loving mother," the older version of Katie answered. Liz Blackburn stepped into the kitchen.

"AJ? It's not often I see you home in the middle of the week," she said.

"We had a little dustup after dinner at a restaurant last night."

"Here's your shirt." Liz handed AJ a plastic bag. "Not another shooting?"

"No," AJ said. She checked the blue denim shirt. "Thank you. You are remarkable, Liz." She hugged her.

"I loved the challenge. Now what's this about?"

"Katie can tell you."

"I'll deal with my daughter. Have more clothing that needs work?" Her eyes sparkled with humor. "Tell me she's not on crutches."

"No one was injured." AJ took a deep breath.

"Hi, Mom. What's up?" Katie walked into the kitchen.

"I brought AJ's shirt back." Liz gave Katie a quick appraisal.

AJ recognized that look. She'd seen it from her own mother more than once. The same slightly tense posture and narrowed eyes.

"Today is Bonnie's swearing in at one o'clock at the Federal Building. Would either of you like to be there?"

"Darn, I can't. I have a meeting. Want some coffee, Mom?"

"I'll take tea, but I have an appointment. I have a card at home that

I'll send to Bonnie." Liz still measured Katie with those mother's eyes, and then turned to AJ. "You need to get ready, don't you? I'll make my own tea after you two tell me what happened last night."

Katie began the story, the young man at Jimmy's and the arrest. "They think the man that keyed my car is connected with the work they've done this summer."

"I see." Liz turned to AJ. "I'll stay with Katie while you're gone, if needed."

"Um..." AJ shot a hopeful look at Katie, who was filling the teakettle at the sink.

"No, and we've had this conversation." Katie raised her chin with a little warning at AJ. "I don't think I'm in danger at this house, but you should know that someone burned two of AJ's vehicles yesterday at the police station."

Liz frowned. "I don't see the connection."

"Me either," AJ said. "There was another fire in town at one of our places the day before that. I don't know if there's a connection between the fires and the shootings, but we're working on it."

Liz held up both hands and shook her head. "AJ, go do whatever it is you have to do."

AJ smiled all the way to their bedroom. Liz and Katie were so alike. They took charge in a nanosecond. She went through the closet and chose a white silk tee with a summer-weight dark gray suit and left for the bathroom. It had been a good breakfast with much laughter over the omelets, which had tasted just fine, thank you very much.

❖

After the ceremony, AJ sent Bonnie off to celebrate and Grace to the office to pick up Tag. She wanted them to scout the house they'd taken down to see if there was a trace of the other Owens brother, then do a drive-by of the businesses they'd found connected to John Owens's operation.

Taking time to thank everyone, she slipped away from the crowd. It was time to let the Milwaukee operation go and concentrate on her new task force, and she decided to begin a serious research of the northern Wisconsin area at the office. She opened the Federal Building doors just as someone called her name, and Peter Adams from Justice caught up with her.

"Do you have time to meet the FBI-DHS coordinator now?" His tan suit and red tie were immaculate against a lightly checked pink shirt. Pete's red hair was trimmed neatly and his pleasant face was clean-shaven.

AJ turned back and walked to the elevators with Pete. The FBI coordinator hadn't returned her call, and she'd assumed she was in trouble over her attempt to contact her. Actually, she'd expected another blast from her own bureau chief.

"There's new information," he said and keyed in his security code.

Margaret "Maddie" Hershey sat across from AJ in Pete's office. Attractive and a few years older than AJ, she wore an expensive white suit and sleek matching heels and gave AJ a warm smile. The office smelled like fresh coffee.

"I was at the back of the room when you presented your case to include Chief Whiteaker's special investigations unit into your task force," Maddie said as she opened the tablet in front of her. "Nice job."

"Thanks." AJ took the coffee from Pete. "My biggest fear is that we'll duplicate your work up north or ruin a thread you're following. I believe we'd be more effective here."

Maddie looked up. "That's so refreshing to hear in this building." She hit several keys and swiveled the tablet so AJ could see the screen. "Clint Weeks. This is my report on his request. Here's his email to me, late last June."

Pete read over AJ's shoulder. "I'll be damned."

"This is why I was at your meeting," Maddie said. "I turned him down, and I'm pretty sure he immediately went to his good friend, your bureau chief, Lawrence Kelly. I don't know why you have a task force—Kelly and I don't talk—but I do have an idea that might benefit both of us. How soon are you going up north?"

"Soon, and I'm for anything that makes more sense than this." AJ held Maddie's gaze. "This whole thing feels off. I could see an assignment or even working with your group, but an entire task force?"

"We did follow up on Clint Weeks's information, although he'll never know," Maddie continued. "Peter, I apologize, but circumstances…" Her voice trailed off and she glanced at him. "We actually believe something *is* going on there. Our people are a little farther south and west, but there's increasing chatter north of Green Bay. I have a rookie agent in Park Falls and he's good. Would you be willing to include him on your team? He's familiar with our setup."

"Let me have a look at him and I'll share what we have so far, but it isn't much." AJ turned to Pete. "Or have you already given her our information?"

"You owe me one." Pete grinned at Maddie before he turned to AJ. "No, I haven't discussed our plan. Also, be aware that Maddie's worked with Charles Ryan."

A bunch of things fell into place for AJ. "If you know Charles then you know I already have a rookie on my team. Tag Beckett."

"Yes, and I know Tag. I did my only tour over there with her years ago, about the first time she was promoted." She glanced at her watch. "My agent's name is Sam Mullins. When I get back to my office, I'll send you his file. How about lunch tomorrow? I'll pick you up at your office at noon. There's a place you need to see, but let's eat first." Then she was gone, the sound of her heels on the marble floors fading.

AJ didn't move for a moment. "Wow," she said. "That was quick. My God, what energy."

"We call her Lightning." He grinned. "Behind her back."

"What's up with her and Lawrence Harvey?"

"When you gave your statement to the police over Ariel's murder last spring, Maddie was with Charles Ryan and Lawrence Kelly in the hallway, waiting for you. At any rate, Kelly gave Maddie a real dressing-down over Clint Weeks's missing daughter and pretty much trashed the FBI's trafficking task force in front of a whole bunch of people. It was a mess, but she didn't flinch, something I really admire about her."

AJ shook her head. "Sometimes Kelly has all the finesse of a rock." She got up, ready to go. "Do you want to meet with us tomorrow?"

Half-standing, Pete said, "No," and sank back into his chair. "Everyone else here knows, so you should too. She's my ex-wife."

❖

Tag placed her phone on her office desk and rubbed her ear, which was sore after all the minutes on the phone. She'd talked to her parents for a long time and finally called Jay Yardly for another lengthy conversation.

Jay's mother was her aunt, her father's sister. She'd married an architect with a thriving business in Toronto, and they wanted Tag's parents to retire on a farm they owned up there. Her folks were considering the move and wanted Tag's opinion. Wisconsin was an increasingly bad place for the Menominee. Most of the young people had already left. Maybe it was time for the older people to get away from the current governor's mess. They talked to each other often during crisis moments, and she felt lucky to have this connection with them.

Last spring, sick at heart after the murder of her friends in Afghanistan, she'd spoken to them and discussed leaving the military. The next week her Intelligence team had stumbled across the information she'd brought home, and that had finalized Tag's decision to leave the military.

Her phone rang. It was Grace, on her way. AJ wanted them to look at the Owens house they'd taken down plus some of the businesses connected to that place. They'd worked on Robert Owens early this morning before Grace had to leave and forwarded all the information to the chief. Thinking about what was ahead of them, she began to clear her desk.

Trafficking was so common in the Mideast that Tag had thought this would be a continuation of what she'd watched for so many years. Much to her surprise, it was highly organized and hard to detect here, hidden behind storefronts, in quiet neighborhoods and in the dark computer sites Grace had picked through this morning. They both knew they'd only scratched the surface, and the new task force would have to pick up where they'd left off.

Chapter Eleven

Grace parked in front of the Owens house, and Tag laughed at the old beater ahead of them on the street. "That car looks worse than AJ's." The man in the car adjusted his rearview mirror and checked them out.

"He knows we're here. The chief posted a car last night." Grace changed out of her heels into running shoes and pointed at the alley and clock tower. "That's where the young boy, Kevin Owens, died, running from this house," she said as she got out of the car.

Tag followed. *Beautiful house and neighborhood.* The hedge wrapped the lawn, and colorful flowers smelled spicy and earthy. She touched the soft grass with a smile and caught up with Grace, who was talking on her phone.

"AJ? The garage door is open at the house and the crime scene tape is down. Is the warrant good for this?" She was quiet, listening. "Okay. We'll check it out."

Tag started to move but froze at a distant sound, anxiously searching the sky. Ice ran through every nerve in her body. At that moment the local news helicopter passed over them and they both watched it. She startled when Grace touched her shoulder.

"What's wrong?" Grace said with a puzzled expression.

"That damned sound...always stops me."

Her face still concerned, Grace turned toward the house. "Come on. Let's see if the door's open."

The back door was unlocked, and they stepped into a large kitchen.

Tag looked past Grace and saw two sleeping bags on the living room floor. Two military duffel bags leaned against the wall beside a pair of military-issued boots. Newspapers were stacked neatly, and a closed laptop sat on a box.

"Someone's been here and picked the house up. We left it in a mess," Grace said.

Tag moved around Grace. A room to their right had obviously been an office. Cords and plugs lay everywhere, but any computer or electronics had been confiscated by the police. There were three bedrooms down the hall, bare but for dirty mattresses on the floor. The house was quiet with a few dust motes floating in the sunlight.

"Seven rooms down here," Grace said. "Let's go upstairs."

They found a long hallway at the top of the stairs, four rooms on each side, with more bare mattresses and another bathroom. There wasn't a mattress in the first room. Just another military sleeping bag. Tag opened the closet. Men's shirts and pants hung neatly inside, including a set of fatigues with "Owens" printed on the standard white tag. The single bathroom was amazingly clean. Shaving equipment neatly lined the sinks. No feminine products she noticed.

"Someone named Owens bunked in that first room, obviously in the military. There are fatigues in the closet, and look at this. The bathroom's been cleaned."

"Those mattresses are victims' bedrooms," Grace said. "This was cluttered and dirty when we were here."

There was a sharp noise downstairs, and they took stairs two at a time, running through the living room, garage, and to the yard, but they found nothing. "This is crazy," Grace said. They retraced their steps, took videos, and closed the doors behind them.

Tag studied the cement garage floor. "Fresh oil spots and tire marks. Something's been parked here recently, and those are motorcycle tracks over there." She looked back at the door. "What did you hear?"

"It sounded like a door slamming." Grace holstered her weapon, turning in a slow circle. "There is no way John Owens would have lived in this house. It's beneath him. Let's check with the chief's man on the street and see if he saw anything. We have to drive by some of the businesses we've connected to this house and then catch up with AJ at the police station."

❖

The chief called AJ as she left the Federal Building. She changed directions and then drove downtown to the police holding area. She parked and checked the area. The last thing she wanted was another shooting or car burning.

The chief handed her papers when she walked into the observation room. "Just talked to the Niagara Police. They have the ephedrine we saw on Jay Yardly's video, but nothing from Clint Weeks. They didn't have a clue what I was talking about."

AJ scanned the papers he'd given her and began to go through the suspect's wallet as Grace and Tag entered the room. "What'd you find at the house?"

"It looks like at least two, maybe three, people there, but let me tell you, John Owens would not have lived in that house. Not his style. Then, when we were upstairs, we thought we heard a door close downstairs. Chief, your guy saw an adult female running from the back of the house and caught them on video. The surveillance is a good idea. We drove by some of the businesses we've connected to the house and videoed that too. I sent you the tape since we're not officially on this anymore."

AJ pointed at the suspect in the box on the other side of the window and continued through Owens's wallet. "As you verified this morning, that's another Owens brother, Robert, three months out of the army. Our victim, Kevin, apparently had two older brothers, both of them in jail at the moment. Look at this receipt. It gives his address as that house, but his driver's license says La Crosse. Here's his army ID, Tag. Think you can get some information out of him and calm him down? All he'll say is name, rank, number, and honorably discharged."

"What about my clothes?" Tag gestured at her faded jeans, worn boots, and army T-shirt.

"He won't even notice. Remember how it is when you come home? Like everyone speaks a different language?"

Inside the box, Tag put her hand on Robert's shoulder and asked about his service in Afghanistan.

"Yes, ma'am," he said and straightened. "I served in Kabul for two years."

AJ saw that Tag had done this before. They said a few more words, and Tag offered soda or coffee. He nodded and she got up.

"Do we have coffee?" Tag leaned into the room. "Anyone want to go in with me?"

AJ shook her head. Every time she looked at Robert Owens she thought of Katie last night. "Grace, you go in."

When they began to talk to the suspect AJ realized it had been a good decision. Grace's easy smile complemented Tag's firm words.

Owens's eyes shifted back and forth, and his body moved constantly. He said he was here to find work, his words spilling out too fast. AJ straightened. If she'd been on the street she'd have thought he was on drugs.

"Look at his teeth and skin." She turned to the chief. "Did we get a blood sample from him for drugs?"

"We should have the results soon. I want to know about the motorcycle," the chief said and went in, taking a seat. "That's a beautiful bike you have, Robert."

"My brother John has worked on that for years. You people better take good care of it because he'll kill me if anything happens to it."

"We don't want anything to happen to that bike or you," the chief said.

"How long are you going to keep me?" Owens scraped his chair back with an obvious look at the chief's uniform, then turned to Grace. "Why are you here? He's police and I understand about the lady last night, but what's this about? You're ATF?"

"We're assisting Chief Whiteaker," Grace said. "Was the victim, Kevin Owens, a relative?"

"My little brother." He shoved forward, defensive. "Granddad gave me permission to stay at that house until I find a job. My older brother, John, owns the place, but look what he did." He made a disgusted sound. "Some kind of sex thing, and now he's in jail and Kevin's dead." He cleared his throat. "He was the coolest little kid. I taught him how to swim, and we played baseball when he got older." His voice wavered a little.

"We were with Kevin in the alley," Grace said gently. "The autopsy said he was sick, but apparently it was untreated."

His eyes skittered away from her. "I don't know anything about that. Don't I get a lawyer?"

"We haven't charged you." The chief stood. "Who is at the house with you?"

"A couple of army buddies, just passing through."

Tag smiled at him and leaned back in her chair. "This is like the army. Hurry up and wait. Let's have more coffee. Maybe we can help."

Grace followed the chief back into observation and they watched Tag string the kid along.

"Look at him. The color and marks on the skin aren't acne, and you know what, Chief? You now have a witness to what went on in the house. The only charges *we* have are the damage to Katie's car and resisting arrest, but now you can use him against his brother about the kids. If it's drugs, let's turn him over to Jock. He'd salivate over this guy, and that would free us up." AJ shot him a grim look.

"You're right, and I see where you're going with Jock. I'll call Charles."

AJ mulled that over in her mind. If Owens had shot at her, how had he missed the first time and done so little damage the second? It could be that the people who'd paid Frog had paid him. She stared at the man, trying to make sense out of him. Why had he keyed Katie's car?

Owens's body was still in constant motion. "I have a handgun, a Glock .22, at the house, but only for protection."

AJ frowned at the mention of the gun. No way was he the shooter. He was too strung out and looked like he'd been that way quite a while.

A minute later, Tag came inside. "How could this kid miss, even with a pistol? I know what he did over there. Those guys don't miss, and what the hell's wrong with him?"

"Did you notice his face? He's only twenty-four but looks a lot older."

"Yeah, and that's some acne he's dealing with. His teeth need work too."

"Good street lesson here, Tag. I'd bet meth. I agree about the gun. He's not the shooter."

"AJ," Jock said, walking into the room. "Got something for me?"

She handed him the paperwork and indicated Owens with her chin. "That's the brother of the victim, the kid in the alley, from the trafficking house that the chief took down."

He looked up quickly. "This guy's your shooter?"

"I don't think so, but he just said he has a Glock .22 at that house. Have ballistics check it. Tag and Grace did a quick run-through of that house but didn't run find a gun. He's staying there. His brother, the primary suspect, owns the place."

Jock watched young Owens. "He's on something, isn't he? Charles said you did a lab test." He looked at the chief. "How do you want to handle this?"

"We haven't said anything about the shootings or drugs. We waited for you," AJ said, glancing at Tag behind them. Jock had ignored her.

"And I have his brother John locked up. The Milwaukee task force will go after him," the chief added.

Jock blew out a breath and rubbed his short hair. "This guy keyed Katie's car last night? That was stupid, but it also means he has her name." He turned back to AJ. "Why don't I take it from here? I'll let you know what I find."

"There's a laptop in the living room at that house," Tag added from behind, but Jock never acknowledged her words.

AJ could see the wheels turning, exactly what she'd hoped for. "Jock, this is me, sharing, and the chief has Grace's video from that house. Both the garage and back door were open and the crime scene tape was down. They thought someone was in the house while they were there, and the chief's guy has video of an adult female running from the house."

Jock jammed the papers in his back pocket. "You have people there, Chief?"

"Just one guy hanging out in a car on the street."

"Why don't you two work out something. We'll be out of town for a while, but Bonnie and the chief will be here," AJ said.

Jock entered the interrogation room, introduced himself, and placed his badge on the table. Robert Owens surveyed the mountain of a man in front of him and muttered something under his breath. AJ was sure Owens was tweaking.

"Wait." AJ stopped Tag and Grace as they started to leave. "Margaret Hershey, the FBI-DHS coordinator, is picking me up for lunch tomorrow, and I'd like you to meet her. She might have another member for our team, so watch for her email. The agent's name is Sam Mullins."

"Margaret Hershey?" Tag turned, hand on the door. "Maddie, right? She did a tour, didn't like it, and went home. Got married."

"She said she knew you," AJ said. "Get Bonnie home safely. Good job today."

The chief and AJ turned back to the window and watched Jock intimidate young Owens for a bit longer. "What about those guys in our parking lot at work?"

"We're still working on it."

"I could swear they were at Jimmy's last night beside an old pickup. Katie said Robert Owens handed them some takeout. I couldn't see their faces, but same body type and height." He nodded. "Watch over Jock for me, will you? Owens has Katie's name, and even though I don't think he's the shooter—"

The chief held up his hand, but AJ pushed on.

"This is different from the mess with Michael." She took a big breath. "And this task force up north feels wrong. You know it does."

"Trust Bonnie and me. I'll walk you to your car." The chief steered her out of the room. "John Owens is in Interrogation, two doors down with the Milwaukee task force. I don't want you in there. He'll know you from the meet you had with him in the gym. Tell me what Margaret Hershey had to say."

Both searched the area and her vehicle again as they walked through the parking lot and talked about working with the FBI in northern Wisconsin. She also mentioned Maddie's comment about "Clint Weeks and his good friend, Lawrence Kelly." The chief laughed when she said they called her Lightning.

"You know about Pete and Margaret?" he said at their vehicles.

"That was surprising, but the energy crackles around her, like… lightning." They both grinned. "How did you know?"

"I'm there so often that sometimes I forget I'm Milwaukee Police. It's one big rumor mill and a fight to see who can get what." He unlocked his vehicle. "Where are you headed?"

"Home to change clothes. If it wasn't for Frog, I'd fight this task force. My worst fear is that someone paid her to go up there to make sure we cooperated. The meeting with Maddie Hershey tomorrow may change everything."

"If I know Maddie, count on it," the chief said.

CHAPTER TWELVE

Sweat trickled down Tag's back as they stood inside Smokey's Bar. With both hands protectively on Grace's hips, she steered her through the wall of music, voices, and packed bodies.

"God, it's a steam bath and I don't see her—"

"There, arm wrestling with a cop." Tag pointed over Grace's shoulder at a table against the wall. People were throwing money down and yelling. Bonnie's face was red, but it looked like she was winning. Tag tightened her grip, tracking Grace's shifting bones and muscle as they moved for a better look.

Bonnie slammed the man's arm onto the table and stood, yelling "Yes!" at the top of her lungs. The group erupted in groans and cheers. Bonnie began picking up the money, but the young cop grabbed her arm.

"You said the best of three."

"That was three." Bonnie shoved the money into her pocket, weaving as she stood. "You won the first one."

"No, it was only two. You're too drunk to remember."

Bonnie held her hands up, shouting at the crowd for confirmation and jammed the rest of the money into her pocket. Tag got her attention, and Bonnie started toward her, bumping her opponent. He didn't like it, and his fist connected with her face. Just that quick, the fight was on.

Tag grabbed Bonnie, but she jerked away and threw her own punch. Another cop shoved Tag, yelled, "Move over, Pocahontas," and threw a punch. He missed and hit Grace in the face, knocking her into Tag's arms.

Tag wasn't sure who hit who or how many, but she and Bonnie ended up with Grace between them, fighting their way out of the bar.

Outside, they assessed the damage. Bonnie had a cut on her jaw, but Grace looked worse. Blood ran down her face from a deep gash across her eyebrow, and she slowly tipped into Tag.

"Damn." Bonnie grabbed for Grace. "Look what you've done."

"Me?" Tag held Grace tight against herself. "I didn't do anything. We could've had you out of there, but no, you had to throw a punch and Grace got hit."

"I don't feel so good—" Grace leaned over and vomited into the gutter. Tag carefully wiped her face with her T-shirt, lifted her into the back seat, and snapped the seat belt.

"I'll drive us to the hospital." Bonnie held out her hand for the keys.

"Fuck you will. You can barely stand up." Tag pushed Bonnie to the other door. "Get in there with Grace and tell me where to go."

"Straight to hell," Bonnie grumbled but crawled into the back seat with Grace. "Take a right at the next light."

Tag and Bonnie sat in plastic chairs in the waiting room in the Columbia Hospital ER waiting for word on Grace. The gray tiled floors stretched out around them, and Bonnie held an ice pack to her jaw. Neither had spoken.

"I never should have thrown that punch," Bonnie slurred.

"Did the doctor check you out?"

"Yes, and I'm okay, but I didn't cheat. That *was* the third match. If Grace is seriously hurt, AJ and the chief are going to kill me."

Tag remembered what AJ had said about Bonnie's crush on Grace. "It was just a bar fight and probably won't be our last. Grace doesn't seem the type."

"Wrong. AJ's been training her for years. I wouldn't want to fight her."

Tag thought of Grace's surprising muscles when she'd held her outside.

A doctor came out of the exam room. Her long lab coat had blood on it. She took a second look at Tag.

"Who's this?" she said, hands on hips.

"Tag Becket, our new agent." Bonnie struggled to her feet.

"Dr. Light, your unit's doctor," the woman said, shaking Tag's hand. "Were you with Bonnie in the bar?"

"Grace and I went to pick her up."

"Then you get to call AJ. Tell her I'm keeping Grace here tonight. I want to keep an eye on a possible concussion."

"Yes, ma'am," Tag said.

"Damn." Bonnie collapsed back to the chair.

"Bonnie, stay where you are until we get this sorted out. Tag, tell AJ to call me on my personal phone." She turned back into the exam room, and Tag pulled out her phone.

"AJ, we're at the Columbia ER. We had a little…skirmish…at the bar. Grace has a possible concussion and stitches. Dr. Light said you should call her on her personal number." Tag heard silverware clatter on a plate.

"What? Where's Bonnie?"

"Right here beside me, but she can't drive."

"Drunk?"

"Yes, ma'am."

"Are you all right?"

"I'm fine, ma'am," Tag said. There was more silence.

"I'll be right there after I talk to Dr. Light."

The line went dead and Tag sat down again beside Bonnie. "She's on her way."

"Christ. My first official day as an agent and I have to call AJ."

"The doctor knows you?"

"AJ and I were injured last spring and spent hours here with Charles and Grace. AJ ended up in surgery. Katie helped a lot."

"You've been friends with Katie for a long time?"

Bonnie nodded and jammed the ice back on her jaw with a grimace. "Since high school."

"And Grace?"

"They've only been here since last September, but she's a good friend." Bonnie leaned back and stared at Tag. "Why?"

Tag shrugged. "I'm going to be working with her and—"

"Give me a break. The only thing I've seen her really excited about is horses. Until you. She's interested, whatever that means to Grace."

She's interested. In me?

"There's a horse ranch south of town. She's out there every chance she has and maybe owns a horse." Bonnie shifted the ice pack. "I've never seen her hurt. This is my fault."

"I'm getting some coffee. Want some?" Tag said and stood.

Bonnie nodded and Tag walked to the coffee machine she'd seen in the lobby. The last time she'd been in a fistfight was beside two young privates in Kandahar. They'd gone into a building looking for a man with a bomb, certain they'd be blown up at any moment. She'd been beyond scared. Tonight, she'd only been angry, and how the hell had she let that happen to Grace?

The machine made a rumbling sound when she put money into it, and she remembered the helicopter earlier at the Owens's house. How long would it be before she got over that damned noise? The doctor had said it was a trigger.

She studied her reflection in the glass. She needed a haircut. She rested her forehead on the glass still feeling Grace in her arms and processed Bonnie's words. *She's interested, whatever that means to Grace.*

As she turned the corner, she heard AJ's and Katie's voices. Grace was right about this assignment. Something was off, and Robert Owens sure as hell felt off. None of the pieces fit. It was like the last time she'd commanded the Dragons, everything spinning sideways and wrong. Her stomach tightened as she tried to keep *that* out of her head. Frowning, she went toward the voices.

❖

"What the hell, Tag?" AJ said.

Tag handed the coffee to Bonnie and came to full attention. "Ma'am, don't blame Bonnie. Someone else threw the first punch."

AJ surveyed her wounded agents. Tag had blood all over her T-shirt and a bruise on her cheek. Bonnie held an ice pack to her jaw with blood on her clothes too. And what was going on? Tag was practically at parade attention.

"What's wrong with you two? It was a damn bar fight," AJ ground out. "And don't call me ma'am."

"Yes…ma'am."

"Now *that* was just mean. And for Christ's sake, at ease, soldier."
Tag blew out a breath and her shoulders relaxed. "Is Grace going
to be okay?"

"So the doctor says. Take Bonnie home with you tonight. Dr. Light
says she's fine, but make sure she's hydrated before she sleeps. Give
her a ride to change clothes in the morning and meet us at the office.
We'll stay with Grace." She took Tag's right hand and studied it, and
then her face. Tag's eyes were pure onyx. "You might want to ice this.
I hope you clocked him good," she said and left for the exam room.

A nurse covered Grace with a blanket, and AJ bent to look at
the stitches. Grace's skin had lost its summer tan glow. "God," she
murmured.

"I feel like crap," Grace mumbled, her normally bright eyes dull.
"My fault. I wasn't paying attention. I need to see Tag. Go get her, AJ."

"Can't. I sent them home to your place. Bonnie feels terrible about
this."

Katie bent over Grace. "Oh, sweetie, those are serious stitches.
I see a black eye in your future. Well, your horse won't care." She
straightened and looked around the room. "I don't like this."

AJ leaned against the bed. "This is only day three, and we've had
two fires and I'm shot, Grace is in the hospital, and we haven't even left
town. I don't like it either."

"What did Dr. Light say?"

"I said I want her quiet and resting until we do more tests. I'm
sure she's concussed." Dr. Light stepped into the room behind them.
"We'll probably release her tomorrow. Grace said you were leaving
town. How soon?"

"As soon as possible. Should we stay here with Grace tonight?"

"No. Go home. I'll take care of her." Dr. Light turned and took
a long look at them. "Have a nice summer? You both look healthy."
She started to leave but turned back. "Wait, I saw paperwork about a
gunshot. Let me see your arm." She unfolded AJ's sleeve and examined
the injury. "Looking good," she said. "How's the leg?"

"We actually had a vacation and did some hiking. I'm fine." AJ
fastened the cuff on her shirt.

A nurse stepped into the room and unlocked the rollers on Grace's
bed, and Dr. Light started for the door again. "We'll talk later or
tomorrow."

Outside, they stood in the parking lot for a moment. "Wonder why Grace needed to see Tag?" AJ said.

"I heard you talking to Tag and Bonnie. You sounded angry."

"Angry? No, just upset." AJ looked at the green lawn and a rainbow of colorful flowers. "Remember last spring when they released me and we stood here?" She put her arm around Katie's waist and tugged her close. "It was foggy from the melting snow and I was so happy to be out of here but hated those damned crutches."

"I took you to dinner to celebrate my bank contract." Katie smiled. "You and those gorgeous daffodils on the table at the restaurant. My favorite time of year, spring."

CHAPTER THIRTEEN

Still worried about Grace, AJ jammed maps onto the corkboard in the office conference room the next morning. She recognized the chief's footsteps before he appeared in the doorway and glanced up. His normally impeccable uniform was...wrong. Even his tie was unknotted.

"I just spent twenty minutes on the phone with the downtown office. What the hell happened at Smokey's yesterday?"

"I heard it was some kind of rumble."

The chief buttoned his top shirt button and tightened his tie. "There are rookie cops with a bunch of injuries riding desks downtown on their first day of duty. Did Bonnie start a fight?"

"That's not what Tag told me. They'll be here soon—"

"We're here." Tag walked into the conference room with Bonnie.

"Damn." He gave them a thorough once-over. "How the hell are we going to report this? You girls have to do the paperwork. I'm not touching it. Where's Grace?"

"Still in the hospital," AJ said.

He gaped at her. "It was that bad?"

"It was," Tag said. "What can we do, AJ?" She gestured at the corkboard.

"Tell the chief about what happened at Smokey's."

"Grace and I stopped at Smokey's to give Bonnie a ride home. She was arm wrestling a young cop. She beat him and he punched her. Heck of a fight."

"You beat him?" he said, and grinned at Bonnie. "Good for you."

"He was a sore loser and he hit me. It all went downhill after that." Bonnie ducked her head.

"We all threw punches," Tag added. "Someone hit Grace hard enough to give her stitches and maybe a concussion."

The chief stared at them. "Okay. I think we'll ignore the paperwork. The fellows downtown would like to do the same. There's damage to the bar too."

"Let me know. We'll help pay for it." AJ shoved a stack of papers that Maddie had emailed to the center of the table. "Tag, I have to keep track of Frog while Grace is in the hospital."

"I've been working with Grace and checked it a few minutes ago. It's status quo."

"How long will Grace be in the hospital?" The chief said.

"I'm waiting on Dr. Light. The tests last night were good, but she's going to have a whopper of a black eye." AJ's phone beeped and she had a short conversation with the doctor.

"She's ready and it's a mild concussion," she said.

Tag headed for the door. "Back later."

"I'll square things downtown." The chief left as well.

Arms braced on the table, AJ stared at one the emails Maddie had sent, a photo of an angelic boy. He had dimples and dark curly hair like Katie. The word "Deceased" was stamped across the photo. He'd only been ten when he died. She drew in a deep breath. Suddenly aware of the quiet room, she glanced at Bonnie's drained and bruised face.

"Are you okay?" AJ said.

"I took a pain pill before we came in. It'll do. The whole thing was my fault, and I feel really bad about Grace in the hospital. Between you and me…" She looked up at AJ. "I'm not very happy about her fascination with Tag."

AJ stopped stacking sheets, turning to Bonnie. She thought of Grace's different, happy face lately. "Grace considers you a friend and that's worth everything. Not only that, but she incites loyalty in people."

"What does that mean?" Bonnie laughed for the first time.

"Look at Jimmy. I swear he'd kill for her."

"That's true, but not counting her horse, Tag's a first."

AJ put her hand on Bonnie's shoulder. "You might be right, but appreciate the friendship. We all need that." She glanced at the clock.

"Let's get you settled. Grace has been working on your office and it's ready."

❖

Maddie Hershey appeared at AJ's office door around noon. She looked younger and more relaxed than yesterday.

"Come in." AJ motioned her into the office. The chief and Bonnie appeared behind Maddie.

"Chief," Maddie said with a big smile for him and then, "Oh, ouch," as he introduced Bonnie and heard the story. "I've never been to Smokey's—"

"Hey," Tag interrupted, carefully guiding Grace inside. "Maddie. How are you?"

"Hey yourself," Maddie said with a closer look. "Don't tell me. You both were at Smokey's with Bonnie."

AJ took stock of her second-in-command. Grace moved carefully and the stitches looked sore with the black eye beginning to bloom. After shaking Maddie's hand and exchanging a few words, Grace disappeared toward her office.

"I'll be right back." AJ slipped past everyone. Dr. Light had said there was no concussion but Grace needed "reasonable" limitations.

Grace was already scrolling across her computer. "You might need to read that information on Maddie's agent before lunch."

"I already read it. Should you even be here?" AJ sat on the edge of Grace's desk.

"I have some fine drugs going on."

"I have to go with Maddie, and I know I'll get a truckload of information. Let's set the task force meeting back a day. You need to rest."

"Dr. Light said to take a long nap and I will. Tag's fixing dinner tonight. Why don't you and Katie drop by for a meal around seven? We'll talk about the meeting after we eat."

"Let me run it by Katie, but okay. Why did you want to talk with Tag at the hospital?"

"Someone called her Pocahontas in that fight yesterday."

"Are you serious? That proves you can't legislate decency."

Shaking her head, AJ turned to leave. "Promise me you'll go home now."

"Thank you."

"For what?"

"For not saying I look fine." Grace managed a smile.

❖

AJ relaxed into the luxurious leather seats of Maddie's white Lexus as they drove down the freeway. She obviously liked to drive and fast, and AJ could feel that energy again. "Nice car," she said as they parked at a downtown restaurant on the lake.

Maddie grabbed her purse, all motion, as she strode across the parking lot. "I like nice things. I fight it, but it's a losing battle." She opened the restaurant door. "Speaking of nice things, that's a gorgeous suit and fits you perfectly. The black makes your hair brighter, if that's even possible." She held the coat out. "Cool. Red silk lining too."

"Katie's mother made this for me. She used to have a business customizing clothing. You should see Katie's outfits." AJ checked the room thoroughly before they slid into a comfortable wooden booth, and she sighed at her own hyper-vigilance.

"I met Katie at the Bennings Bank's city volunteer luncheon in July. She's a force to be reckoned with, not to mention interesting... and adorable." Maddie smiled and picked up her menu. "You're a lucky woman."

AJ patted her heart. "She lives here."

After they'd ordered, Maddie continued. "About Charles. I've known him for a long time. He and I ran a sting for the FBI when I got out of the army years ago. When you left the military, he pointed you out and was always talking about you.

"I've kept an eye on you since you were injured in Los Angeles during that horrible FBI assignment. You actually met me in that Virginia hospital before he sent you home to recuperate, but I'm sure you don't remember."

"Not a good moment for me." AJ blinked. All she remembered of that hospital was pain and a foggy mind.

"You recovered and did an excellent job here. Charles is still bragging on you."

"Seven dead and one of them by my own hand? That's nothing to brag about."

"It couldn't be helped," Maddie said as the salads arrived and they took a few minutes with the food. "Have you finished with your therapist about Ariel?"

"The last appointment was the day I was shot. How's that for irony?"

"I suppose, but you've put together one of the best small groups in the country." Maddie picked up a salt shaker. "I worked with your therapist to build the new task force, which brings me to the next point. If we work together, I need to talk about who is going up north with you. I know you and Tag and Sam, if you decide to take him, and that leaves Grace. Charles won't talk. He said to ask you."

AJ frowned. "Do you mean yesterday's fight in the—"

"No, but her eye looks terrible, doesn't it?" Maddie took a moment with her salad. "I know you have some idea what's ahead of you, everything from abuse and rape to murder. We call it labor and human trafficking or modern slavery, but even that's kind. As the person in charge, I need to know that Grace can handle this."

AJ leaned forward, and then it hit her. "How did you know?" she said in a low voice. Only she and Charles knew about Grace's childhood, and they'd never told. Nor had they discussed it with Grace.

"After Ariel, you have to ask?" Maddie met her eyes.

"It never occurred to me. First of all, I trust her with my life. If anything happens to me, she could step in and never miss a thing."

"I'm not talking about her record. It's spotless. I need the personal stuff from you. You've worked together for years. You'd know. What about her relationships? Or has she had a reaction to a situation that made you wonder or go back over the moment? I read those awful records from Children's Protective Services in Phoenix. It was like reading one of my victim reports up here. Her father...not to mention her uncles. God."

"Charles and I spoke with her grandparents. It *was* terrible." AJ scrubbed her face. "She spends all of her free time at a horse ranch here and is a critical part to my group. Some have shown more than a passing interest in her, but there have been no relationships." She frowned down at the food. "The only person I've seen her show any interest in is Tag."

Maddie's brow furrowed and she muttered, "huh," appearing to think about AJ's words. "Grace is like Tag. So trustworthy that it almost sets your teeth on edge to question her. Still, I need to. Did you ever read the psych evaluation on Ariel?"

"Only after I'd shot her and it was too late. It had to be the drugs."

"It was, but that's the point. We go so fast every single day, and law enforcement is so big that we miss things. Sometimes a task force depends on the details. Like Ariel. Or Grace."

AJ straightened. Now she knew why Charles had called her house. "I'll talk with her. Tag's cooking tonight, and we're having dinner with them."

"Let me know." Maddie popped a slice of tomato into her mouth, chewing thoughtfully. "Pete told me you've found another Owens brother."

"I suspect Robert Owens is involved, but my gut says he's not the trigger. We turned him over to Charles's man, Jock. He has a serious drug problem."

"How're you doing with the shootings and the fires?"

"I'm so alert *I'm* practically on fire. We have no idea who's shooting at me or who burned Home Base and my agency vehicles, or if they're even connected. I even hate to talk about it." She scanned the restaurant again, trying to calm herself. "Let's talk about Sam Mullins. I see he's forty-seven years old, six foot tall, multilingual, a graduate of MIT. Wife deceased, and he's an engineer?"

"We're the same age. He lost his wife to cancer and it changed his life. He's a hiker and a climber, and I've liked him from the moment I met him. He's a natural leader."

"Let me meet him. Sounds good."

"Also, when Tag came back, stateside, I tried my best to get her, but she applied immediately for the ATF."

"It's personal," AJ said. "I've read her entire background that's available, but—" She didn't want to say that she felt Tag was hiding something. "What do you know?"

Maddie shrugged. "Enough to know I could have used her. Also, as I'm sure you know, that last op with the Dragons was terrible. They lost practically half of the unit and she spent time in the hospital. Of course they gave her a medal but then transferred her to Intelligence and that was a shame. She's a great leader in the field. Have you ever seen that many medals and recommendations?" Maddie pushed her empty plate away. "You said Grace seemed interested in Tag. I've never seen anyone so...pursued...as that woman." She shook her head a little. "What was Tag like in the field?"

"I thought she was the whole package. She has great instincts, was decisive, superb in a crisis, and I've never seen anyone so trusted. It was remarkable. Off-duty, she was funny, open, and warm." Maddie gave a little laugh. "Her martial arts skills are ferocious." She raised her eyebrows at AJ. "Charles said you're the same."

AJ thought of her party and Tag's fist hanging in the air over Jock. "Who knows, but it doesn't make any difference. I still have to teach it."

Maddie's phone rang and she frowned at it. "I'm sorry. I have to take this." She took the phone toward the door, and AJ watched her talk with a fair amount of animation and gestures. Finally, she ended the call, then made a call of her own and returned, apparently not very happy.

"Sorry. I thought I'd turned it off." She took a drink of water and composed herself with a smile. "Any special reason you prefer undercover work?"

"It's usually simple. I want to be the only one I have to worry about, but this is different." She thought of Frog. And Katie. "Look. What I'd really like is to stay here and track the X-Girl murder. It's day four of my new so-called task force and I hardly have enough information to have a meeting."

Maddie nodded. "I understand, but they're not going to let you stay here." She looked around the busy restaurant. "You'll do it because you believe in what we're doing, something you share with Tag, plus your ability to lead. People listen when you speak."

AJ shook her head. "Charles also said Ariel and I were alike, and look how that turned out."

Chapter Fourteen

Maddie pulled away from the restaurant at about Mach one. AJ pushed back into the seat with a deep breath.

Maddie finally pulled into a small parking lot. They looked across the well-tended yard and huge, century-old house, a part of a large estate on the bluffs of Lake Michigan. Hannah's House was the finest rehabilitation center in Milwaukee. Charles had helped AJ place Frog here before she'd tucked her into Home Base.

"This place always makes me think of Edgar Allen Poe." AJ pointed at the roof. "Look at those crows. When it's cold, they gather around the chimneys."

Maddie searched the ornate gables above them. "I never thought of that," she said and rang the bell.

Jaelyn, the home's director, answered the door. She smiled when she saw them. "Good to see you, Maddie. And you too, Allison. Tell Katie thanks for the donations and keeping our name out there."

"We appreciate your work," AJ said and meant it.

"We've had a sudden uptick of residents, and I'm swamped. I'll be in my office if you need me." Jaelyn's PA, Ozzie, was suddenly beside her with an armload of paper.

AJ stopped them. "How many new people do you have?"

"There was a big fire north of Ashland Avenue, and we took the surviving girls and women. Seventeen in all, not counting the children, and we're scrambling."

"The big house downtown by the bakery? That was important to me. Does Milwaukee Arson know you have them?" AJ knew it had to be Home Base.

"They brought them here. You were involved with that house?"

"Last winter and spring. Have you talked with the DEA? Charles Ryan?"

Jaelyn gave her a sharp look. "Oh, Lord. They're part of that? Tell him to call me."

"How do you know Jaelyn and her PA?" Maddie said as they walked down the hall.

"She's a friend of Charles. I had a young girl here, a CI, and she did very well. This is a great place."

Maddie entered the last door at the end of the long corridor, a small room lined with bookcases, newspapers, and magazines. She held her hand up for a scan at an inside door. When they entered, AJ came to a stop in front of walls of computer screens. Men and women wore headsets, working on the computers in front of them.

"Hannah's House allows us this space, our on-the-move offices. It's sealed. No one can hack this place, and we can speak to our people in the field instantly." She named off locations of several of the screens. "The next room is sealed as well. If you can't find me, you'll know I'm here." She did another hand scan, went into the next room, and tossed her bag on a large desk in the corner. "Grab that chair and I'll give you the background."

The room hummed with fast, intense conversation. No one paid any attention to AJ.

"Over five years ago, Hannah's House began to lose residents. They'd just disappear. Then different shelters in the area began to report the same problem, and other Midwestern states spoke up with much the same. I was in Oregon up to my ears in undocumented workers, and my chief gave me a heads-up. I began to watch the numbers. Milwaukee shelters worked with police and our local FBI, but no one could account for the missing people, mostly young women at that time. Finally, city police stopped a van full of young girls, some as young as ten. The cop, a smart guy who now works for us, wisely advised them of a missing taillight and let them go. He notified our local group and they tailed them to Wausau. Four months later, I was reassigned here. DHS came in when Canada reported some issues." Maddie pushed her hair back and activated her computer. "Charles and I met here before you relocated last September, but a word of caution. Chief Whiteaker knows about Hannah's House, but not this, our office here."

AJ nodded to show that she understood. "Grace worked on human trafficking when she was in our cyber division and she's been helping me research."

"How did she handle that?"

"Very well." AJ turned, still taking in the office. "So, this is... what?"

"Our Ground Zero. Yes, I have an office downtown, but my PA runs it." Her eyes sparkled with interest as the huge monitor on her desk came alive. "I'm going to show you where we are right now, this day at this hour."

"Wow," AJ said. Cities and towns were underlined on a map with numbers below them.

"These are the rescued or deceased victims from this area, some of which I sent you." Maddie put her finger on the first column. "This shows data and dedicated agents."

"How big is this area?" AJ pointed at the screen.

"We work in quadrants, depending on what's there and how many agents are available. Also, victim data and persons of interest." She gestured at the office. "This is the reason I wanted Tag to work with us. Her computer skills." She turned to a young guy in T-shirt and jeans at a nearby desk. "How fresh is the coffee?"

"I made it about twenty minutes ago."

"Want some?" Maddie said. "I do. Take it black?"

AJ nodded, engrossed in the map before her. As Maddie had said, their focus was more to the south and west of where her people would be.

"Will my group be on this map?"

"Right here." Maddie touched Niagara, and the color changed to red. "I'll enter the information once you're up there. Here's Sam." She touched Park Falls on the map, and the computer went to another page with Sam Mullins's name and columns of data. "When you call me from up there, no matter what the reason, this will light up in the other room on their computer dedicated to your unit as well as this computer."

She tilted the monitor for a better look. "It's not as complicated as it looks, although I wouldn't call it simple. You need this when you have this many people in the field and two separate agencies. This is speed and it works. It took us years to get these systems going, but now we have quite a few of them in active areas."

"My operation's small and we'll be closer to the Crooked Lake area, not Niagara."

"True, but closer to Canada than anything we've got. I'm hoping you'll find how they feed north to the border. That's a win-win for both of us." Maddie swiveled her chair to a different monitor. "A large part of the problem was that they got organized on computers before we did, so we had to scramble to catch up. Here are the adults we've found that enable and manage this gigantic operation in Milwaukee and up north. They use men and women, working girls, pimps, and others. Trafficking includes security, transportation, even cosmetics, hair care, clothing, cooking, health care, everything you can imagine. You must have seen some of this working with the chief this summer, like that house you took down." AJ nodded again and Maddie pointed at her computer. "Even a whisper goes on here. The hard thing is the children. When they bring them in they keep them for years. Honestly, years, but sometimes they escape or we find them. Here, read the first case."

AJ became absorbed in the carnage, lost track of time, and soon over an hour had passed. She shoved back. It was worse than she had thought.

"More coffee?"

AJ shook her head. "Do you have water? I've never read anything like this. What is this?"

"Chaos," Maddie said, handing her a bottle of water. "Enough for today?"

AJ pulled in a big breath. "Yes."

"Let's show Tag and Grace this network. If it goes well, I'll explain my proposal for your team." Maddie stood. "Want to take a break and step outside for a bit? There's one last thing."

They walked out to the grassy area in the center of the complex, and the fresh air almost made AJ stumble. She took a drink of water to wash away the bad taste in her mouth and sank down on a bench.

Maddie stretched with her hands above her head. "I know they call me Lightning behind my back at work, but fighting this is the only thing that keeps me sane. For what it's worth, we've made quite a bit of headway in the last two years."

"You said there was another thing to talk about."

"That phone call I had at the restaurant earlier? Tag's on-base Intel division discovered something in Afghanistan. One of her ex-Dragons is now an FBI agent on the East Coast, and Tag contacted her. They took it to the next level. That phone call was my chief informing me that I'll be Tag's contact here, but I don't have all the information so I can't tell you any more other than I'll be working with her separately from your group."

AJ stared at her. "Will it interfere up north? Is she in danger?"

"No to both questions. I want to talk to Tag first and will tell her that you know as much as I know, which is next to nothing. Only Pete, Charles, and Lawrence Kelly know about Tag."

"Can I let Tag know that you mentioned it?"

Maddie nodded and AJ was sure that this was what Tag had been hiding. She held up her phone. "I need to text Katie about dinner tonight."

"Okay. Meet me over there at the residents' craft store. Have you been there?"

"I saw it when my CI was here, but I've never been inside. I'll meet you there."

Maddie walked toward the other side of the wide green lawn, and AJ sent Katie a text to call. A few seconds later, her phone rang.

"Hi, love," Katie said. "Where are you?"

"North of downtown." Warmth shoved at the cold churning inside her. "How's your schedule tonight?"

"I've only got one more meeting and then I'm clear."

"Grace wants us to come over. Tag's cooking."

"She's out of the hospital? That's good news. What time?"

"Seven." AJ watched some small birds at a feeder, trying to tuck a smile into her voice somehow. "It's really good to hear your voice."

There was a moment of silence. "You sound…odd."

AJ closed her eyes, listening to Katie's breath. "Love you."

"Me too. Honey, are you okay?"

"Now that I've talked to you."

AJ disconnected and took a deep breath. Several young women played with toddlers on the grass, and she recognized some of them from Home Base. It took quite a bit of paperwork and money to be here, and she wondered about that.

She remembered Frog here. Now she was up north, alone, except for Greg and Jeff watching over her. Could this get any worse? She thought of Grace. Of course it could get worse because Maddie was right. Parts of Grace's life was similar to what she'd just read. She walked across the yard, heart aching.

Tiny bells rang when AJ entered the craft store. After the sun's heat, the store was cool with subtle lights and a hint of incense. Maddie was talking with one of the girls behind the counter, and AJ walked down an aisle, needing something, anything, to distract her. A glint caught her eye and she bent over a jewelry display.

A ring reminded her of Katie. Tiny, inlaid spring green leaves circled the silver band. Gold rimmed the edges. AJ motioned at one of the clerks and smiled when it shone in her hand. Spring was Katie's favorite season. She checked the size. She looked up, right into Maddie's smile.

"Something special?" Maddie said.

"It reminds me of spring. And Katie."

The clerk held up the ring. "A Door County artist consigns her work here. There are bracelets, necklaces, and more."

AJ held out her card. "I want this ring and it's the right size. Do you have a nice box for it? It's a gift."

"The artist makes the boxes out of real wood. You'll love it."

Maddie peppered AJ with stats all the way home. "The FBI estimates human trafficking is worth over thirty billion annually in the US, and involves over three hundred thousand victims taken into some form of prostitution—as I said, we call it slavery—every year." She glanced at AJ. "Shocking, isn't it?"

"God," AJ said and scrutinized the parking lot as Maddie pulled into the spot next to her agency vehicle. "Tag picked up the British *Guardian* on the plane on the way home. According to them, Milwaukee is a hub for human trafficking. Is there any truth to that?"

"Honestly, I can't argue because of the declining economy or high unemployment rate here. Industry has been leaving this state like rats on a sinking ship, all of which feeds our problem significantly." Maddie rubbed her forehead. "I can't deal with it nationally. It stops me from thinking straight, so I concentrate on Wisconsin." She took a deep breath. "One more thing. We keep a few of our rescues at Hannah's House, and I'm scheduled to see one tomorrow. We can turn Tag and

Grace loose on the computers and then include them in the victim's meeting. I'd like to see Grace in this situation, if it's okay with you."

"I'll see how she feels tonight. She won't be in the field up north, by the way. She'll coordinate the computers and our little group, so you'll be dealing with her most of the time. Tag and I will work the town…and your Sam, if he's a go. Chief Whiteaker, Bonnie, and the rest of the team will stay down here. Do you want a look at our plan when it's completed?"

"You're offering? I have to fight for every piece of information I get downtown."

"That's why Charles put us out there, away from the downtown offices."

Maddie stared out the front window. "The single thing Pete shared with me was how angry you were when you found yourself with a task force."

"I feel we're doing a personal favor for a political friend, which is crap." She changed the subject. "When can I meet Sam?"

"He'll be in town tomorrow and I'll set something up. I'll let you know."

AJ nodded and opened the car door. "Wait. Are you working on X-Girl?"

"Absolutely, and I have a small team devoted to that victim, including my best profiler. Tell Chief Whiteaker they're meeting with the Milwaukee task force tomorrow."

Maddie left, and AJ walked to the chief's office. "Got a minute?"

"How bad is it?" he said.

"Worse than I anticipated…than *we* anticipated." She took the chair in front of him and slid out of her shoes with a sigh. "First, tell me about the Owens boys, and God, I need coffee."

"Jock found Robert's gun at the Owens house. No prints although it's been fired recently and the lab's working on it. He's got the kid in the hospital already." He handed her a cup of coffee. "Still don't know if Robert's the shooter. Or the arsonist."

"Damn it," she said, and then told him about some of the cases she'd looked at but never mentioned the computer rooms. He loosened his tie.

"I may take up smoking again," he said. "I didn't know the girls from Home Base were there, and I don't think Jock does either."

"I'll call Charles to let him know Jaelyn's expecting a call from him at Hannah's House. Why don't you and Bonnie go with us tomorrow and interview the Home Base girls. Grace, Tag, and I will stick with Maddie. When we have the team meeting here, you lead the Home Base part of the discussion. We're going to have to stay tight on this one."

He gave a little snort. "Talking to downtown makes you paranoid, doesn't it?"

"Yes, and another thing. Maddie said to tell you that she has a small team working on X-Girl, including her best profiler. They'll be talking to the Milwaukee task force tomorrow."

"That's good news. I've been hoping they'd help that new task force."

AJ's arm was healing, but it hurt right now. She picked up her shoes and padded across the hall to her office for ibuprofen. The closest she'd ever been to anything this big was the undercover assignment in Los Angeles. It had broken her, but she wasn't broken now. She was angry. She set the little wooden box on her desk, opened it, and held the ring. Smiling, she anticipated the moment with Katie, and then, with a deep sigh, leaned forward and called Charles.

❖

AJ's bones ached with stress all the way home. Charles had urged her to talk to Grace, something she didn't want to do. She parked, surprised to see Katie's SUV already in the garage. Lively violin music floated by her as she opened the door and walked up the steps through the kitchen to the deck. Barefoot, in a Milwaukee Brewers T-shirt and cutoffs, Katie was playing something AJ didn't recognize, but it was happy music and it made her smile. She waited until Katie lowered the violin. She cleared her throat, and Katie turned just as AJ put her arms around her.

"Play some more," AJ said, her mouth against Katie's ear.

"That's an old Civil War tune my grandfather used to play." The lowering sun outlined Katie, and the slight breeze tousled her black curls. "Um, we have time before dinner. How about a shower? Together." Katie pushed closer.

AJ slid her hands under the T-shirt and pulled in a quick breath.

Katie was braless. She slid her hands down into the cutoffs. "You're commando," she said breathlessly, her entire body tightening. Jesus, she wanted her.

Laughing, Katie pulled her into the house, leaving clothes all the way down the hallway with groans and laughter. Fully in charge, Katie pinned her against the wall, her warm mouth and fingers tracking every single sensitive inch of AJ's skin. Completely aroused, AJ could only hear their ragged breathing but managed to get them to their bed. They shared a final shattering climax that left them both breathing hard. Katie rested her head on AJ's bare stomach, slick with sweat and sex, her breath tickling her skin.

AJ was so relaxed she felt seconds away from sleep. "Your mother is going to kill you. You threw my suit on the floor."

"No. She'll just make you another." Katie pushed herself up to an elbow, her hand drifting across AJ's hip. "When we talked today, I swear I felt your skin against mine. Is your arm okay?"

"I think it fell off when you threw me on the bed."

"Ha. We threw each other."

AJ gently pushed curls back from Katie's face. "I love you," she said. "Wait a minute. Don't move." She scrambled up and over Katie, searching for the gift in the kitchen. Katie was propped on the pillows when she came back.

"I found this today," she said. "For you."

"The wood is beautiful," Katie said, running fingers over the deep reds and browns of the wood shaped like an apple. A faint gold shone under the colors. Katie opened the top and her eyes widened. "Oh…"

"It said your size. I get to put it on you." Katie held out her hand, and AJ slipped it on the ring finger. "I thought of how you love spring—"

Katie shoved her back, stretching out on top of her. "It's beautiful. I love you so much."

"It's hopeful, Katie, and—" AJ saw tears in Katie's eyes. "Wait, don't cry."

"It's only happiness, sweetie." Katie curled up and held her hand out, admiring the ring.

"See the leaves?" AJ leaned over her. "You like it?"

"So much I can't even talk about it." Katie sat up. "You sounded odd on the phone."

"This damned assignment is going to kill me. I just know it. We were at Hannah's House today—" AJ stopped. She couldn't talk about it. "I saw part of what I'm going to do up north."

Katie studied her. "I know you can't tell me things. We've been through this before. Say what you can."

"It's really ugly." AJ's stomach twisted again. "Margaret Hershey is the FBI special agent in charge I'll be working with. Could we have her here for a meal? She said she met you at a volunteers' luncheon at the bank."

"She might have. I coordinated one this summer. Is this someone I can talk to if I need to reach you?"

"Absolutely," AJ said. "Let's take a shower and tell me about your day." She pulled Katie up against her. "Promise me one thing."

"What?" Katie leaned back, her face still serious.

"You'll wear underwear tonight."

Katie tossed a grin over her shoulder and wiggled her naked body as she walked away. "Maybe."

She heard the shower begin in the bathroom, and walked down the hall, picking up their clothes. "And we don't have the shooter yet," AJ whispered at the floor.

Chapter Fifteen

Shortly after AJ and Maddie left the office, Tag reminded Grace of the doctor's orders to rest. "I can barely stand up," she said, handing Tag a list. "Will you do the shopping?"

Tag wandered through the nearby monster-sized grocery store, soaking up the smell of fresh produce and fruit. The huge meat selection stopped her in her tracks. She took her time with the shopping. Even waiting in line had been a kind of joy. On the way home, she stopped at a roadside stand for fresh corn on the cob from a local grower. They talked for a while about his in-city farm, something she'd never seen in Milwaukee.

Her phone rang as she returned. Much to her surprise, it was Maddie notifying her that she'd be her contact in Milwaukee over what they'd found at the base in Afghanistan. She didn't have all the information as of yet so they'd have to talk later.

Ice crawled up Tag's spine. What they'd discovered in Intel had been verified. Would America understand or even pay attention to this new information? AJ was right. The nation's temperature was boiling.

She focused on the groceries and began to put them away in Grace's well-organized kitchen. She had looked forward to cooking a meal and concentrated on a tossed salad. Afterward, she changed into jeans and a T-shirt and then headed outside to clean the grill. She worked until she heard music from the kitchen.

Grace, barefoot, swaying to violin music, was setting the table. She looked much better, and Tag could smell her shower soap.

"Great music." Tag absorbed the sight, her heart tumbling into a little free fall.

"That's Katie playing."

"She plays the violin?"

"Oh, does she ever. She won a competition with that one. The song's over four hundred years old."

"It's beautiful." Tag gathered what spices she needed. "Hungry?"

"Starving, and the sleep was just what I needed." Grace's light rose tank top and white shorts draped her body deliciously.

Tag deliberately turned away and glanced at the clock. It was past five o'clock. "Are Katie and AJ timely?" If they were, she should start the ribs now.

"Most of the time, but last spring, after AJ's surgery and Ariel's death, things changed. Once we get up and running, she'll change." Grace arranged salt and pepper shakers beside salad dressings.

"I've heard about her martial arts skills."

"She pushed me into my black belt." Grace laughed a little. "I *pushed* back, but she kept challenging me, and it was worth every minute."

Tag rummaged for meat tongs. "You said you've known her four years?"

"It was my first job out of Cyber Crime, chasing drugs up from the South. Jock was with us too. I had to learn about the drugs and the people who used them as I went. Crazy." She placed salad bowls on the table. "Did you read our so-called meth manual? Parts of this state are flooded with it."

"Yeah, last night, trying to keep Bonnie awake. I also read the new task force notes. Where's the rest of the assignment?"

Grace gave a frustrated sigh. "That's all we know, Frog and the girls. The Bureau is usually clear about a task force, but not this one. It's driving us crazy."

Tag took the ribs outside. This group had worked together a long time. She felt their respect and trust for each other, and she sensed Grace did not trust easily. Tucking her Dragon necklace into her T-shirt, she thought about the women she'd commanded. They'd been close like AJ's group. Their loyalty to each other had been unbreakable until that day that had shattered them forever.

She tossed a pinch of salt into the barbecue sauce and added brown sugar and chopped peppers. Grace knew much about her, but she knew little about Grace, other than what she'd seen here. She drew a line at using computer skills on coworkers or friends. A lot of women had pursued her, but Grace certainly wasn't one of them. Still, Bonnie had said Grace was interested yesterday at the hospital.

She walked to the railing and traced the river at the end of the long lawn. The almost-evening sun behind the lush maple and oak trees and the long stretch of green grass reminded her of home. This was why she was back in Wisconsin. She planned on working for this country she loved until someone stopped her. The balcony doors opened.

"Lovely, isn't it?" Despite her injured face, Grace's eyes were that unusual blue again. "Those ribs smell delicious. Your recipe?"

"My father's special sauce. He swears it tenderizes the meat."

"If it's as good as it smells it's going to be great. I'll put the corn on." She went back inside, leaving her beautiful smile embedded in Tag's mind.

She loves flowers, Tag thought, inspecting the potted, rich red geraniums around the railing. There were plants inside too and lots of books, not to mention all the music discs in her office. The art was colorful but thoughtful like the large brass statue of a horse in the bathroom for towels plus some small statues on end tables. Art, music, and books meant a wide and curious mind to go with that lovely body and marvelous face.

Grace stepped outside again. "Here they are," she said with a loud whistle, waving.

"Where'd you learn to whistle like that? I could never master it."

"Two older brothers," Grace said. "I'll get the door."

Tag set the ribs away from the flames, tucking that information about Grace's brothers into her memory along with everything else. She could see AJ's bright hair as she and Katie walked across the parking lot, leaning into each other, laughing, both wearing plain summer dresses. Tag frowned. This morning AJ had worn a professional black suit, appearing completely in charge, even a little dangerous, but now she was wearing a dress? She was certain AJ didn't muscle or threaten to set the pace and direction of this unit. Subtlety was more her style.

There were voices and laughter in the kitchen and Katie stepped outside. "Hi, Tag. Wow, that smells good."

"Ribs, with my father's sauce."

"I can smell spices." Katie leaned over the barbecue. "Yum."

"You have a big family?"

"Five of us. Three girls, two boys. I'm in the middle." Katie held the platter. "Here, I'll take them inside."

The kitchen was empty. "AJ and Grace needed to check something in her office before we eat. When they stayed with me last winter they'd huddle in my office. There are things I can't know and that's fine." Katie took the salad out of the refrigerator. "We brought wine."

Tag held the bottle up to the light, sending deep red lights over the counter. "Does it bother you to be left out?"

"Only when it involves AJ being shot, and then I want everything I can get my hands on." She reached for the glasses. "How about your family?"

"Two girls and one boy. My brother won't go near a stove. Since I'm the middle kid like you, cooking was a priority. Both Mom and Dad taught me."

"The other girl's the oldest?"

"No. Emma's the youngest and bright as a star. Got her veterinary medicine degree in Madison and started a clinic at home." Tag took a drink of wine. "She can be trouble because we all spoiled her, but she's super with animals. I hear she's a good vet."

Katie tasted the wine and smiled. "What about your brother?"

"He's a military pilot and I'm sure he'll retire in the air force."

"Smells great in here," AJ said, following Grace into the kitchen, flashing Katie a look so warm that Tag blinked and stepped back a little.

"No talking about my eye or stitches," Grace said, setting the corn on the table.

"What eye? You have stitches?" AJ grinned.

"Did you read the Bren Black book I gave you?" Katie said to Tag, passing the salad.

"I finished it last night while Bonnie slept." Tag started to laugh. "I've been in a lot of helicopters, Katie. Bren Black would have to have been made of rubber. You can't make those maneuvers while you're in the air."

"Are you talking about the sex…or how she flew the helicopter?" AJ buttered corn and laughed.

"Either, although one can always hope about the sex scenes," Tag said over the laughter. "It's not a bad story. Just a little impossible."

"So you laughed at it, like AJ?" Katie's face was still mischievous.

"Honestly, yes," Tag said. "However, the mystery was good."

"Ha." Katie taunted AJ.

AJ grinned. "She's right. The storyline's solid."

More conversation about books and movies wound all the way through the meal. It was the most Tag had heard Grace talk about anything, and was she imagining Grace's eyes on her constantly? She made coffee and they all sat back, relaxed and full. Suddenly, Grace gave a little yelp and grabbed Katie's hand.

"Where did you get that gorgeous ring?"

"AJ, today." Katie beamed and held her hand up for everyone to see.

"Oh," Grace murmured. "AJ, you have good taste."

"I do. There she sits." Face flushed, AJ pointed at Katie.

Tag grinned at AJ's embarrassment. "I'll take care of the dishes while you two work. How about a movie, Katie?"

"Only if you let me help clean up. We can choose the movie together." Katie stood. "Those ribs were out of this world. What was the kickback in that sauce? Peppers?"

❖

AJ moved her chair close to Grace's desk. "Before we begin, I need to tell you what I saw and learned with Maddie today. The girls from Home Base are at Hannah's House."

"What? That's expensive. Who did that?" Grace looked up.

"Jaelyn said Milwaukee Arson brought them to the facility. I talked to Charles and he'll call her about Home Base. The chief and Bonnie will handle those women and keep Jock in the loop. Some of the survivors from the FBI-DHS operation are there. I'd like you and Tag to go with me to see them…if you're up to going. Tomorrow?"

"Right now I'd say yes, but I'll know more in the morning. I want to make sure it's not the drugs talking. Those survivors need special care."

AJ leaned back in the chair. "How long have we known each other?"

Grace cradled her coffee cup in her hands. "That's odd. Tag asked me the same question."

"Tag's good with people, isn't she?"

"She has great instincts." Grace tilted her head in a question. "And you and I've worked together long enough for me to feel as if you're edging up to something."

"It's your childhood, Grace." AJ held her breath and they stared at each other.

"My childhood?"

"Federal agencies are on a new tack, and the incident with Ariel was one of the things that started all of this. Background checks are being scrutinized, our group came up, and Maddie asked about you."

"I don't understand."

"She has your entire background, from birth to present." AJ plowed ahead. "I'm sorry. Not just for the intrusion into your life but that Charles and I never discussed it with you."

Grace made a small sound and turned away.

"Maddie felt this assignment might not be a good fit for you, and believe me, after what I saw today, I'm even worried about myself."

"My father and uncles…I was so young." Grace almost whispered. "I still miss my mother. Finally, when I was eleven, she got us to my grandparents. My father killed her when I was twelve and he died in prison." She met AJ's eyes. "But you know that, don't you?"

"Charles and I talked with your grandparents when we shifted you to the team. We made the decision to leave it alone because…" AJ looked out at the growing dark, trying to find the words. "Because you're so good at everything you do."

"You talked with my grandparents?" Grace quickly wiped her eyes and muttered, "Ow."

"I need to warn you before you see what I saw today. Brutal is a kind word. Maddie might talk with you too. On the bright side, you're going to love their system. Tag will too."

Grace stared at the floor. "Does Katie know? Or the chief?"

"Only Charles, Maddie, and I know. If it gets too hard, you have to tell me."

Grace slumped. "Not Tag?"

"No, of course not."

"I checked myself out when I worked in Cyber Crime. I've had a ton of therapy, but my dreams usually let me know. So far I'm good."

AJ searched Grace's face and decided it was the truth. "More crap news. No one can prove young Owens is my shooter. Jock found the pistol. No prints, but it's been fired recently. The lab's testing it, but I'd bet someone else is involved. Check the chief's notes on this. We all have to watch our backs, Grace."

"Damn, I knew it. I felt it." Grace stood with a quick shiver. "I'll get more coffee and then let's begin working on the meeting."

AJ stopped her from leaving. "Wait. Let's talk about Tag."

"What?" Grace sank back into her chair.

"You knew about me and Katie long before I did. You were right." Grace pushed her hair back, her face beginning to flush.

AJ grinned. "I've never seen you laugh like you do around her. She gets your full attention, and that's new too. I'd be happy to talk to—"

"God, no." Grace waved her hands. "I hardly understand what I'm feeling and I haven't even known her a week. There's been no one, especially a woman…" Grace went quiet, her face bright red. "I didn't mean to say that."

"Um, I don't know how to respond," AJ said.

"Right. I'll get us fresh coffee," Grace said and left in a hurry.

AJ wiped her sweaty hands on her dress. "Jesus," she muttered. Still, it had gone better than she'd anticipated. Now she knew what Grace preferred. No one…until Tag.

Grace placed the cups on the desk and lifted her one good eyebrow at AJ. "You're going to make me miserable, aren't you?"

"You were relentless at Katie's last winter."

Grace made a face at her and turned to the computer. Once again, AJ noticed that Grace shared Katie's delicate, feminine appearance… until she stepped onto the mat. She'd earned that black belt and knocked her down more than once. Another crazy day, AJ thought with a deep breath. She'd been a mess when she'd gone home today. The unexpected sex had wiped her mind clean, and she felt more focused than she'd been in days. "Did you buy that horse you've been training all summer?"

"Yes." Grace turned the monitor on her computer so they could both see it. "Why?"

"I want to use Crooked Lake Resort as a base. When Katie and I were up there on vacation, I noticed horse stables. What if you put your horse there for some horse reason?"

Grace laughed. "You're going to have to be more specific than that."

"While the rest of us are out in the field, you need something besides computers as a cover. See what I'm driving at?"

"I could be a computer contractor on a special project and I brought my horse with me," she said. "We could use the stables for a meet, instead of something public like the resort."

"Or you could ride somewhere to meet us. We did some hiking and I saw places completely out of the way."

"I like the idea." Grace brought up photos on her phone. "Here's my horse."

AJ looked at the small black horse. She knew a lot about farm animals, but they hadn't had horses. "What's his name?"

"*Her* name is Crow. It's a mare, a quarter horse, and loaded with energy. I had a heck of a time training her, but she's finally settling down." She took the phone back, smiling down at the photos. "How would we get her up there? I'd need a horse trailer. Should I call the resort?"

"You do the calling. We'll pay for everything, and lease a pickup. You've transported horses?"

"Forever, and I can rent a trailer at the stables. I even have a dream pickup. Do I get the truck I want?"

"Just walk in and lease it. I'll give you the blind card so you're not tied to us on the lease. Does the stable here know you're ATF?" AJ said.

"No. Everything's under my personal account."

"Good. I thought you'd like this idea. Also, Maddie will have Sam Mullins here so we meet him before we leave. If I know Maddie, it'll be fast." AJ grinned at Grace's happy face. "Then, I thought what if I have Tag work with Jay Yardly? People might know her in Niagara, and I don't think it's wise to have her work for a delivery service. I'll bet Jay could find a place for her in his office, computer related. That leaves only Sam and me working for Henry Adams and less attention to us as a group. We'll all have rooms at Crooked Lake."

"Great idea. Yes. My own pickup." Grace pumped her fist in the air, then frowned. "Crap. I forgot to tell you something. Yesterday, at the Owens's house, I lost Tag for a moment. She spaced out on me when a helicopter flew over."

"What do you mean?"

"She didn't even hear me talking to her."

"Maybe it's a battle memory or…hell, I don't know. I'll get on top of that psych eval."

Grace left for more coffee, and the sounds of the movie crept down the hallway with Katie's and Tag's laughter trailing behind. AJ counted in her head. If the doctor released Grace, they could be at Crooked Lake in a few more days, but first, she had to talk to Tag about what Maddie had told her today. It could be tied into the helicopter thing.

CHAPTER SIXTEEN

The two FBI go-to rooms at Hannah's House were noisy the next day, but Grace and Tag were oblivious, riveted by the computers. Maddie stood behind them, instructing, while AJ read a victim file.

"Wait. Grace, see this?" Tag pointed at the computer screen. "Look how fluid it is." Grace leaned over for a better look and Tag pulled her chair close.

"Think you can navigate this?" Maddie grinned.

"Bring it on," Grace muttered, typing furiously, tucked next to Tag.

Maddie glanced at AJ and indicated the office next to them. Once the door closed, she turned with a smile. "You're right about those two. Are they even aware of it?"

"I spoke to Grace last night and I think she's confused, but it would be a first for her. I haven't talked with Tag."

"They obviously love the system, a bonus for me. They almost drooled. Of course, Sam will be there too, if you say so." She handed AJ a cup of coffee. "How soon will you leave?"

"Hopefully, after the task force meeting tomorrow and Grace is cleared by the doctor. Did you get my email last night with the outline of our plan?" Maddie gave a quick nod. "I also spoke to Pete's uncle in Niagara. Do you know the family?"

"I spent a lot of time up there with Pete." Maddie wheeled a chair around and sat down. "I like where you've placed Tag and Grace in the community."

"Did Pete mention my CI in the group we're following?"

Maddie's eyebrows shot up. "You have someone in that group? I didn't know that."

"It's Frog, the young girl I had rehabilitated here, but something's wrong. The night she left she told me that two policemen paid her five thousand dollars to go undercover. The money's in her bank, but we have no idea who paid her. It was a cash transaction."

"Did you notify the Bureau? Or Lawrence Kelly?"

"It's in the task force notes, but I didn't talk to Kelly."

"Well, hell. I don't like that."

"And we still don't have the person or persons that shot me or set those fires. The chief, Bonnie, and Jock will continue on those problems, and that's everything right now." AJ set her cup down. "You're welcome to come to our task force meeting."

"No. If you okay Sam and he's there, that's enough. Grace appears to be feeling better, but those stitches and her eye look terrible."

"Good drugs, she says. We talked about her childhood and I mentioned your name. She thinks she can handle this, but if you want to say something privately, go ahead." AJ held up the file she'd read while Maddie worked with Grace and Tag on the computer. "This is awful. This man and woman may have been doctors, but a C-section on their kitchen table?"

"That's who I want you to see today. Sandra was the first real victim I spoke to when I came here. The owners bought her for sexual purposes only. No children. She was sixteen, and she's thirty-one now." Maddie gave a little shiver. "I've been with her quite a bit but can barely get a word out of her. She'll speak if she's in pain, but that's it. You're the first new people she'll see, and I'm interested in how she'll respond. There's also a little girl named Happy we're working on. She was seven when we rescued her a year ago and will barely speak. We'd like to get Sandra and Happy in the same room and try to create a relationship. We have a bunch of doctors working on those two."

"Tag and Grace should read this before they meet Sandra."

"Did you see what happened when they arrested the doctors who 'owned' Sandra? The local judge let them out on bail and they disappeared. This was the case that brought the DHS in, and we believe they're out of the country."

"One last thing," AJ said. "You said you have one of your best groups working on X-Girl meeting with the Milwaukee task force today. Will you keep me posted on their progress?"

"Of course. That meeting's happening right now, and it'll help the new city task force here with that murder, not to mention a lot of other things. I had to get clearance to do this, but they saw the value."

Tag and Grace walked into the office and AJ handed Grace the file. "We're going to talk with this victim, so read this file and then we'll go upstairs to meet her."

When the elevator door swung opened, a female doctor waited for them. She opened a door to a bright, airy room with a bed, sofa, and television. A desk and chair sat in the corner. The windows were open and AJ smelled the fresh air. Someone was humming.

"Sandra, you have company. Maddie's here."

A short blond woman in a simple blue housedress peeked around the corner, searching their faces. She smiled when she spotted Maddie.

"How've you been?" Maddie gave her a hug. "Have you eaten lunch?"

Sandra nodded, her pale blue eyes focused on Maddie.

AJ leaned against the wall beside the door. Tag and Grace sat on the couch. Maddie kept Sandra's attention, talking easily and smiling. Sandra suddenly turned and gave Grace a long stare with a small step toward her. Grace straightened but held Sandra's gaze. It was so quiet in the room that AJ could hear them breathe. Grace's eye bloomed purple in contrast with the yellow T-shirt she wore.

"Are you all right?" Sandra's voice was unused and rough.

Grace nodded with a shallow breath.

"What did they do to you?" Sandra rasped.

"I'm okay now." Grace's voice was clear but soft.

Sandra reached out and touched her face. Grace held still and calm.

"Are you sure you're all right?" When Grace nodded again, Sandra turned away, sat in the chair, and stared out the window. Her short blond hair was dull, even in the sunshine.

Maddie motioned for them to leave. Standing in the hallway, Grace looked unsure and Tag placed her hand on her back.

"That's the first time she's done anything like that," the doctor said with a longer look at Grace. "What happened to you?"

"Someone hit me in a bar fight. What just happened?"

"She actually interacted with you," Maddie said and turned to the doctor. "Maybe we can bring Happy up for a visit soon. What do you think?"

"I'll make sure I'm available. That was a moment. Thank you." The doctor smiled.

"I don't understand," Grace said.

"I think it was your black eye and the stitches. Sandra had a lot of stitches." Maddie turned toward the elevator. "Let's go see the other victim. Happy is an eight-year-old we saved last year. Her story is different than Sandra's, but unfortunately not uncommon. Her parents sold her to a handler when she was three." Maddie punched the elevator buttons.

"Her parents *sold* her?" Grace turned to Maddie with a disbelieving expression.

"A handler trains children to sex. A good handler in this business makes more money than I can even talk about. They can go anywhere, live anywhere, be anyone." Maddie held up her hands. "That first case you read yesterday, AJ? They were all negotiated by a broker. The victims were taken by an abduction crew and sold to a buyer online after the broker vetted him. The whole transaction took less than a few days. We lost those victims but arrested all of the adults –the broker, the crew, and the buyer."

The doors opened to the main floor and they walked down a long hallway toward children's voices and laughter. Maddie opened a door to a dark room. "We're hidden here."

They each took a chair and watched about eight or nine little children, most playing in three large sandboxes. Sunlight streamed across them from large windows, and the colors in the room brightened everything. AJ estimated most were between five and eight. One little girl, a truly beautiful child, was alone at a tiny table coloring in a book, her back to the other children. She had loose brown-gold curls. The loner, she thought.

"Can anyone pick Happy out of this group?" Maddie said.

They all pointed at the solitary little girl, her thin shoulders hunched as she colored.

Maddie nodded just as a small boy carried a ball from the sandbox to Happy at her table, rolling it across the book and colors, and into her lap. She was up in a flash. She hit him and sent him sprawling to the floor. He screamed and an adult appeared, separating the two. Happy stood, little fists at her side, glowering at the adult and the crying boy.

"A few months ago, she'd have been on top of that kid, pounding him," Maddie said. "She seems to have progressed to a simple leave-me-alone phase. She doesn't have many words, but she certainly knows the word *fuck*. Her swearing still shocks me. Some of the best child psychiatrists in this country have studied her in the last year, and most are unsure if she can be salvaged, but I'm not quitting. All the doctors call her a *feral child*." Maddie's phone chirped with a text, and she looked up with a smile. "Sam's here. Let's have lunch together, down the road. I have a place for him to stay, but he's yours, AJ, from the moment you say he'll work."

AJ watched Grace, intent on the little girl.

"What do the doctors mean...*salvaged*?" Grace turned to Maddie.

"Good question, but I'm going to continue with both her and Sandra." She checked her watch. "We have to go."

After the introductions, AJ sat next to Sam Mullins at the restaurant. Her first impression was that he liked women and enjoyed talking to them. She was rarely wrong on that. He ran a hand through his thick, short brown hair when he turned to answer a question from Maddie, and he had done his homework. He thanked her and Tag for their service and asked Grace how she was feeling. Maddie had described him perfectly. He had a fit body with big hands and moved easily, comfortably.

AJ asked about his military experience. His eyes lingered on Maddie before he turned to AJ.

"I didn't like it." He smiled, not the least apologetic. "I enlisted after I graduated from MIT and was a part of Desert Storm. When my tour was over, I came home to the private sector as a micro-electronics engineer, married my girl from college, also an engineer, and we were happy as clams in Arizona." He took a breath. "I assume Maddie has explained the rest?" He looked around the table and they nodded. "Okay then," he said and leaned back in his chair.

AJ again noticed his voice and pleasant appearance. People would talk with him easily. She would be working with him every day and didn't want an experience like Jock.

"We have our task force meeting tomorrow morning," she said. "You'll meet everyone else then. You've read our notes?"

"Yes, but it looks as if you're right at the beginning. Is that correct?" AJ nodded and he continued. "This is what I've been doing in Park Falls. Things were quiet when I left, but I have an odd feeling about that place. Too many people that didn't look local." He sent another look down the table to Maddie.

AJ checked out the busy restaurant. She watched a young couple move to a table and had an idea about how to present herself and Sam to their fellow employees at Adams Delivery Service up north. Sam blended easily. Tomorrow night would be a good time to have Maddie and Sam to the house for dinner. She began to eat and the entire plan came together in her head. It would work, but she'd have to explain to Katie.

AJ sent Tag and Grace home after the meal with Sam and then decided to work alone at her home office. She changed into shorts and a T-shirt and put together a simple but favorite broccoli and chicken casserole, got it in the oven, and let the harsh day settle inside her.

She wandered outside to the backyard in the last of the sunshine before she went to work. The ground was dry, so she picked up the hose. They could use some rain. Would Katie have time to take care of the yard? When she was recovering at the beginning of summer, she'd planted new flowers and shrubs. The guy down the street owned a nursery and she'd used his services. She pulled out her phone and called him to set up a time to begin regular lawn care. He said he'd do it personally since he was a neighbor.

She jotted down a list of things around the house to talk to Katie about and opened her laptop to go over the Niagara and Crooked Lake area. Tag had called Jay Yardley that morning and he'd agreed to give her a job. It felt like things were coming together.

The scent of food from the kitchen caught her attention and she checked the time. Katie was late for some reason. She got up, set the oven on warm, and checked her phone. There was nothing from Katie, and she went back to work, lost in the information in her laptop.

Much later, she rubbed her eyes, ready for tomorrow's meeting. She realized it was full dusk and grabbed her phone. Where was Katie? A wave of panic washed across her. She dialed Katie's number, but it went directly to voice mail and she thought of all the possibilities. It was after seven o'clock and unlike Katie not to check in if she was going to be this late. She tried Katie's phone again, but this time the phone was off.

"Okay, that does it," she said, racing to the bedroom. She slid into jeans and boots and secured her weapon. She turned the stove off, covered the casserole, and engaged their security system. As she turned, Katie came in the garage door.

"God, that smells good. I'm starving," Katie said, hanging her bag on the kitchen chair. The smile slid off her face when she looked at AJ.

"I didn't know where you were and it's so late and I panicked—" After a moment, AJ laughed softly. "I am so dumb."

"No, you're not, but something's wrong." Katie studied her. "You're wearing your weapon." She looked around the kitchen nervously. "Did something happen?"

AJ bent, her hands braced on her knees, heart racing. "I didn't know where you were."

"I told you this morning I had to drop off my SUV to repair the damage from that Owens kid. My uncle gave me a loaner, a luxury sedan. That's probably why you didn't hear my car in the garage. You can't even hear the motor."

AJ straightened. "Want some wine before you eat? I'll drink first to calm myself."

Katie lifted the casserole lid and inhaled with a smile. "Let's do both. Drink and eat. This smells wonderful. My phone died and I couldn't call." She put her phone on the charger, undid AJ's holster and laid it on the counter, and wrapped her arms around her.

"I feel stupid. I tried to call, but your phone was off and—"

"I wasn't home and it's dark. I know. That's happened to me…a couple of times." Katie took silverware out of the drawer and began to set the table. "Let's sit, enjoy the wine, and tell me what you can about your day."

CHAPTER SEVENTEEN

Pacing in the chief's office, AJ adjusted her weapon under her suit coat the next morning, waiting for him to get off the phone. They had to address the Milwaukee task force later, and she'd chosen a caramel brown suit, white tee, and deep brown ankle boots for a professional appearance.

"We hit gold," were his first words when he hung up. He laid out yesterday's interviews with the women from Home Base at Hannah's House and handed her the sketches of the two men involved with the two women that had perished in the fire. The victims had worked with a police artist, and the sketches appeared to match the two men that had been here the day of the fire. Best of all, everyone had reported a Confederate flag tattoo on one of the men.

"If it's them, it's murder," AJ said. "I wish I could get these sketches to Frog. What if they were the two men that gave her the five thousand dollars? Is that too much of a stretch?"

"We thought of that too."

"Anything on Robert Owens?" she said as they walked down the hallway.

"Jock said he'll see me today."

AJ placed her coffee and pastry by the chief at the head of the table just as Jock stepped inside the conference room.

"Do you mind if I sit in?" It was the first time he'd ever asked, and she smiled, pointing at the chair beside her. "I sent you and the chief an email on what I found on the men at the Owens house."

"Thanks. Get some coffee and something to eat," AJ said as she counted heads. Twenty-eight people including the DEA, FBI,

Milwaukee Police, and her ATF were in the room. Law enforcement should work together like this more often, sharing information.

Bonnie was talking—no, flirting—with a young blond cop, and AJ thought that was a good thing. Tag had her arm casually over the back of Grace's chair, listening to something Sam was telling them. AJ looked at them again. Tag always seemed to be reaching for Grace. The childhood they'd discussed briefly skated across her mind as well as Grace's odd reaction to the victims yesterday at Hannah's House.

Darn, she was hungry and realized her stomach was reminding her. Munching on the pastry, she checked her notes. She still hadn't talked to Tag about Maddie's surprise, the Afghanistan connection. She'd have to get to that before they left for northern Wisconsin.

She'd spoken with Jeff and Greg this morning. Each had a room at the motel near Crooked Lake where Frog and the girls were living, but things were *quiet*. That *quiet* puzzled her.

The chief handed out copies of the sketches of the two men identified by the Home Base women and began the meeting, repeating what he'd told AJ.

"Let's begin with the recent shootings and two fires," the chief said. "First, our security videos from here and Jimmy's Restaurant appear to match the eyewitness sketches from the Home Base survivors. The one important thing that stands out is the man's tattoo."

The chief's young, cute cop waved the papers. "I talked to these dudes at the Copper Penny when I pulled the late shift two nights ago. The bar would still have the surveillance." She held up one of the pictures. "This guy did most of the talking and asked how long we'd been here. He said he's grown up in Milwaukee and never remembered a police station here. This one with the tat was friendly, but I was in uniform." She sent the chief a grin.

"After the meeting, run over and ask if we can have their videos." The chief brought up Robert Owens's mug shot on the big plasma TV in the room. "Anyone recognize him?" When no one spoke up, he detailed the incident involving Katie's car, his connection to the house they'd taken down, and Jock's involvement.

"Damn. Tell me it's not Michael's drugs again," one of AJ's men said.

Jock responded. "No, not Michael's group, but there are drugs involved. I've got Robert Owens, this man, in rehab, and I'd like any of you to keep me in the loop if you happen to run across something—anything—involving him. We believe he's involved with the two men in those sketches. I'm the DEA primary here, so get in touch with the chief, Bonnie, or me. The chief has all the information we found." He held up the sketches. "Thanks for any help." He left the meeting. AJ watched him go, wondering about his new professional attitude. Something had changed.

"I'll be very brief," AJ said and stood. "As most of you know, we have a task force up north." She pointed at the maps on the wall. "This is where we'll be, and I expect it to take most of September. The FBI has had a well-publicized ongoing national human trafficking investigation for years, and we'll work with them so we don't cross paths. FBI agent Sam Mullins will be a part of our group." She pointed at Sam and he raised his hand with a friendly smile. "Four of us will be undercover, tracking a specific group of women that might have been sold for sex. As we gather information, we'll pass it back here. Bonnie and the chief will update the feed, so keep in touch. The DHS came in when Canada reported traffic up there, so stay alert out in the city. You never know what you'll stumble over."

She paused as everyone studied their tablets. "One thing I want to point out. Human trafficking crimes are just below what is spent for terrorism, plus hours logged tracking all of this. I've included information from the Department of Justice, both local and federal, and I want you to treat this much like we did Michael's task force. We're after information, so keep a low profile. We need names, people missing, the businesses involved, or anything else you hear. There are people out there making millions simply by sifting through the general population, and all ages and genders are involved. Don't forget that Milwaukee has a new trafficking task force and they need information too. Once again, report to the chief, Bonnie, or Jock...oh, and Grace and I will have our appearance altered a bit." Comments and laughter followed, and she grinned.

"Here's what we know right now. We have twelve females in a motel near Crooked Lake about a half hour south of the Michigan border and we have a CI embedded in that group. Ages are between eleven to mid-teens. Jeff and Greg from our group are at that motel, so we've got that much. I wish I had more, but you can bet we will soon, and that's it."

Chairs scraped as people stood and left. AJ opened the box on the table beside her, handing out a phone and credit card to each of them with a slip of paper. "Here's your room numbers at Crooked Lake Resort. Tag will be working with Jay Yardley. Grace will be there as a computer tech on a local business assignment. Sam and I will be working for Adams Delivery Service. Grace and I will have our names and appearance changed, but everyone else carries their real names, including Jeff and Greg." She stopped for a drink of coffee. "These are new phones that only the six of us have, programmed with only our numbers. No other names are on those phones and no apps."

Grace held the credit card in front of her. "This is my name? Gabrial Frank?"

AJ tossed her own credit card across the table. "Well, look at what I've got. Anne James. At least our initials fit so it'll be a little easier to remember."

"Just two different names out of six including Greg and Jeff. That's easy."

"If we slip and call you AJ, no one will notice," Tag added.

"Greg and Jeff say the twelve girls are in three rooms at that motel. Every day it's the same routine. One of the women drives into Niagara in the morning, gets breakfast or whatever, and brings it back. Then, a repeat performance around four o'clock in the afternoon. About every other hour during the day, the adult women take several of the girls outside for a short walk down the road. Greg and Jeff are gathering video although we're going to set up our own surveillance when we get up there. No one has contacted this group or come to the motel."

AJ shook her head. "I can't believe we're going up there with just this, but we are. We'll leave as soon as the doctor releases Grace and stagger our arrival times. Grace, you'll go first with the horse, check into the resort, and then do the horse thing. Tag, you'll follow about an hour behind her. Sam and I will share a car later that same day. When Sam and I check in, I'll call each of you that night. On the first day, use room service when you get hungry. Stay away from the dining room, but I do recommend their food. Since Katie and I were just there, I don't want to risk being recognized, so I'll sneak in with Sam as if we're a couple."

Grace looked up. "Have you told Katie about your plan with Sam?"

"Of course." AJ smiled. "She'll meet Sam and Maddie tonight. We're having them over for dinner."

"I'll bet that was fun," Tag said with a laugh.

"No, it wasn't, but she's okay now. Grace, you and Tag come over to the house tomorrow. Katie's sister, the one that owns the hair salon, is going to do our hair."

Grace frowned, running her hands through her long brown hair. "I just had it done."

"Don't even start. It's just a month and you get your horse and your dream truck. Are you picking it up today?"

Grace sighed. "Yes, later. I'm going back to Hannah's House after we're done here and see how things worked out with Sandra and the little girl. I've already talked with Maddie. She'll meet us there, and I can keep in touch with her while we're up north."

"Sure." AJ studied Grace's face. "How do you feel? You see the doc tomorrow."

"I'm much better, and Tag will go with me. I'll stop for my truck after."

"Let me know." AJ began taking the maps off the wall. "These maps are on our phones. I'll be at the Milwaukee task force with the chief this afternoon if you need me. We'll look over video and information about Robert Owens and those two men. If we need help, I'll let you know."

Tag pointed at her own hair. "I could use a cut too. Do you think Katie's sister...?"

AJ nodded. "Consider it done."

"Nice suit, by the way," Tag added as she turned to go, hand on Grace's back protectively. The chief watched them too and turned to AJ, eyebrows raised in a question. She only smiled.

That evening, Katie and Maddie talked in the kitchen. They'd bonded almost immediately over the roast chicken. Apparently, Maddie loved to cook as much as Katie. AJ took the time to talk with Sam, walking around the yard, looking at the plants and shrubs.

"I fought terrible depression after my wife died," he said, bending over a special ground cover curving around the grass. "Then, a stroke of luck. I met Maddie." AJ waited to see if there was more, but he added nothing, so she covered the silence talking about her time in Ecuador. Finally, Katie called them inside.

Later in bed, she remembered what he'd said about meeting Maddie and told Katie.

"She told me that Sam was staying with her," Katie said. "I wondered, but we got into a discussion about herbs and recipes and never went back to that."

"Maddie said she had him covered down here, but it never occurred to me she meant *staying with her.* We probably shouldn't tell anyone."

"Aren't you glad we don't have to worry about that?"

"God yes, unlike Grace and Tag—"

Katie shot straight up in the bed. "What?"

AJ looked at her, realizing she'd never mentioned this. "Some of it is work-related, but I talked with Grace the night Tag cooked those great ribs. Grace turned bright red. It's the first time I've seen her genuinely interested in anything…besides horses."

"And you didn't think to tell me?" Laughing, Katie punched her in the shoulder.

"Hey…ow. You're stronger than you think." AJ rubbed her arm and then stretched out on top of Katie. "I wasn't keeping a secret. I just happened to notice them…in meetings, working together, and other times. Grace made my life a living hell over you last winter and spring. I'm going to pay her back, believe me. Watch them tomorrow when your sister's here." She started to say more, but Katie stopped her with a super-nice kiss and the subject was forgotten.

CHAPTER EIGHTEEN

AJ set the drill down and tested the back gate. It was the last house repair on her list to be done before she left, and she put the drill away in the garage.

Laughter filtered into the garage from the deck, and she walked into the kitchen to see what was up. Katie was describing something with her hands, causing her sister and mother to howl with laughter.

She turned away, missing Katie already. *At least the shootings have stopped* rolled through her mind just as Katie put her arms around her.

"How do you do that? Know when I'm having a moment?" She leaned back into Katie.

Katie tightened her arms. "I'm a witch."

"One of the good witches." AJ grinned. It was true. Katie was the only one who could make her mind fully settle, and that actually was magic.

"Quit messing around, you two. I need your help," her sister grumbled behind them, gathering things off the counter.

AJ backed away, thinking of the victims at Hannah's House. They hadn't had any magic in their lives. Unless, maybe Maddie. Yesterday, the Milwaukee task force had nothing but great words about Maddie and the help her group had given them as they'd gone over all the videos.

"Come on. It's time to begin." Katie grabbed her hand and gave her that teasing smile that mirrored her mother's.

"Want to change clothes? We're talking major overhaul here," her sister said, placing bottles, scissors, and other things onto the table on the deck.

AJ straightened. "Wait. I just want..."

"Not what I had in mind," Katie's sister said with an evil grin. "You're mine."

AJ swore good-naturedly and sat on the stool.

About an hour later, she stood and undid the cape. Even her eyebrows felt battered. Now she was *almost* a brunette. Her hair was layered and shorter, the color of medium oak. She washed her face in the bathroom and stared at herself in the mirror. There were streaks of very light yellow, like the memory of being blond. Maybe it was the eyebrows that made her face appear longer and her eyes bigger?

"I like it," Katie said, stepping inside. "Not what I'm used to, but it's really nice." She walked around her. "It makes you look softer, but you'll never disguise those eyes. I love you, no matter what color your hair happens to be."

AJ sighed. "I know it'll grow out." They heard voices in the kitchen. "There's Grace and Tag. I'm going to change clothes." Katie ruffled AJ's hair, placed a kiss on her cheek, and left with a grin.

AJ tossed the clothes in the hamper. She wanted pizza and beer for dinner. Lots of beer.

Grace and Tag stared at her as AJ turned in a circle in front of them.

"Holy hell," Tag finally said. "I'd know the eyes anywhere, but..."

"I'm afraid," Grace said, shrinking back toward the door. "I wouldn't recognize you at first glance, maybe even a second. I'm hiding at home afterward."

"First you're having pizza and beer with us. Then you can go home." AJ pushed her toward the deck.

"Another lamb to slaughter," Katie said and introduced Tag to everyone. Grace had met them all when she stayed with Katie last winter and spring.

"Let's feed everyone pizza and beer after this mayhem," AJ said to Katie.

Katie only grinned with another long assessing look. "This is the most fun I've had since last night," she whispered in her ear. "Look.

You're right. Tag can't keep her hands off her, and see how close Grace is?"

Katie's sister ran her hands through Grace's long, dark brown hair, and everyone was quiet as a long swatch of hair fell onto the deck. AJ felt the anticipation and peeked at Tag, who looked absorbed in the scene. Katie's sister worked steadily, constantly moving Grace's head to look at the shape. Now it fell just below her ears, and she ended up with a much younger, tousled look. Then came the color.

Finally, Grace stood, stamping her barn boots and brushing off her black T-shirt and snug well-worn jeans. It was an amazing transformation. Grace didn't look a day over twenty with much shorter light blondish hair, including her eyebrows. The sun glinted off her bright hair. Grace was pretty, even with a black eye, but at this moment she was beautiful.

They all clapped and Katie's sister grinned and bowed.

Grace looked at the group. "How bad is it?"

"Come with me," Tag said, leading Grace to the bathroom. The rest of them waited, and then it came. The scream.

"What did you do?" Grace demanded of Katie's sister. "I look twelve and I'm blond. Even my eyebrows."

"It's beautiful," Tag mumbled, totally bemused, but Grace didn't look reassured.

"Okay, okay," Grace said. "Mission accomplished. No one will recognize either of us."

"Wait." Katie grabbed her phone, pushed AJ next to Grace, and took photos. Tag had her phone out, taking pictures.

"Enough," AJ finally said. "Tag, sit. She's going to give you a trim too." She called in the pizza order just as the doorbell rang, and she hustled down the kitchen steps to the door. To her surprise, the chief stood there, out of uniform. She could count on the fingers of one hand the times she'd seen him in casual clothes.

He stared at her, equally startled. "AJ?"

"I know, quite a change. We just finished. Come on inside."

He followed her in and they all settled at the kitchen table as AJ did the introductions. He was still staring at both AJ and Grace.

"No one will recognize either of you." He turned to Katie's sister. "My youngest is looking for a new hairstylist. Where do you work?"

AJ smiled at Katie. Her sister had her own shop that did quite well, especially with the younger crowd. The chief tucked the card into his shirt pocket and looked at AJ. "Something came up and we need to talk. Tag and Grace too. Can we use your office, Katie?"

"Do you want to stay and eat with us?" Katie said.

"I'm on my way somewhere and I'll be in meetings all day tomorrow, so I thought it would be wise to speak to these girls now. They'll be gone soon."

Katie's smile dimmed, and it made AJ's stomach clench.

In the office, the chief handed AJ a thumb drive. "From this point on, your offices are locked at work, and I'm glad you took the maps off the wall in the conference room," he said. "Bonnie and I ran the last three days of security at the station this morning. Those parking lot men have been there, twice. The first time, around three in the morning two days ago, and again this morning about the same time. Oddly enough, they didn't go into any of the offices or the conference room. They simply walked the hallway and looked into our offices, then they were out the door to the parking lot. We have their pickup truck license plate, and Jock ran that. I don't know what the hell's going on, but I won't stand for this. I'm on my way to the watch commander's house and we're going to have a few words."

AJ stared at the video on the computer. "I don't understand. We've never had anything like this happen, have we?"

He shook his head. "Tag, thanks for the information on Owens and his two friends from the military. We would never have gotten that deep on our own. Have you read her notes, AJ? They're both using an alias here and employed by a nursery service, planting trees."

"I planned on talking with her today," AJ said. "I'll review it and leave you an email."

"Let me know when you're leaving. Ladies, you look amazing." He grinned and left.

Tag sat on the edge of the desk, staring at the floor. "We had this problem constantly on base. It's hard to spot."

"At least they caught this," AJ said with a deep breath. "Wait until we're up north, out of our comfort zone. You know what that's like, Tag. And, Grace, remember Arkansas?"

"What happened?" Tag said, looking at both of them.

"Grace and our GPS had a little misunderstanding," AJ said. "We were lost for at least half a day."

"You exaggerate," Grace said. "It wasn't more than an hour...or three."

"Not by the time we retraced our miles." AJ stood to go. "I smell pizza. Let's remember to ask how long the color will last on our hair."

"I don't know," Grace said, tentatively touching her hair. "But it'll definitely alter my wardrobe."

AJ looked at her. She was right. Of course it would.

"What did the doctor say, Grace? And is your horse ready?"

"I'm good to go but still have to take meds for a few days, and yes, I have the pickup and the trailer. I called the stable up north too."

"Let's eat first and then, Tag, show me what you found on Owens and his friends."

Later, Tag and AJ went back to the office to look at the information. Tag took a healthy drink of beer and tapped the screen on AJ's laptop. "I talked with these two men's commander last night. The names they're using here are the names of men who have been dead for over a year. I sent him their photos and he came right back to me. See their real names? They served with Robert Owens." She tapped the screen again. "I don't know why they're using those names since they both had honorable discharges. They're breaking the law using false IDs, Social Security numbers and more, but this is your call."

"Did you put this on our notes to Maddie?" AJ said. "I know you've been talking with her."

"Maddie said she talked to you about my situation. Want to talk about that now?"

"I would have expected that in our first conversation. In my office."

"I was under orders, AJ." Tag's face was carefully neutral.

"I understand, but someone should have notified me. Okay, just tell me what's going on."

"We stumbled on some intelligence last spring. I took it to my commander and he put us on it, full-time. We went back and checked it out, but then none of us were sure what to do with the information, including my commander. It's going to be political. They sent it up the line and we ended up talking with one of my ex-Dragons that now works for the FBI on the East Coast. What followed was intense, to say the least. It won't interfere with what I'm doing here, but it's damned serious." She walked to the office window, her back turned to AJ. "That's all I can say right now."

"All right. Keep it between the two of us. Don't share with Grace or anyone else. I'll let Maddie know we've talked."

"Fine." Tag paced a little. "It really is a big deal and scares me to death."

"Tag, I felt something was off, right from the beginning." AJ stood and locked her desk. "Back to our assignment up north and the two men. If we arrest them now, we lose our connection to whatever it is they're doing here. I think we'd be better off just tracking them. I'll talk with the chief and let you know."

CHAPTER NINETEEN

Four days later, Tag got into her car at Jay Yardley's office in Niagara and sat for a minute. Was this even real? She was actually here, in northern Wisconsin. Last weekend's meal with her family still felt like a dream. The familiar smells of the house, their voices, even the squeaky front door sifted through her memory. There had been so many moments when she'd been sure she'd never see them again.

She drove toward the Crooked Lake Resort where the task force was staying. AJ had placed her and Grace in the business suite, a large meeting room in the middle with a bedroom on each side. All of their computers were on the long desk in the big room with a large table for meetings or group meals. It would work well for their purpose.

The motel where Frog and the girls were being held was less than a quarter mile from the resort. She slowed a bit for a better look at the place. After midnight last night, she and Sam had tricked out the place, giving Grace many angles on her computers.

In the daylight, the motel looked a bit run-down, but the parking area was clean, the grass mowed, and the colorful flowers well tended. The old box truck was there and another vehicle. A new black Lincoln sports sedan.

After she topped the hill ahead of her, she pulled off to the side of the road and dialed AJ on their group phone.

"Tag?" AJ said. Tag could hear her shift the delivery van.

"There's a new car at the motel."

"About time," AJ said. "I'm at the gas station on the north side of town. What's the quickest way to get there?"

"Take a right at the first big intersection with all the lights. That road takes you past the motel. I'm on my way to the resort to change clothes. The new car has a rental license plate."

"I've got a delivery at the motel. I'll see it. I want a meeting in your suite around seven o'clock tonight. Find some pizza and beer for us," AJ said and disconnected.

Tag looked at the roof of the motel in her rearview mirror. She had lost girls in Afghanistan, but she was not going to lose this group. She stared at the phone. She'd heard nothing from Maddie about her possible testimony in Washington DC regarding the information her group had found on base. She'd done what they'd instructed—stay quiet and as out of sight as much as possible. She dialed Maddie but got her voice mail and left a message.

Tag pulled back onto the road and turned toward the stables. Grace might be there. After being together every day in Milwaukee, the days up here apart had been an adjustment, and she missed her. Grace's new pickup was there, a big reddish-brown Dodge. She'd been over the moon with this truck, like a kid at Christmas when they'd shopped at the dealership.

Tag grinned at the memory and got out of her car, feeling the tiny bite from the cooling sun. Autumn was on its way. The sumac in the woods and the trees around the lake were beginning to turn. Afghanistan might have had trees but nothing like the ones that surrounded her now. She loved this land she'd grown up on with all her heart. With a deep breath, she imprinted the scene on her mind.

The sound of hoofs echoed through the stable. Grace and Crow raced around the ring in an ever-tightening circle. Grace was golden in the sun against Crow's shinning black. She pulled the reins and the horse skidded to a stop, but Grace's agile body hardly moved. She rubbed the horse's ear and then nimbly dropped to the ground. Crow's ears perked up. Grace patted the horse's neck and turned, shielding her eyes against the sun.

"Hey," she called out.

"Having a workout?" Tag grinned.

"Long day at the computers and I needed some fresh air. How was your day?"

"Lots of people, but I had some quality time on Jay's office computer. Not a bad day but busy. I'm on my way to shower and change clothes. AJ wants a seven o'clock meeting. I'll order pizza. Do we have beer?"

They walked back to Crow's stall and Grace shoved the horse inside. "I made a run to the little grocery store down the road and picked up some things, including beer. Hope you like apples." She jammed her gloves into her back pocket and turned with a smile that left Tag breathless.

"You know I do." She rubbed Crow's nose, letting the horse get her scent. "Can I give her an apple?"

"She'd love it. Go ahead."

Tag laughed as the horse snapped it up. She picked up a second apple, and Crow shifted toward her, pushing Grace into her, a full-on body slam.

"Darn it, Crow," Grace said and reached for a brush with another lean against Tag.

Tattooed by the firm body and breasts against her, Tag's heart stuttered. "I'd better go clean up," she said, stumbling a little.

"Don't use all the hot water." Grace grinned, turning to the horse with the brush.

❖

AJ swung the delivery van across the road into the motel parking lot. She'd intentionally scheduled this as the last stop of the day and engaged the van's security camera. She placed cartons on her pushcart and entered the lobby and office. A plump matron, older with gray hair, stood up behind the desk as she entered.

"Can I help you?" she said with a friendly smile.

"Adams Delivery," AJ said and placed the clipboard on the counter.

"Where's our regular driver?" the woman said as she checked the order on the clipboard.

"Oh, I don't know. I'm new." AJ shook her hand. "Anne James."

"Donna Seesom. I own this place. We'll see each other a lot. Adams Delivery is my lifeline."

"I'm new to the area and the job," AJ said as she checked the cartons with her tablet.

"Are you staying in town?"

"No, at the resort, but we're looking for a place. Any recommendations?"

"Are you interested in buying?"

"Well, maybe. We wanted to leave the city, so it's a possibility."

"I have a place between here and Niagara. Four-bedroom ranch with a nice big yard." She pointed out of the window behind her. "I'm redoing this place so I can live here."

"Just starting, I see." AJ looked at the grassy area behind the motel that backed into the forest. There were piles of new lumber and construction equipment.

"We've begun on the inside of this place." She signed the papers and handed the clipboard to AJ. "I was born here, moved away, married, and now I'm back. Must be karma." She grinned. "The house I'm selling belonged to my parents. I came back from Green Bay after my husband died."

"It's a beautiful area," AJ said and grabbed the handles of the cart. "If we want to see your house, who do we contact?"

"Oh. Me, of course." Donna laughed. "I'm not a real estate agent, but there's a For Sale sign in the front yard."

"Write down the address for me and your number on there. We'll take a look at it."

The woman wrote the information on a notepad and handed it to AJ. "I'll look forward to it. I put both of my numbers on there."

AJ backed the van out of the lot and drove toward Adams Delivery to clock out. That woman looked like someone's grandmother, not a part of anything as dark as trafficking, but who knew? She'd talk to Henry Adams and his wife before she left work. Grace would have the video with the new car's license plates on her computer.

Sam opened a beer and slouched into the chair. Grace sat in front of the computers, and Tag stretched her long legs onto the coffee table. They were waiting on AJ or the pizza, whichever came first.

"How does your eye feel?" Tag said.

"I saw the doctor the day after we settled in here and had the stitches out."

Grace turned so Tag could see. The black eye had faded, and her skin shone as it had when Tag first met her. The stitches were gone, leaving a thin red line intersecting the eyebrow in their place. Tag remembered Grace's body against hers at the stables and swallowed hard. "It's almost gone. What do you think, Sam?"

"I agree, but remember I've only known you with a black eye." He squinted at Grace. "Probably all that time in the sun with Crow."

"And while I was enjoying that sun today, I met your sister." Grace grinned at Tag. "Why didn't you tell me Emma is the Crooked Lake Resort veterinarian?"

Tag straightened. "I didn't know. We were all so happy to see each other that all I know is that she's got a new boyfriend. He's a vet too but from Iron Mountain."

"She's shorter than me," Grace said. "Her eyes are really dark, like yours, but her hair is about the same color as mine."

"It's her hairdresser," Tag said with a laugh.

"No way," Grace said. Sam laughed at them as AJ walked in with two boxes of pizza. She set them on the long table in the middle of the room.

"What's funny?" she said, opening one of the boxes. "I met the delivery guy in the elevator. Now he thinks I'm you, Tag, but he'll never know. I paid in cash."

Grace leaned over the food with a happy sigh. "We were laughing because I met Tag's sister today at the stable. She's the resident vet here."

AJ opened another box and raised an eyebrow at Tag.

"I didn't know, but no harm done." Tag grabbed a slice. "Emma only knows I'm working for Jay. Grace was laughing because Emma's a blonde. I teased her at the family dinner, so I got to hear all about her hairdresser."

"After our experience with Katie's sister and our hair, I'll believe anything," AJ said.

Tag checked AJ's appearance. It definitely was a different look. Less business, certainly more casual.

"How's things at Jay's?" Sam said, leaning over the pizza.

"He has me out in the country. It's a week-long mini-poll for the state as the governor ramps up for another run."

AJ shook her head. "I haven't met a single person that likes him."

"Jay didn't have a choice, and he's not happy. He said I came along at a perfect time. When it's over he'll find something else for me."

"What kind of questions are you asking the people you interview for the poll?" AJ took another slice of pizza. "Anything our group can use up here?"

"Not really. Just general questions like how each home is doing, are they happy with the economy, what about education and health, those kind of things. Oh, and do they have any suggestions to help Wisconsin." Tag laughed. "Most say they'd like a new governor."

Grace put her pizza down and turned to a computer. "There's an online questionnaire from the newspaper too. Several other groups are doing these questions as well, and they're publishing the results."

AJ balanced herself on one knee on a chair, reading the article. "The newspaper is published once a week, right?"

"I bought a paper today to read later," Sam said.

"Grace, what did you find out about the tags on that new car at the motel?" AJ sat down next to her.

"You won't believe it. It's a rental under the names of our parking lot guys, the ones we think burned our vehicles and Home Base. I forwarded everything to the chief. They used the same fake names they were using in Milwaukee. Here's the rental information. They used John Owens's house for an address."

AJ studied the screen. "Damn. That means they're tied to Frog's group." She took another bite. "The chief is still working on that."

Grace hit a few keys and checked the motel surveillance.

AJ took a beer from the well-stocked refrigerator. "Here's what I found out at the motel." She related the conversation with Donna Seesom. "Put this information on the computer," she said and handed Grace the handwritten note the woman at the motel had given her. "Sam and I talked with Henry Adams and his wife when we clocked out. They knew the owner of that house that's being sold, John Badger, and they don't believe Donna Seesom is his daughter. They thought the daughter had died." She looked at Sam. "Didn't Henry's wife say there was a car accident years ago? The husband owned a construction company and died in the nineties. The widow, Mary Blanche Badger, was a nurse at the local hospital, so you should be able to track her easily. Tag, work with Grace on this. You can casually ask Jay about this woman and her house and her so-called parents. I don't want to alert anyone we're looking at her."

Tag watched AJ again. She hadn't just changed her appearance. There was a softer way she interacted with people. The way she walked, almost always behind Sam.

"I didn't see Greg's or Jeff's vehicles at the motel. They're not there now either," Tag said.

"They're meeting with the DHS in Iron Mountain, but they'll stay at the motel. Have you talked to the DHS, Sam?" AJ turned to him.

"Yes, in Park Falls," he said, "but this is different. I've never seen a truckload of kids. It's like they're waiting for something to happen. Maybe they were waiting for these two guys?"

AJ nodded. "Remember what Maddie said, how they gather their victims? What if that's what these two men do? Find and abduct people?"

"And make a lot of money off the abduction," Sam said and shook his head.

"I saw it in Afghanistan." Tag made a disgusted sound. "That money's everywhere. I've seen kids like Maddie's victim, Happy, or women like Sandra. We can't feed people, but by God we always find money for sex. Or weapons of mass destruction."

"How much of what you did in the military was involved with this?" AJ said.

"It wasn't our focus, but I saw it constantly. It was their country, not mine. Intel says America's one of the top destinations for the world's sex trade. That so disgusts me."

AJ nodded and yawned. "Girls, get on Donna Seesom. Sam, scour the newspaper. It's right in front of us, but we just haven't recognized it." She picked up her bag. "Tag and Grace, remember to leave your inside doors open so you can both get to the computers." She smiled at them. "I need a shower. See all of you tomorrow."

CHAPTER TWENTY

Worn out, AJ tossed her phone on the bed and left a trail of clothes all the way to the shower. She let the hot water pour onto her face, across her tired muscles, and let go of the "Sam's girlfriend" personality.

The charade had worked. People at Adams Delivery Service saw her and Sam as a couple, exactly what they'd intended. They'd worked through this on the drive to Niagara. Sam probably knew more about Katie than he should, and she certainly knew a lot more about Maddie. If she'd ever had a brother, she'd have wanted someone like Sam.

She settled by the window studying the lake. Someone was having a party at the beach bar, and laughter drifted up through her open windows. Even the little lighthouse at the far point of the lake was operational tonight, something that made her smile. She and Katie had taken a boat out there to see the decorative building, a smaller version of the real deal. The house behind it looked like a beach house on the Atlantic, something she'd grown up around.

She thought of the suite where Grace and Tag were staying. Everything fit. It was perfect for the computers with the big middle meeting room, long table and desks.

Last month, she and Katie had made reservations at the last minute and it had been the only space available. They'd stepped inside with their bags and just stared. It was huge. And empty. They'd both laughed, going across the kitchen with the industrial-sized refrigerator, sinks and cooking bar, not to mention the king-sized bedrooms and—

Katie. Her mind rewound and she grabbed her personal phone. There were three unanswered texts, including one from yesterday. The first two simply said *Around?* but the one sent less than an hour ago was not happy. *Where are you?* she read.

"You promised," Katie said, picking up right away.

"I'm sorry."

"I miss you and worry. Are you okay?"

"It's still quiet, but we may have caught a break today...and, again, I'm sorry."

Katie sighed and then her voice brightened. "One thing that I know will make you smile. The lawn guys showed up and did a great job. I even gave them a beer when they were done."

"That's good. This place feels so wrong without you. I'm looking at the lake and the lighthouse and just came from the suite where we stayed. I miss you too."

"Well, I'm in bed, going over notes for tomorrow's meeting, and I'm not washing these sheets until you come home."

They both laughed at that. "I still have a bunch of work too," AJ said, staring at her laptop on her desk. "I haven't even checked my email and I have to call Maddie."

"Don't forget to check in tomorrow."

They said a bit more and then regretful good-byes. AJ pulled up the photo of Katie on her phone, the one she'd had in Little Crane Lake last spring. She stared at it for a long moment and then opened her laptop.

This whole thing was going way too slow. Sitting back in the weeds wore on her, but she didn't miss the anxiety and nightmares. Or the shootings and fires. And there were the girls and Frog. Someone had to watch over them.

"Crap," she muttered after reading the chief's notes. Nothing new there either, especially no information on X-Girl from the Milwaukee trafficking task force. When she talked to Maddie, she'd ask. She was anxious to hear what Maddie had to say about the new car and the two men at the motel. She reached behind her for the group phone to call, still thinking about Katie and the yard guys.

"What guys?" she said out loud, scowling at the phone. The man down the street said he'd do it personally. She logged onto their home security, backed it up a couple of days, and began to page through. There they were. Two familiar men in an old pickup with a lawn mower and tools. What the hell. It was the two men who were now at the motel down the road. She swore at the video and called the chief, then sent him the security videos.

She froze the last frame. Katie. Standing on the deck in little purple shorts and gray T-shirt, handing them each a beer and, damn it, they were looking at her like she was a meal. She sent another copy to Grace.

❖

Tag leaned back in her chair. "Got it," she said to Grace, pointing at the screen showing the death certificate for Donna Seesom.

Grace looked at the information on the computer. "And here's the tax information on her so-called parents' house, the one she's selling. I don't know who she is, but she's not the daughter. That's just like those men at the motel with the fake names."

Tag held up a beer. "Want one?"

Grace nodded, typing. "I'm sending this and the certificate you found to the group and the chief and Maddie." She finished and propped an elbow on the desk, studying Tag.

"What?" Tag said, catching the look.

"I didn't hear you come back last night from the motel with Sam. Those were good angles, by the way, and we still haven't talked about your parents' meal last weekend. Was it fun?"

"I really loved the meal with Mom, Dad, and Emma. Jay and his wife were there too. I can't tell you what that meant to me. Will you come down and meet my folks?"

"Absolutely," Grace said, but a trace of confusion passed across her face. "This is a first for me," she continued as if she were thinking out loud.

Tag understood two things at that moment. This was brand new for Grace but not because she was a woman. It was simply new, and Grace was trying to figure her own feelings out. The scent of the stable and leather and the outdoors drifted around her as she waited for Grace to say more, her heart beating hard.

Grace took a deep breath. "I don't even know how to talk about this."

Tag took Grace's hand, but the computer chirped and a little red devil bounced across the screen.

"What the hell?"

"It's my *AJ Alert*." Grace opened the file. "Oh my God, look. Katie and those two guys from the motel. It's AJ's security video. See the date? Why did those men mow their yard?" Grace reached for the group phone just as it rang. "I see it," she said to AJ and put the phone on speaker.

"Want to go to the motel with me and shoot them?"

"The phone's on speaker and Tag's here. Let's all go."

"I'm in," Tag said. "Why were they at your house?"

AJ snarled. "The owner of the nursery, our neighbor, said he'd take care of the yard personally. The fucking truth is we can't do anything. I called the chief and sent this to him." They heard her take a deep breath. "We think those guys worked for him. What are the odds of that? Remember the information we found that said they worked at a nursery? Damn, I hate this. I have to call Maddie, so talk to you later. Guess I can put my gun away for a while, but when that moment comes, I get dibs." She disconnected.

Grace ran the video again, stopping it when Katie handed the men the beer. "No wonder she's cranky." She turned, her face a little dreamy. "I was there for their first kiss."

"You were...where?"

"By the exit sign at the Copper Penny. I was with Katie and her sister, watching Michael at the back of the room. Charles had driven AJ and Bonnie back from Little Crane Lake. They were both injured and high on pain pills. I'm not sure AJ intended for that to happen at that moment." Grace cut Tag a look. "It'll always stay in my mind."

Tag reached for Grace's hand again.

"You were saying..."

Grace tilted her head with a deep breath but kept looking at Tag. "I don't know what to say to you. I've never met anyone like you."

"I have an idea," Tag said, inching close, framing Grace's face with her hands. "See how this works." She kissed her softly and carefully, heart banging against her ribs.

Grace's blue eyes were wide and startled and a shade of blue that Tag still couldn't identify. "Much better than words," she said and licked her lips. "Could we do that again?"

Tag did just that, every piece of her body shaking. Somewhere, something was thumping, and that quickly turned into banging.

"For crying out loud." Grace tossed her pen across the desk and moved toward the door.

AJ and Sam strode into the room. "The cops or maybe a fire truck are at the motel. See the lights down the road? Look at the computers." AJ turned. "Grace, take your truck down there and call us. Neither Greg nor Jeff is picking up."

Grace grabbed her weapon and keys and was gone before Tag could move.

"Tag, pull up all the angles on the motel so we can watch," AJ said.

Hands still shaking, Tag brought up live shots from the motel. She could still taste Grace's lips.

"I was on the phone with Maddie when the sirens went by. Didn't you hear them?"

Tag shook her head, and Sam pointed at a group of girls huddled in the doorways.

"There's Frog," AJ said.

"Has Maddie seen any of the video from here?" Sam said.

"Yes, and has three of them identified, four including Frog. That gives me hope." AJ turned to them. "Tag, talk with Jay. See if we can trust the cops. Or if you don't want to use Jay, see what you can find out while you're doing that survey thing. Didn't you say you know some people here?"

Tag nodded. "Two that I went to high school with, and I've spoken to both of them. One's an artist with a little shop in town, but the other's a doctor at the hospital. I'll get in touch with her. And there's no problem talking to Jay." She turned and put her friends' names on her personal computer notes. "I think Jay's kind of jazzed over this whole thing, believes it's for Clint and understands I don't want the family to know. All I said at our meal was that I'd be working for the government soon."

"Clint Weeks's grand opening of his Niagara Inn is within two weeks. It's all over the newspaper I bought," Sam said, watching the video.

"Damn," AJ said. "That means we'll have a couple hundred new people in town to deal with. Great." Her phone rang and she put it on speaker.

"There's at least one body," Grace said, slightly breathless. They watched the EMTs wheel a gurney to a waiting ambulance.

"There's Donna," AJ said, pointing at the woman talking to the sheriff's deputy, animated and angry. There was only the ambulance and two sheriff's SUVs. "We're watching the feed, Grace. Can't see... oh, we've got you."

"They're really arguing," Grace said. "That woman's hanging in there and— hey, get your hands off me." They all heard a man's angry voice and the phone went dead.

"Christ," Tag said, reaching for her weapon in the drawer.

"Hold on." AJ put a restraining hand on Tag. "Wait for it." Grace spoke to the sheriff's deputy and put her hand out. It looked like he had her phone. They said a few words and she stepped back. He moved at her aggressively, and suddenly, he was on the ground.

AJ shouted, "Atta girl, Grace." The officer stood, obviously furious. Grace said something and he pulled his fist back, but she made another quick move and he was on the ground again. The man scrambled up and charged at her, but she turned quickly, sweeping his legs out from under him, and he was down for the third time. Grace shook her head and got into the back of his SUV.

AJ turned to Sam. "Take the car down there, but let this play out. If they ask, tell them you just stopped to see if you could help. Don't forget she's 'Gabrial' and be alert for Greg or Jeff. Show the sheriff's men your paramedic ID if you have to."

Tag sagged back in her chair, feeling useless. "Why'd she get into his SUV?"

"Because we need to see law enforcement up here." AJ put a hand on Tag's shoulder again. "She's trained for this. I'm not kidding when I say she's my best success story. Trust her. If the cops detain her, do you think you can get Jay there as her lawyer?"

Tag tipped back in her chair, not used to waiting. Her phone began to ring, but AJ grabbed it before Tag could get her hands on it.

"Don't answer. What if they have her phone and want to see who picks up?" Tag's phone went silent and AJ's began to ring. "Grab that number, Tag. Put it on the computer."

Tag had the location up in a heartbeat. It was the sheriff's phone number.

CHAPTER TWENTY-ONE

Tag followed Jay into the sheriff's office south of Niagara. Much to her surprise, Aaron Youngbear stood behind the desk.

"Evening, Jay. What's got you out this late?" And then his face split into a huge grin. "Tag, I'll be damned. When did you get home?" Grinning, Tag shook his hand. "Aaron. Good to see you. I finally left the service and am doing some work for Jay." He was one of her brother's best friends since they were kids, and it was good to see him.

"So, you're both here for what?" He looked at them, puzzled.

"You have my employee, Gabrial Frank. She's one of my computer women," Jay said.

Sergeant Youngbear raised his eyebrows. "That little lady that was shooting video at the motel works for you?"

Surprised at Jay's quick lie, Tag hung back. He was usually all suited up, but now Jay wore a faded Green Bay Packer T-shirt, jeans, and neon-green running shoes.

The sergeant laid papers on the counter. "You sign the papers while I'm getting her. Deputy Miller said she did some damage."

Grace did some damage? Tag looked around the station. It was immaculate and the flagstone walls gleamed.

Jay reached over the counter for a pen. "Wonder what he meant by damage?" He paused his writing and looked at her. "This might cost some money."

"I'll pay for it, or she will. Get her phone back and anything else these fellows took."

The metal door slammed and Grace stepped out with the young deputy. He had fresh bruises on his face and rubbed his jaw.

"Mr. Yardly," he said, shoving Grace toward them.

"Deputy Miller." Jay nodded. "What's happened with my employee?" He handed the paperwork over and took a long look at Grace.

"She was videoing us at the motel down the road from the Crooked Lake Resort. No one authorized that. Did you?"

"No, but I doubt it was criminal. She probably wanted to put it on social media."

Grace hung her head and smartly looked embarrassed.

"So it's a draw, right?" Jay regarded both men. "She'll want her phone back and anything else you might have confiscated."

The deputy tossed Grace's phone and keys on the desk with a loud clatter. "There'll be no charges, but she'll have to stay away from that motel. One dead is enough for this night." He rubbed his face again and stared at Grace. "Where the hell did you learn to fight like that? A pretty little girl like you should be out on a date with some lucky guy."

Tag clenched her fists. *Stupid little sexist.*

"There's a body?" Jay looked up.

"Already transported to the hospital," Deputy Miller confirmed. "Christ, that was terrible."

"Miller, leave it alone." The sergeant turned to Tag. "Let your brother know I said hello, and give my regards to your parents."

Jay held the door and the three of them walked outside into the cool dark night. Tag glanced at Jay. She'd remembered Grace's undercover name but hadn't told him about the ambulance or the body. He was frowning as he held his car door for Grace. Tag started to follow, but stopped as she heard the sound in the night air. The *whomp, whomp, whomp* of helicopter blades grew closer. "What the hell," she said, fighting the familiar panic, grabbing for control.

Jay looked at the sky. "That's just Judd's personal ride home from Madison."

They watched the helicopter pass over them.

"Who owns that?" Tag said.

"The CEO of Marine Bio-Tech, the plant over that hill. They're working on clean water. It's a facility the state built three years ago. Clint's the majority investor."

Tag concentrated on her breathing and wiped her sweaty hands on her jeans.

"My truck's at the motel," Grace said from the back seat and snapped her seat belt.

"I recognize you now," Jay said, looking at Grace in the rearview mirror. "Your lead agent in Milwaukee was right. I wouldn't have known you. I know you're trying to help Clint, but you might want to stay away from that motel from now on." He gave a short laugh and nudged Tag's shoulder. "Maybe I'm having a midlife crisis, but this is the most interesting thing I've done in years. My wife thinks I'm having an affair." He parked at the motel, now dark and quiet.

"Kathleen's smarter than that." Tag grinned. She'd always liked Jay's wife, who was also a lawyer.

"Normally, yes, but she's stressed as hell over the new house we're building."

"You're building a new home? Where?"

Jay gestured toward the lake. "Over there, on the north side of the lighthouse next to that little cottage. I think I'll turn that smaller building into a new law office for both of us now that the kids are in high school." He turned in the seat to Grace. "What happened here, at the motel?"

"I was driving by, saw the ruckus, and stopped," Grace said and got out of the car. "That older woman that manages it and the deputy were having one heck of an argument."

"What older lady?" Jay said. "A man from Wyoming, a friend of Clint's, owns the place. Well, maybe he hired her and I just hadn't heard about it." He grinned. "I'll catch it on the town's grapevine tomorrow and let Tag know. Thanks for letting me play, ladies."

"Do I owe you anything?" Grace took her keys out of her pocket.

"Not so far. I'm sure the damage mentioned was to young Deputy Miller's face. I don't think that has a monetary value," he said.

Grace shook his hand through the open window. "Thank you, Mr. Yardly. I appreciate your help."

"It's Jay, and don't hesitate to call if you need help again." He held up a hand. "Wait. I told them you were my employee. I'll put you on my list at the office so we're all covered with the sheriff. Tag says you're a computer whiz, so welcome to the firm." He grinned again and drove away.

Grace drove toward the resort.

"You okay?" Tag finally said.

"Of course. Call AJ. Tell her we're on our way and we're sweeping this truck once we get there. Damn. We'll need new phones."

"We ran the phone number when the sheriff's department tried to use your phone so we knew. We watched you on the computer. That deputy never stood a chance. Nice work." Tag dialed AJ on her personal phone. When she hung up, she laughed. "You should have heard AJ watching that live feed. She was yelling at you to hit him again."

Grace's mouth twitched with a little smile. "Three times. Three times I knocked that dummy down and told him to stay down. He didn't even realize I got into his SUV willingly until we were driving to the station. I wanted some information on the dead person, but he wouldn't give it up. Whatever happened at the motel really upset the deputy." She took a deep breath and laced her fingers with Tag's. "That was fun, but you were the best part of my day."

Pulse racing, Tag glanced at their hands. That beat down in the parking lot confirmed she had a lot to learn about Grace and had been every bit as ambushed as the deputy. She brought their interlaced fingers to her mouth and softy kissed Grace's knuckles. This had been some day.

❖

AJ waited for them in front of the computers. Sam returned and confirmed the motel had gone quiet. She sent him off to bed and then called Maddie to finish their phone call. She told her about the motel, the sheriff, Grace, and how Jay had helped.

"Maddie, we have tons of information on Clint Weeks, but what do we have on Jay Yardly?"

There was a moment of silence. "Not much. I knew him when I used to hang out up there with Pete. Nice guy, smart, and a good rep as a lawyer." AJ could practically hear her think. "Huh. Let's do a run on him down here. I'll get back to you," Maddie said. "You'll have your new phones tomorrow at Adams Delivery. I gotta run. Later, girl."

Next AJ left messages on Jeff's and Greg's personal phones. Both had responded. They'd been scouting Clint's new facility where they'd do some finishing work until the place opened. They'd meet AJ there tomorrow morning.

While she was waiting, she reread Tag's data on the two motel men. Somehow Tag had managed to talk to people that had served with both men and Robert Owens. Tag must have some serious cred. None of the three men had done any more than work in Transport in Kabul, and outside of shooting commendations, they'd simply served their time. They had no marks on their records either, and all had honorable discharges.

Swiveling her chair slowly, she looked around the room and the two beer bottles and chairs, nestled up to each other. No wonder they hadn't heard the sirens. Grace's eyes had been a brilliant blue. Maybe it was time to meet Grace's horse and have a little one-on-one at the stables.

One of the computers had the tax information on the property Donna Seesom was selling up on the screen. AJ scrolled through recent property transactions in the area, spotting Jay Yardley's name. She wasn't sure where the acreage was that he'd purchased, but she'd find out. It looked like it was out by the little lighthouse.

Grace came through the door at that moment, her face shining. Tag followed with an odd look on her face. They both laid their group phones on the desk near AJ.

"No information on the dead person," Grace said, taking a drink from her beer bottle.

"Good job," AJ said. "Tell me what you both saw."

"There were sheriff's vehicles and one ambulance at the motel. Was that Donna Seesom?" Grace took another quick drink.

"Yes. Did you find out what she was so angry about?"

"She didn't want them interfering with what was 'a personal and unfortunate accident.' She actually shoved that deputy around, the little jerk I tangled with. I saw Frog when I drove in, but they moved the girls inside, and I didn't see the body. It was already bagged."

"So the sheriff's department might not be aware of the girls?"

"They never mentioned them," Grace said. "That deputy that you saw was really upset over the body and so were the EMTs. Something's off about that body."

AJ shook her head. "It looked like he didn't even realize you'd gotten into his vehicle. When did that hit him, and how's his face?"

"He yelled at me all the way back to the station. More than his face is bruised, but he killed the phones. Tag said you caught that. My truck's clean. We swept it in the parking lot." She took a deep breath. "What do we do now?"

"I talked to Maddie. We'll have new phones tomorrow. Also, Jeff and Greg scouted out Clint's new place. They'll put in on our link. Grace, let's meet at the stables around two tomorrow afternoon." AJ shoved herself out of the chair. "Where'd they take the body?"

"To the hospital. Jay said he'd have information in the morning. I'll call you when I've talked to him," Tag said. "The sergeant at the sheriff's is Aaron Youngbear, a good friend of mine, so that's an another person I can talk to."

"Good. Speaking of Jay, he's on that list." AJ pointed at the computer. "He just bought some property."

"Yeah," Tag said. "He told us on the drive back that he and Kathleen are building a new house out by the lighthouse. That was odd because he never mentioned it at our family dinner. Also, he's going to put Grace on his employee list to cover his presence at the sheriff's tonight." Tag's personal phone rang and she checked it. She raised her eyebrows at AJ and moved toward her bedroom. "I'm beat. Think I'll turn in. I'll let you both know what Jay finds out." Her eyes lingered on Grace.

AJ nodded and turned to Grace. "See you tomorrow." Grace didn't answer, and AJ saw that she was examining the knuckles on her hand with a faraway expression. "Nice job tonight," she added.

Grace looked up with a smile. "What? Okay, tomorrow at two. Wait." She looked toward Tag's bedroom. "We were coming out of the sheriff's and a helicopter went over. Tag stopped dead cold, lost to us. Know anything about that?"

"No, but I heard a helicopter here, while I was waiting. What do you mean, 'lost'?"

"She just seemed to…go away. It's the second time I've seen her react to a helicopter like that. I told you about the first time at the Owens's house."

"Why don't you just ask and let me know," AJ said and left. Walking down the hallway to her room, she put the information into some kind of order, and had an idea. The next step should be to contact Frog. Those girls were still taking their daily walks, according to Greg and Jeff. She'd do some running in the morning.

CHAPTER TWENTY-TWO

The next morning AJ ran down the road through scattered patches of ground fog. Jeff had called to let her know Frog and her group had just left the motel parking lot for their daily walk. AJ thought it would take about twenty minutes to reach the girls. The ground fog would help. They wouldn't see her until she was right on them. She picked up her pace a bit.

She topped the hill, hearing girls' voices, and she sprinted toward the group. There were screams and yells as she angled her body, just missing them. She intentionally tripped to the ground off the road. The woman in charge hurried over to see if she was okay, and AJ sat, head in hands, until she heard Frog's voice and looked up into her face. Frowning fiercely, Frog stopped and her eyes widened. AJ held out a hand and Frog grabbed it, helping her to stand.

"I am so sorry." She bent over, hands on hips, catching her breath. "I was out on a morning run. Everyone all right?"

"We're fine," the woman said, checking each of the girls. "Are you sure you're not hurt?"

"Positive." AJ held out her hand, introducing herself. "Anne James, room five-one-five at the resort." She looked down the road. "Where are you from? I haven't seen any houses out here."

"We're at the motel. That way." The woman pointed behind them.

"I know that place. I work for Adams Delivery and make stops there." AJ looked at the girls. Only Frog looked at ease. They appeared to be any age from ten to thirteen and not too clean. Their hair was not brushed, clothes didn't fit, and they all looked afraid, clustering around the woman. Hungry and tired, AJ decided.

Mission accomplished, she thought, running back to the resort. Frog now knew she was here, what name she was using, and where she was. For that matter, Frog had probably recognized Grace last night despite her new hair color. She'd have Grace go over that video and watch Frog.

Back in her room, AJ showered, thinking of the number of times she'd trusted Frog's instincts. Depended on them. Both she and the chief thought she'd make a great cop if they could ever find the time to develop her. But not yet. The kid was still reckless and needed more training.

Dressed in her delivery work clothes, she sent Grace a to-do list and reminded her of their meeting. She opened her door to leave just as Tag was about to knock.

"Have a minute?"

"Almost. Jeff helped me stage an accident down the road this morning. I ran myself into Frog's group that walks every morning and got my location and name out there for the kid. It was amateur, but you do what you can. If I know Frog, she has Grace identified from last night. You'll like her, Tag." She picked up her bag. "What's up?"

"That call I got last night was from Washington. They may need me to testify soon. They notified Maddie too."

"Crap. Do you know when?"

"No, but they said soon. Maddie wasn't too happy either."

"It'll sound better if you tell Grace and Sam when you know for certain. I might leave too many unanswered questions if they asked me."

Tag nodded and leaned against the door. "Could we talk about Grace?"

"Not like I didn't notice, but just not now. I'm late." She shouldered the bag. "Keep me posted about the Washington thing. Sam says the new phones from Maddie are at Adams Delivery, so pick yours up on your way into town. I'll deliver Jeff's and Greg's phones to them at Clint's new place. They're doing some finishing work on the building. Since Clint's not in town I'd like to see if we can hide some cameras there. Any ideas about that?"

"I'll talk Jay into a tour this afternoon when he's in the office and let you know if he heard anything about the body last night."

"I'm meeting Grace and her horse at the stable this afternoon.

I'll deliver her phone." AJ shut the door behind them and they walked down the hall together.

"This is so slow and I'm used to moving fast. How are you doing?" Tag said.

"Same problem, but I have a feeling things are about to pick up."

❖

AJ parked the van in front of Clint's lodge on the south side of Niagara. The building looked huge. A gigantic red neon eagle flew across the front of the lodge, and she stared at it for a moment. It would be seen for miles.

She carried the box with the phones and her clipboard inside. To her right, a grounds crew worked on new shrubs, and a truck with sod in the back was parked by the trees. It reminded her of the two men staying at the motel, the ones that had been at her house with Katie.

She went up the broad steps and backed through the stained-glass doors.

"Anne," Jeff called and she looked up. He was hanging above her on some beams, holding a roll of tubing. "Stay right there. I'll come down."

She took in the beautiful plush lobby, all done in various reds, accented with blacks and browns. "Got time for a quick idea of the layout?" she said as Jeff opened the box and stuffed the phones in his cargo pants.

"Sure. Greg and I are finishing the neon drivers for the big signage on the front. How'd you do with Frog this morning?"

"Perfect. She has my name and room number." They walked to the middle of the first floor. "Think it's possible to install some cameras here? Tag will be in here this afternoon with Jay and she'll have some ideas too. Compare notes." AJ saw Greg walking toward them and nodded, turning to go.

A man in an expensive suit walked inside, holding hands with a young woman. As they went by, she stared down at her clipboard so the man wouldn't get a clear look at her, but she got a solid look at the young woman.

He said a pleasant "Good morning" as they passed each other, and she responded in kind. Three steps later, her brain woke up. That wasn't a woman. It was a young girl, possibly twelve or so, dressed to look older with makeup. "Holy shit," she said under her breath and glanced over her shoulder. The man was talking to Jeff, gesturing at the ceiling. She sat in the van for a moment, thinking. What was that? When she talked to Grace this afternoon, she'd ask her to surf the internet and see what could be found up here about young girls made up to appear older.

❖

AJ parked beside Grace's pickup at the stable and called Maddie on her new phone.

"Thanks for the quick phone turnaround. I'm just delivering Grace's."

"Ask her to put anything, any detail, she can remember from last night, especially names, on our computer thread. Also, Pete's helping me with Jay Yardly. He always has a handle on that area. Have you seen the lighthouse on the lake where Jay is building?"

"Katie and I took a look at it when we were here." AJ looked around the stable to see if anyone was outside. "Tag said Jay recognized Grace from our meeting in Milwaukee but believes we're working for Clint. You and Tag talked about Washington?"

"Yes, but if she has to go we can't do anything about it."

"I agree. In other news, I contacted my CI up here this morning and also got a good look at Clint's new lodge. We're starting to get into the scene here."

They ended the call, and AJ got out with her clipboard and box for Grace. She looked around the area and at the lake. Spring was Katie's favorite season, and AJ felt a quick pass of loneliness. A door closed nearby and Grace walked toward her. AJ handed her the box and had her sign the paper just for show.

"Let's go meet Crow." Grace tossed the phone box in the bag she had slung over her shoulder. "Tag's sister, Emma, is in the office, just an FYI."

"How are you feeling? Anything left over from the concussion?"

"We're meeting to discuss my health?" Grace said with a smile.

"No, but it's important. Think about Tag and the helicopter."

"Do you think that's it, an injury?"

"Not necessarily an injury but I think it's something she brought home with her, and we still don't have her psych eval," AJ said as they stopped at a large stall.

"Here's Crow," Grace said, picking up a saddle.

AJ touched the velvety nose, but the horse shied away.

"Hold still. Stubborn girl," Grace said, pushing the horse with her shoulder. "I saw you leave on a run this morning."

"I intentionally ran into Frog's group as they took their morning walk, and it worked. I got my name to her and where I am at the resort. Those girls are so young." AJ went quiet as they walked to the arena. "They were afraid and didn't look well taken care of."

Grace looked away, a sad expression on her face. "Well, I'm sure. I watch them on the computer and they just trudge along, heads down."

AJ couldn't find the words to say more. Finally, she said, "How's it going with Tag?"

Grace brightened and sagged against Crow, smiling. "Last night was special." Her smile transformed into a dreamy look.

"What do you mean?"

"I kissed her. Or she kissed me."

"Well that's, um, are you—"

"It was wonderful. I loved it."

"Just a kiss?"

"Just. A. Kiss?" Grace drew the words out with a happy sigh. "I feel like a teenager. It was spectacular." She did a quick little dance. "I don't know what this is, but it sure is fun. I've never had anyone look at me the way she does. She's so steady. It's like she's inside me. I'm kind of floating right now—"

A sharp crack whooshed by them and Crow reared, then ran. AJ pulled Grace to the ground, and tried to crawl on top of her to protect her. The next shot came, and she could hear Crow's hoofbeats racing away.

"Crow," Grace cried out and scrambled out of AJ's grasp. The next shots hit the ground right behind Grace's boots as she ran. People spilled outside, yelling and pointing to the hill. Something flashed behind the pines.

A slender blond woman led Crow down the aisle into the stall. The similarity to Tag was undeniable. She had to be Emma.

"I have her, Gabrial. Who the hell would shoot your horse or you?" She stared at AJ. "Or you? Is everyone okay?"

"Crow's shot?" Grace stumbled, racing to the side of the veterinarian.

"Let's look at the damage," Emma said. She opened her doctor bag and pointed at Crow's haunch and the blood.

At the sight of blood, AJ had to look away, her body still racing with adrenaline.

"Okay, Crow, okay," Grace murmured, rubbing her neck, taking the reins from Emma. Eyes desperate and filled with tears, she looked at AJ. "What the…?"

AJ's heart sank. She was positive the shots had been intended for Grace, not Crow.

"Emma, this is someone from the resort. Anne James."

Emma tossed a glance at AJ. "I saw you drive up in your Adams van when Gabrial and I were talking about the little mix-up at the motel last night. She says you're ex-military. So is my big sis." She applied something to Crow's skin that caused the horse to move quickly away, but Grace held Crow. Emma stepped back. "She's just grazed," she said with a relieved breath.

AJ placed her hand on her heart. "That scared me. Does this happen up here often?"

"No, thank God, but that was a pretty good tackle you performed out there," Emma said with a little grin directed at AJ. "Police are on their way. You'll have to talk to them. Did you see anything out here? The shooter?"

"I thought I saw something up by that double stand of pines." AJ turned to Grace. "I heard about the stuff at the motel too. What were you doing down there?"

"Coming back from town. I should have minded my own business. My bad."

Emma was shorter and curvier than Tag but had the same eyes. Even their voices sounded similar. "The sheriff didn't charge you?" she said to Grace.

"No. Thank heavens for your sister. Tag got Jay to help me."

Both of them worked through the charade of the story, and then the cops were there. After identifying herself, giving her statement, and answering all questions, AJ left and drove toward town, calling Tag on their group phone. This was going to be a problem in so many ways.

❖

Tag was leaving Clint's building when her new group phone rang. She saw it was AJ.

"Just leaving Clint's," she answered. "Greg gave us the tour. Jay has people coming for the grand opening, and he's been there a lot. He also gave me some news on last night's victim from the motel, a thirteen-year-old girl, but they haven't done an autopsy yet. I'm going to contact my friend, the doctor."

"Do what you can," AJ said.

"I had breakfast at the local diner but heard nothing, so someone's keeping it quiet."

"Well, I may as well make your day." AJ pulled in a breath. "I delivered Grace's phone at the stable, and while we were out in the ring with the horse, someone took four shots at us. Grazed the horse, but your sister was there and was a big help. I wouldn't have had a clue—"

"Is Grace okay?" Tag interrupted and pulled off to the side of the road.

"Only the horse was grazed. Emma said it was nothing serious. It was a pistol. Again. I had to talk with the local police. They let me leave right away because I'm just the delivery person, but they were still talking with Grace when I left. I told them I'd just delivered a package and asked to see her horse while I was there. Let Jay know because he's her 'lawyer' and all that."

"Did you and Grace manage the cover with Emma?" She gripped the steering wheel.

"We did fine, but I tackled Grace in the ring when she ran after the horse, trying to get her out of the line of fire."

Tag toyed with her Dragon necklace, stomach tight. "I'll avoid the stable. It'll complicate things. I'll cover myself with Emma over last night at the sheriff's, but I need to talk with Grace first."

"All right. I'll call Maddie's office and get this on the record."

"Who were they shooting at? You don't look anything like you did in Milwaukee." She wiped her sweaty hands on her pants. "Damn. It was Grace, wasn't it?"

"I thought so, and it was probably connected to last night. I did run into that group of girls this morning, but I'd lay odds it was Grace they were after."

Tag drove back to the resort and changed into a faded UW Badgers T-shirt, well-worn jeans, and some thick socks. It was quiet next door, and she assumed Grace was still at the stable. Just as she slid into her boots, there was a loud *whack* against the wall that separated the rooms, followed by some loud curses. She cracked the door and peeked into the large middle room.

Grace was knocking things off the desk and table, and swearing. Tag inched into the room.

"Are you okay?"

Grace whirled on her. "You heard what happened with Crow?"

"AJ called me on the way home."

"Those cops weren't the least bit concerned that Crow got hit. Emma was a big help." Paper scattered around Tag like a handful of snow.

"That's not what I asked, Grace. Are you okay?" Tag stood deliberately in front of her.

"I'm fine. Thank God they're the worst shots in the world."

"Good enough to hit AJ in Milwaukee." Tag knew Grace was in shock, and she gathered Grace's shaking body against her. She soon realized Grace was crying. She brushed tears off her face and held her tight again. "Hold on. I've got you."

Grace drew in a big breath. "I guess it's only fair you get to see my first temper tantrum in years." Grace wrapped her arms around Tag with a deep breath. Someone knocked on the door. Grace stepped back impatiently, calling out, "Come in."

Sam walked inside but stopped when he saw the mess on the floor. "AJ said to stop here first," he said and picked his way through the debris. "She's changing clothes." He took a long look at Grace. "You okay?"

"I'm fine, but Crow's not so good. I know it's just a scrape, but damn it all to hell." She began to pick up the papers on the floor.

"I don't know if you should be at the stable now." He sat on the couch.

Tag sat beside him. Thank God he'd said it. Now she didn't have to.

Grace turned, angry again. "You don't get to say that. I'm not staying away because some dummy has a gun. Everybody in this country has a gun, even kids, and I'm not—"

"But this is the third shooting," he interrupted as AJ came through the door. "Not that I'd argue with you about guns."

"That's enough," AJ said, rummaging in the bar for a bottle of water. "Arguing doesn't get us anywhere, and we all agree on the gun issue. What did the cops say, Grace?" She surveyed the room and cocked an eyebrow at her.

Grace stared at her for a long moment and then took a deep breath. "They called just before Tag got here. I have to be in Niagara at nine o'clock tomorrow morning. That's all I know."

AJ nodded. "Tag, did you talk to Jay? After the business with the sheriff last night the cops will know something about *Gabrial*, and we don't want to blindside him."

"I called him after you and I talked," Tag said, watching Grace stack papers on the desk. A dark feeling crept through her. Before she could stop it, the image of Jane, her next in command Dragon, flooded her mind, running toward her in a hail of gunfire. She went down. Tag closed her eyes with an inner groan and got up for water. "Jay wants to go with you in the morning, Grace," she said. "The local police contacted him about the shooting." She turned to AJ. "Did you talk to Maddie?"

"No, just her team, and I gave them all the information." AJ rubbed her eyes. "Call Emma now and see what she has to say."

Tag dialed her sister on her personal phone. Emma was still at the stable, checking on Crow.

"I ran into Gabrial when I got home," Tag said. "I heard what happened out there."

Emma recounted the story but hadn't seen anything outside. She didn't have a clue why anyone had shot into the arena.

All the time she talked, Tag watched Grace put the room back together. Her face was calm and empty, her temper gone. Or hidden.

"Okay, I need some food," AJ said when Tag was done. "Sam, why don't you and I go down to the dining room and get something? Give these two a breather." She touched Grace's shoulder. "Order from room service. You need food too."

After they'd gone, Grace sat in front of the computers and rubbed her forehead, eyes closed. "It's me, isn't it?" she finally said. "They were shooting at me."

Tag grabbed the room service menu. "Let's get some food and talk about this."

"You order. I'm going to shower and change into clean clothes." She left for her bedroom and Tag picked up the hotel phone.

CHAPTER TWENTY-THREE

The Crooked Lake resort's homemade chicken soup and roast beef sandwiches were out of this world. Tag sat with Grace at the little table by the window, knees touching, and watched darkness cover the lake. Even the faint scent of Grace's shower soap was soothing.

"Help me out here. I don't want to talk about guns or people shooting at me," Grace said. "I'd rather talk about those little girls down the road or Maddie's progress with Happy and Sandra in Milwaukee. She gives me updates on those two."

"How're they doing? I worry that Happy's too wounded to recover."

"So far, their biggest accomplishment is that Happy now uses a fork to eat and not stab other kids with it," Grace said. "They're making marginal progress with Sandra and Happy together, but I've never seen the word *anger* used so often." She sighed and pushed her empty dishes to the side. "That was really good. Thanks. Would you make some coffee? I've got a headache and took some aspirin after I showered. God. Even my feet hurt." She stretched out on the long leather couch in the middle of the room. Tag went toward the coffeepot. "Your sister's really funny when she talks about you. Calls you tall, dark, and handsome." She laughed for the first time.

Tag gave a little snort at the tease in Grace's voice. "I could return the favor, but I'll be the good big sister. Our house had a lot of laughter, but we worked hard. Coffee will be ready in a minute. Move over and I'll rub your feet."

Grace plumped the decorative pillow and placed her feet in Tag's lap.

"Mom and Dad met in college, and both say it was love at first sight. I think it still is." She grinned at Grace. "Dad's typically English, a little on the short side, and so is my brother. Mom and I have Granddad's Swedish bones, but our skin and eyes and hair are all Menominee. Actually, she's taller than Dad, but they're both in great physical shape and still work hard."

"Do they have animals on the farm?"

"Sure. Chickens, two cows and a pig or two. Used to have sheep, but they didn't do well for some reason. They always sent *me* to look for the sheep," Tag said with a laugh. "We had an old beat-up ATV for the pastures, and I loved driving it but hated those sheep."

"No horses?"

"Not now. They gave them to the kids ranch just outside of town."

"A kids ranch? That's cool. When we go down there could I see it?"

"Emma does a lot of work there. See, I'm being the *good* big sister."

"You are good, Tag, and that feels wonderful." Grace groaned as Tag rubbed the other foot and kept on talking about being the middle child of English-Menominee parents. Soon, Grace was breathing deeply, sound asleep.

Tag stared at the dark night and then at Grace. Tag brushed her tousled hair off her forehead. She liked it blond as well as its natural dark brown. She traced her fingers across her shoulder and down to the hip. Her anger that someone had shot at Grace was like a slow burn. Tag got up and went to Grace's bedroom to find a blanket.

She turned on low lights and closed the drapes. She'd never been in there. The room smelled like Grace. Suddenly, she stopped, staring at the poster above the bed.

"I'll be damned," she said. It was the recruiting poster she'd posed for when she'd led the Dragons. Where on earth had Grace found that?

She looked at the books on the bedside table and picked up *The Last Unicorn* that she'd found in Milwaukee, the one with the photo of a young Grace inside. The other books were all about survival. She picked one up and looked closer. It was about sexual abuse. An expensive wine-colored leather notebook lay open beside the bed. Tag bent closer and saw a list of names in Grace's unique vertical writing. There must have been at least twenty or twenty-five names, all beginning with "Dr." followed by dates. Tag studied the dates. Some were fifteen years ago. She frowned, seeing telephone numbers beside them. How long had Grace been involved in this?

She covered Grace with the blanket and sat down at the computers. She checked the motel, still thinking about Grace's bedroom. She hadn't seen that Dragon poster in a long time.

The motel looked quiet. She thought about her Dragons. She couldn't get them back but she could fight for these girls that were held down there. She backed tonight's video up a couple of hours and went over it slowly. The new Lincoln had been there, and she watched it drive out of the lot. A few minutes later, a girl came outside and slipped something inside Jeff's pickup. Was that Frog? It looked like the girl with the spiky hair that AJ had pointed out last night.

There was a quick rap on the door, and AJ stepped inside. Tag pointed at the sleeping Grace on the couch.

"I think I just saw Frog on here putting something inside Jeff's pickup," she said.

"You did. Jeff's meeting with her right now, behind the motel. Can I see the computer?" AJ stopped at the couch, tucking the blanket over Grace's shoulder. "God. I can't believe someone actually shot at her," she said. "I'm angry."

"I am too," Tag said. They both sat at the desk, watching the motel video. Finally, Tag sighed. "What the hell is going on here?" She gestured at the computers. "I mean the motel, Clint Weeks, all of this?"

AJ took a deep breath. "I've fought this assignment from the beginning," she said. "Let me show you the Bureau's first email to me when Katie and I returned from up here." She brought the document up on the screen. "Grace has read this too."

Tag read it. "It doesn't say anything other than 'forming a task force.' Well, it mentions this general location and Frog's information, but nothing specific."

"It was the lack of specifics that had me calling Lawrence Kelly. Of course we argued. He said I'd get the rest later, but I never have. Now he tells me to work with Maddie. I wanted to stay in Milwaukee and work with the new task force and X-Girl." AJ got up for coffee. "Then, after we had that meeting with Jay and Clint, I decided it was a political favor, and I was really pissed. Any thoughts on this?"

"It's muddy. We're just going through the motions, all for Clint

Weeks. And we haven't connected Weeks to the girls in the motel," Tag said. Her voice carried some anger. "I understand the shootings and fires in Milwaukee were serious, but now one of these girls is dead."

They both looked at Grace.

"Did she finally realize she was the target? Not Crow?"

"Yes, but she wouldn't talk about it. She said she had a headache."

AJ tapped her coffee cup with her fingers. "I was afraid of that. Grace handles crisis differently than anyone I know." She shook her head. "First, I need to hear what Frog tells Jeff. Maybe we'll have something new. Still, I agree that it feels like babysitting. I have that nagging suspicion it has nothing to do with Clint or his grand opening. It's something else altogether."

Tag sighed. "What does Sam say?"

"We talked about this over dinner tonight, and he agrees with what we've just said."

Tag stretched her arms above her head. "Let's say we are here because of Kelly's friendship with Clint, but that's just the surface. You're right. Maybe the problem is something totally different." She stood and began to pace. "And what about the Owens brothers and the two motel guys? What if they're connected in another way than what we've found? I'm concerned that the chief and the task force down there haven't dug up any new information."

AJ looked at Tag. "It's hard for me to connect the fires and shootings back to my bureau chief—"

"Exactly," Tag said.

"Let's see what Frog gives to Jeff tonight and then what the police tell Grace in the morning. We'll have a group dinner here tomorrow night. We need to talk about the direction we're taking." AJ rubbed her eyes. "This morning you said you wanted to talk about Grace."

Tag nodded and sat back down. "I was really frustrated when I got back to Milwaukee after all that crap in Washington. Believe me, Grace is the last thing I anticipated. All I wanted was to come home. Then wham, there's Grace. All that brains and beauty, and she somehow stretches my normal, the way I usually meet a woman. This is so odd. Something about her makes me want to talk to her." Tag shut up, embarrassed. "She says she doesn't know how to talk about it."

AJ nodded. "I've always said she's unaware of people's attraction to her. Then, all the time we were walking out to the arena this afternoon, all she talked about was you." She stared at Tag for a moment. "Here. Let me show you something." She flipped one of the screens to her own files. "Grace found John Owens in Milwaukee at a fitness gym and I went in there as a seller with her. She was the 'product,' so to speak." AJ ran the video she'd looked at with the chief at the office. "Watch Grace during this whole conversation."

"You were trying to sell her?" Tag frowned when the video stopped.

"We were trying to learn the market, the language, winging it. Owens was so greedy and arrogant, and you saw the way he treated her. Exactly like a 'product.'"

"Look how innocent Grace appears," Tag said, touching the screen. "Has she always been that way?"

"Pretty much as far as appearance goes. It's like there's a step missing." She laughed a little. "She was onto Katie and me, right from the beginning."

"She never talks about her family, and yet she asked me about mine tonight. I don't want to get into her business, but—"

AJ's phone pinged with a text from Jeff. "Jeff's on his way up. I'll take it down to my room so we don't wake Grace. Watch the computer, will you? I'll come back when he's done and we'll talk again." And she was gone.

Tag saw Jeff leave the motel in the dark night. The black car was still gone. She took a deep breath and stared at Grace. It was something between them, whatever it was, and she wanted more.

❖

The clock said 10:17 when Jeff knocked on AJ's door. She'd just texted Katie and sent lots of hearts.

Jeff wore a baseball cap over his dark hair and tossed a paper on her desk. She'd made coffee and offered him some.

"How's Frog?" AJ said.

He touched the paper but smiled. "She's good. You've seen the building materials at the motel, all that wood and equipment? They're not exactly *remodeling* like Donna Seesom told you. They're rebuilding the center of the inside, where Frog and the girls are located. The middle four rooms. Greg and I have seen men there, lumber being moved, and were going to ask, but the time's never been right. Here." He held up the paper. "Look at Frog's drawing."

AJ leaned over the pencil sketch.

"She thinks they're designing a new front entrance here. He touched the drawing. "It'll be like stepping into a bar. You can have a drink and go down the hall to the private rooms." He sat down beside her. "I gave her everything I could. Our schedules, what we're doing and so forth, but didn't tell her about the FBI's private phones that we use. She saw Grace last night and of course you this morning. Also, the delivery van."

AJ studied the paper. "It looks like a private club. Do I have this right?"

He nodded. "She says they're bringing more people here next month. There's room." He adjusted his cap and ran his hands through his hair. "The final thing? She didn't know who Clint Weeks was when I mentioned him."

They stared at each other under the weight of that information. Finally, AJ said, "Did you talk to Tag today when she and Jay came into Clint's lodge?"

"Yeah, but Greg did the tour. I've seen Jay in there a lot. He was talking to that man with the little girl, the one dressed up to appear older. That was weird."

"I saw them too. What happened to that young girl?"

"That man handed her off to one of the suits that hang around there and they disappeared into the dining room. Never saw them again." Jeff stood. "That's it. Oh wait, is Grace okay?"

"How'd you know about that? I was with her."

"We heard it at Clint's and Frog knew about it too, but only that it was a shooting and she called Grace 'Gabrial' once. That was interesting."

"That could have come from the cops, the sheriff, or someone at the stable," AJ said, feeling as if this was turning sideways. "Put everything you can think of on Maddie's thread on the computer. Good job, both of you. How do those girls look to you?"

"Terrible," he said. "Underfed and afraid. Used." He jammed his cap on, pulling the bill down hard. "If I could do anything it would be to put them all back into that truck and drive away. Greg says the same. They're just kids."

The minute he left she called Maddie's private number and told her everything.

"My God," Maddie said finally. "I'm home and on my second glass of a very fine wine, thank heavens. I have a morning meeting with Chief Whiteaker at the Milwaukee task force. I'll call you afterward."

"Grace has to meet with the Niagara Police tomorrow morning. I'll have that for you when we talk again. Anything on Tag's trip to Washington?"

"Hell no. That's such a mess, and the election's just around the corner. I have no idea what they're going to do. I'll talk to you tomorrow."

Chapter Twenty-Four

L eaves drifted past AJ the next morning as she walked across the loading docks at Adams Delivery looking for Sam. It was a perfect September day, missing only one thing. Katie. She absently rubbed her hand across her heart.

Sam was stacking boxes by his van. She yelled at him to wait. If they traded some deliveries, she could stay in town and keep an eye on Grace at the police station.

"Hey," he said. "I was just going to call you. I had to stop at the bank and saw one of the motel guys with Donna Seesom in an office there. The man wore a suit and actually looked very businesslike. What if it's connected to what Frog reported?"

"That's a thought. Be sure and put it on the computer."

He nodded. "I stopped by the lodge on the way in and talked to Jeff about last night. That thing at the motel is weird. They should use the house Donna is trying to sell for a private club. It's isolated, out in the country, and would take a lot less to refurbish."

AJ blinked. She hadn't thought of that.

"Maybe that's why they were at the bank," he continued. "What if they're thinking of two locations? Or maybe they need the money for the work they're doing."

They readjusted deliveries, and as he drove away she had a thought. It might be a good idea to call Donna Seesom and ask to see her house. At the very least, they could go through the place. It might even add pressure on the Seesom woman.

❖

Tag stood inside the police station listening to Jay joke with the young female officer at the front desk. Grace stood beside him, very straight in her black suit and dressy boots, calm and poised. Tag felt that little "ping" she'd gotten the first time they'd met at the Milwaukee airport, and she placed her hand on Grace's back.

Leaning backward into the hand on her back, Grace murmured, "I like that," and turned with a smile that reached her incredible blue eyes. "Is it true the Menominee are 'People of the Tree'?"

The question was completely out of the blue and a million miles away from the Niagara Police Station.

Tag grinned. "You have the most interesting mind."

"I found some things online and meant to ask last night, but…" She quirked her mouth. "Sleep got in the way."

"It's true," Tag said. "The Menominee were here hundreds of years before the Europeans and managed the trees. White pines and sugar maples mostly. It's one of the healthiest forests on Earth. It grew into a business after this area became a state, and the Menominee—"

"Gabrial, Tag, follow me," Jay interrupted. "We're meeting Lieutenant Lithscom, the man in charge. Remember Deputy Miller at the sheriff's? That's his cousin. The Millers and Lithscoms have been law enforcement here for decades."

An older, tall man with dark, graying hair opened the office door, and Jay introduced them. He looked nothing like Deputy Miller, but Tag certainly remembered his face. She took the chair at the back of the office. Lithscom never smiled. He completely ignored her.

Over an hour later, they sat at the local diner, hungry and unhappy about the meeting.

"Thanks again, Jay," Grace said, reaching for her iced tea.

"Wait until you get my bill," Jay teased her. "I love it that they have no idea who you really are, but I wish they had a clue about the shooting. Lithscom's crap attitude doesn't help."

"Yes, but he knew Gabrial decked his cousin. I almost laughed when he said, 'You're the one that had Deputy Miller on the ground?'" She dabbed hot sauce on her plate of ribs. "Bet the family hotline is sizzling after he had a look at you. He'll give his young cousin a hard time." Her smile faded. "I certainly remember him."

"We barely speak unless we have to." Jay shook his head, disgusted.

Grace dug into her chicken salad. "What's the story?"

"He killed a man outside of our high school when he was a young cop here," Tag said.

Grace looked up. "Did he shoot him?"

"The victim was a Menominee who drank too long and hard here in Niagara. Lithscom chased him all the way back to Keshena and cornered him in the parking lot at the high school as the football game ended and the crowd was leaving. He drew his gun and shot him in front of everyone." He bit into his sandwich. "I was in college, but Tag and her family were there."

"We were all getting into our cars, including the victim's family. Lithscom never even paid attention to any of us. The Keshena Police were there, but he warned them too," Tag added, then stopped eating and stared at the front of the diner, giving Grace's leg a little nudge. Luckily, Jay had his back to the cash register.

AJ stood at the checkout with several boxes on a cart. Right ahead of her was one of the men from the motel with a young girl beside him. AJ was turned away from them with her head down, studying the clipboard in her hands. She slid a glance at Tag and Grace before she turned away to the manager. The place was busy, and she pulled it off easily. Grace's hand briefly covered Tag's hand under the table.

"Everyone took cover," Jay continued the story. "I'll never be able to look at him without thinking of that. He isn't shy about his feelings for the Menominee. Any time he can create a problem down there, he works at it. I salivate every time I get him on the stand in court."

Tag changed the subject, keeping Jay's attention. "I caught a ride into town with Gabrial and left my car at the resort. Do you need me this afternoon?"

"Actually, here's what I'd like from you two." Jay wiped his hands on a napkin and stood. "Take Gabrial to my office and show her our computers or whatever you think she should see. I've told my staff that I'm thinking of upgrading so she can pose as a company rep for a new system. That way, when it gets around town that I was seen with her, it'll look like she belongs to my office."

"It's the least I can do." Grace smiled at him, and Tag grinned watching him react to that smile. She knew exactly how she felt.

"Then all 'fees' are covered," he said and stood to go. "I have a meeting in Iron Mountain. I'll be back this afternoon."

Later, in Jay's office, Grace ran through the home site and a list of his clients. Everyone was introduced to "Gabrial Frank," and she did a credible job asking the right questions. Her interaction with Jay's employees intrigued Tag. She listened carefully to everything they said to her.

Grace bumped her with her elbow. "You told me to remind you to make a phone call."

"Thanks, I forgot," Tag said and dialed her friend Dr. April Stewart at the hospital about the autopsy results on the young girl from the motel. After a brief conversation, they agreed to take a coffee break at the little shop around the corner.

❖

The doctor was easy to spot in the crowded café. April Stewart was the only person in scrubs with long black hair over her shoulders and skin that matched Tag's. She reminded Grace that April was the head of the hospital's pediatrics department. Tag introduced Grace as "Gabrial," but April didn't take much time for small talk.

"I have to be quick," she said, checking her watch. "As to what you called about, something's off. Officially, it was an overdose, the usual mixture of local drugs, but our gossip says a lot more. There was evidence of rough, severe sex and some kind of mutilation. My gut says they're covering this up." She raised her dark eyebrows over a sip of coffee and looked at Grace. "My grapevine also says a woman was at the motel that night and got arrested by the sheriff's department. Jay was involved...and you?" She lifted an eyebrow at Tag and left the question hanging.

Grace spoke before Tag could say a word. "That woman was me." She faced April. "I was on my way back to the resort, saw the ambulance and sheriff's vehicles, and stopped. It was just curiosity but a dumb thing to do."

April gave them both a shrewd look. "I was in Keshena with my folks and ran into your parents, Tag. They said you'd be working with Jay for a while but you're going to work for a government agency?"

Tag thought a little honesty would work here. "I'm just taking a little rest before I have to get back to full-time. Gabrial is Jay's consultant while he changes his computer system."

"I see." April leaned back into the booth. "Have you seen Jay's new office and home he's building out by the lighthouse?" She turned to Grace. "You'll be out there?"

"I don't know. I've only looked at his system and it's doable, so far." Grace took a long drink of coffee and looked out into the crowd.

"And I ran into Emma yesterday morning. She's got a new honey," April said to Tag. "She hasn't changed a bit, has she? Goes through men like Kleenex."

Tag laughed. "My mother keeps me informed. We had dinner and Em seems happy. I'm proud of her work too."

April checked her watch again and stood. "You're a lot, Tag. Emma's always fighting to keep up with you." She tossed some money on the table and bent, holding Tag's necklace in her fingers for a closer look. "What's this?"

Tag moved away from April's fingers. "My unit's Dragon necklace that we all wore."

April let go of the silver chain and ran a finger down Tag's neck. "Gotta go. Nice to meet you, Gabrial, but I'd stay away from that motel if I were you. I'm trying to get this one out for dinner, but no luck so far." She gave Tag a mischievous smile and left, threading her way through the crowd.

Grace blew out a breath. "If one more person tells me to stay away from the motel…" She gave Tag a long look. "You know her well?"

"Ah, we were young and in college. She went her way. I went mine."

Grace grinned and gave her a light punch on the shoulder. "Should we go back to Jay's?"

"Let's go to the resort. I'd like to check some things on the computers."

"I'm going to the stables to check on Crow."

"Can I go too?"

"I was hoping you would."

❖

The day held on to its beauty as they checked the horse. Grace read the notes Emma had left and put a lead on Crow, walking her out into the ring.

"Stand here, beside me," she said to Tag. "I want to see how she runs." She urged the horse forward to circle around them. A little breeze picked up and the horse trotted away, tail up.

"She looks great, Grace."

"And that's a big load off my mind." Grace turned slowly with the lead held firmly. "Who do you think shot at me?"

"No idea. It's the same question as why someone shot at AJ in Milwaukee. Where are the trees that AJ and the police talked about?"

Grace pointed up the hill. "Those two tall pines are where Lithscom said they found tracks."

Tag scoured the area. As far as she could see, no one was there now, but there was plenty of cover to be had.

"So…what do you have against helicopters?" Grace said.

"What do you mean?" She turned and faced Grace.

"Twice. Two times. I've seen you freeze when there's a helicopter above us. Once in Milwaukee at the Owens house and the other night at the sheriff's office here." Grace kept turning slowly with Crow, her voice calm.

"I can't get past the sound of them. It was our last day as Dragons," Tag said, the word stumbling out of her mouth and every muscle in her body rigid. She looked up at the sky. "This was all in the notes when I arrived."

"It was there, but just stats. It was only who was there, a kind of vague description of the action, and that was it."

"After we were ambushed, we ran toward the incoming helicopters, people going down all around me. My second-in-command, Jane, was running toward me. I had one of the medics, one of the first hit. I got there and turned as Jane went down. She didn't make it, and I almost didn't either. It's the one thing I still have nightmares about. I think I have a handle on it, and then, wham, it gets me."

Grace stood very still, a sad look on her face. She dropped Crow's lead and hugged Tag hard. "I'm sorry," she whispered, her breath warm against Tag's neck.

"I don't talk about this. Maybe I should." Tag swallowed hard. "When I was recovering in the hospital, I had a great therapist, but that was a long time ago. I'm never prepared. The sound of a helicopter brings it back in a heartbeat." She held on to Grace, heart racing. It still hurt worse than anything she knew.

They stood for a moment, unmoving, until Grace picked up the lead and reined the horse back. "Let's go back to the resort."

❖

AJ used her private phone to dial the number Donna Seesom had given her, but a man answered and she hung up. She called Sam and asked him to call the same number in about twenty minutes and, if Donna answered, set up an appointment. Driving toward her next delivery, she tried to remember the information they'd found on the computer, the taxes and assessment of Seesom's house, but her memory was fuzzy. She called Grace and pulled over to the side of the road, jotting down the numbers as Grace gave them to her.

"Sam and I are trying to set up an appointment to see Donna Seesom's house that she's selling. It might make us a little late, but I want a meeting with everyone tonight. Did you see Sam's notes from this morning and the bank? Oh, and how'd it go at the police station?"

"I read Sam's notes and am adding the police information right now," Grace said. "They found footprints and shell casings but they don't have a clue, and I don't think they cared much. That cop we talked to, Lieutenant Lithscom, has quite a history with Jay and the Menominee. Good cover in the diner, by the way."

"Is Tag still with you?"

"Yes," Grace said, lowering her voice. "She just went to change clothes. I talked to her about the helicopter business, and it's exactly what you said. Something she brought home." She raised her voice to normal. "You want me to remind Greg and Jeff about the meeting tonight?"

"I do and I'll get back to you if we get an appointment to see that house tonight. You were asleep when I was there last night. Everything okay with you about the shooting yesterday?"

"It just scared me," Grace said, and AJ heard her pull in a breath. "I left some information on our private email for you. Talk to you later."

AJ pulled out onto the road, thinking about Tag's conversation about Grace last night. It had left her staring at the dark for a long time before she slept. If Tag had been unprepared for Grace, she had not been prepared for either of them. And she hadn't been prepared for Grace's childhood either.

Sam called her back and confirmed a six o'clock meeting at Seesom's house. "Let's have a meal at the meeting tonight," he suggested.

They left it there and ended the call.

Chapter Twenty-Five

Tag changed her clothes and opened her bedroom windows. A pine-scented breeze slipped into the room. She stretched out on her bed, listening to Grace on the phone, and the conversation at the stable replayed in her mind. The image of her Dragons and helicopters swiped her memory one more time, and she shifted, feeling restless.

"Tag," Grace said from the doorway. Gone was the professional black suit, replaced by jeans and a T-shirt with the word *Wild* across a running horse. The bed tilted a little as Grace settled down beside her. "I'm sorry. I shouldn't have intruded."

"It's not your fault. It's my own stupid mind." Tag turned to her side. Her eyes lingered. "No apologies."

"I've never been in a battle. Never even been shot at like that until yesterday." Grace pushed up on an elbow, fingers tracing Tag's hand. "I'm still sorry."

Tag shifted closer, catching Grace's light fragrance. "Are there things you don't talk about? Things you never say to another living soul?"

Grace stretched out on her back, face turned away. Something changed and the air went flat. "Of course," she finally said.

"This is mine. The thing I never talk about." Tag's mouth was dry, and she licked her lips. "That therapist in Afghanistan said I'd know the right time and person. That's why I told you. It felt...right." She touched her heart. "Right here."

"Your heart? That's romantic."

"Right," Tag said with a grin.

"Romantic...as in love?" Grace turned, sneaking a look at her. "I don't know if I've ever been *in love* but I've been *in like* a lot. Does that count?"

"Of course it counts. *Like* is important and makes you sparkle." Tag reached for Grace's hand. "And I really *like* it when you sparkle."

"I've never done this before, lain on a bed and talked..." Grace gestured at the bed.

"I get to be a first?"

"In lots of ways." Grace topped her words off with a blush.

Tag inched closer. "Maybe that's why it feels *right*."

"This feels—"

The phone began to ring in the other room, and Grace bent with a quick, shy kiss. "Come with me. I made some coffee." And she was gone, running toward the phone.

This feels...what? Tag's heart thudded. If she stayed here on the bed, Grace would come back and that would lead to something she didn't think either one of them was ready for. She didn't quite understand what Grace did to her. It was more than just the need to touch. She needed to share words and ideas.

Teetering emotionally, she hauled herself upright. The timing was wrong.

She entered the room just as Grace ended the phone call.

"AJ and Sam are posing as buyers, meeting with Donna Seesom at that house she's selling. She wants a meeting and dinner here with all of us after they get back." She held up a cup of coffee.

"I want to look at Maddie's new information," Tag said and took a sip of coffee. "I care about those little girls." She smiled and Grace's face relaxed. "I'll add what April said today to the computer, but also, show me Frog. She's important."

"Frog's a recovering addict and, as far as we know, still clean. You'll like her. Look. Maddie's group found three more names. That's over half of the girls, including Frog." Grace sped across the keys until she found Frog's information, and they read the notes together, including the time Frog had been at Hannah's House and Grace had worked with her.

"She's nineteen? That's old for that group even though she looks younger. Most are ten to fifteen. That girl that we saw in the diner this morning couldn't have been over thirteen, and did you see how afraid she looked? Did you find anything on the girl dressed up older that AJ saw at Clint's place?"

Grace nodded. "I'm into the surveillance they already have in place." She hit a few more keys and went over to Clint's new lodge. "Here's yesterday's video."

Tag could see they only had basic video running, but it showed AJ leaving, passing the man and the girl, then later an older man guiding the child toward the back just as Greg and Jeff had said. Jay was on video later talking to that older man. That caused Tag to pause.

She knew Clint's security would sharpen the surveillance to a room-by-room camera soon. She checked the calendar. Not much time until the grand opening. She reread some of Frog's information and went on to Maddie's notes about the girls she'd identified. Two had been sold by parents, but the rest were all abducted from the Milwaukee area, mostly from foster homes. That surprised her. She'd expected out-of-state kids and said so to Grace.

"I had the same thought, but Maddie's system is huge and she's had some success. These girls are so young they'll be reported by schools, parents, or the foster system. If they were older, there'd be less chance of finding them," Grace said. "God, who'd sell their kids?"

"Why don't we just go get them and take them back to Maddie?"

"Both AJ and I have asked the same question, but Maddie says to wait and see what develops."

"But that little dead girl can't wait," Tag said. "This is just wrong."

Grace sighed, nodding, and turned to the clock, scanning the room. "AJ and Sam are at Seesom's by now. I've got to get this place ready for the meeting." She moved to the table and began to clear off the things they had scattered across it.

AJ and Sam stood next to Donna Seesom in the spacious living room.

"It's beautiful," Sam said. "Is this your furniture?"

"My parents did a lot of entertaining," Donna said. "He did the wood, but she did the colors." She pointed at the long beams across the low ceiling. The whole room was light blue and green with deep brown accents. The furniture leaned toward formal and appeared hardly used.

AJ let Sam do most of the talking. They'd already been over most of the structure questions like the age and quality of the furnace and cooling systems, the roofing, plumbing, and appliances.

She had liked the kitchen and smiled to herself thinking of Katie taking this tour. The bricked-in oven and huge stove in the kitchen would have made her scream with joy. Not to mention the large carpenter-style wooden table. The colors there had been deeper as well. It was a working kitchen. Someone had liked to cook.

Sam was right. Whoever was redoing the motel should have located their "club" here. Each of the four bedrooms had a bathroom and made the motel look cheap. She wandered into the even more formal dining room while Sam kept Donna occupied over the window frames. The house appeared to have been recently cleaned. There wasn't a speck of dust anywhere.

AJ took a more thorough look at Donna Seesom. To be fair, she did look like a much older version of the real daughter in the high school yearbook they'd found. Since both so-called parents were deceased, most of the people in town had only their memory to depend on. Neither Henry Adams nor his wife had seen her since she was in her twenties. Right now, Donna seemed nervous and a little edgy, and where was her car? When they'd driven up she'd been standing in the empty three-car garage, no vehicle in sight.

"Do you mind if I take a look at that beautiful deck?" AJ asked.

Donna jerked around, mid-conversation, and nodded at AJ.

AJ walked outside, turned slowly, noting all the exits. She looked at the surrounding forest and the sky. The day was quickly draining into night. The place was perfectly isolated, and Crooked Lake was less than two miles away. Her mind tracked back to the motel. This was a puzzle, she thought, walking back to Sam.

Donna was handing Sam the papers with information on the house, including the finances. Sam looked at AJ.

"Not what you expected?" Donna looked at them with an unsure smile. "I'm trying to sell it as quickly as possible."

AJ goggled a little at the figures and put her arm around Sam's waist. "We'll talk it over, but I would have expected to pay considerably more for an acre and a house like this."

"Most would." Donna nodded. "Wait. You haven't seen the family room in the basement." She bustled off toward the downstairs stairway. That cinched it for AJ. Donna was stretching out the time, trying to keep them here as long as possible. They followed her down the steps.

It was a shock. The entire basement was redone into an enormous game room, complete with a huge fireplace. There were two pool tables and several televisions. AJ opened a door into a computer game room. More amazing, the games were up-to-date, something a real gamer would enjoy.

"I'd like nothing better than to see a family live here and enjoy all of this." Donna picked up *Call of Duty* and *Grand Theft Auto* stacked on a table and turned them over in her hands. Something was off. AJ realized Donna had no idea what she was looking at. She'd probably never played a game in her life. The computers were up-to-date as well, and AJ wished either Tag or Grace were with her.

"Did someone live here recently?" AJ said, shuffling through the latest PlayStation games.

"No. No one's been here."

AJ pointedly checked her watch. "We have another appointment. I noticed you don't have a car. Would you like a ride?"

Donna shook her head. "No. I'm fine. Someone will pick me up." She sounded disappointed and walked away.

AJ had Sam drive when they left so she could take a closer look at the papers. Suddenly he said, "Holy shit," and they both laughed. The house was priced at exactly half of what they'd both guessed before they'd arrived. Hundreds of thousands of dollars less.

"Wait until the rest of the group sees this," AJ said, holding up the papers. "Did you get the feeling she didn't want us to leave? I felt as if she was trying to keep us there."

"She was nervous, jittery, the entire time we talked," he said. Right at that moment, the new black Lincoln sports sedan from the motel drove by them, headed toward the Seesom house.

Everyone except Greg was at the table when AJ and Sam arrived. It was a simple meal but plenty of fried chicken, a variety of vegetables, salads, and potatoes, all served family style.

AJ grabbed a plate and asked, "Where's Greg?"

"Something's wrong at the motel. He stayed to see what's happening," Jeff said. Grace got up and opened the computers.

They could see the girls lined up outside with the two adult women. Greg was leaving the office with one of the two men from Milwaukee, both of them gesturing at each other. The man stormed over to Greg's pickup, opened the doors, and checked the back. Greg shook his head, got inside, and pulled away. The man turned and yelled at the girls. Donna Seesom was not there, nor was the black Lincoln.

Grace backed the video up to when the black car left. There was nothing for a few minutes until the man ran out of the office and banged on the girls' doors. The girls looked upset as they lined up outside and the man yelled at them. Greg came outside and followed the man into the office. AJ didn't see Frog amongst the girls.

None of the girls moved while the two women walked in front of them, talking. Grace fast-forwarded the video. "What the hell," Tag said and sat back down at the table just as Greg walked inside.

"You won't believe this," he told them. "Frog is missing."

CHAPTER TWENTY-SIX

A J felt everyone take a breath. "What do you mean?"
"Didn't you see it on the computers?" Greg said. "He yelled
across the parking lot and asked if I'd seen the kid with the spiky hair.
I told him no and that I was on my way out to dinner. He ran across the
pavement, checked my truck, and ranted about the 'punk kid' who'd
run away. I just stood there, acting puzzled in my 'less is better' mode."
Greg shook his head and began to pile food on his plate.

"Did you see her today?" AJ said, passing dishes around.

"No. Did you, Jeff?"

"I haven't seen her since last night, but I did see that new black
Lincoln leave tonight after I came home from work. I know for sure it
was the guy with the tattoo—we call him Tattoo Man and so does Frog.
He was driving, but it was already too dark to see if anyone was in the
car with him."

AJ looked across the table at Sam. "We saw that car on the way
back from Seesom's house, but as you said, it was almost dark. That
road ends at her house. The other man, not Tattoo Man, yelled at you?
Donna wasn't back?"

Greg shook his head. AJ addressed everyone. "All right. Before
we do anything about Frog, I need your opinions about what we're
doing here. What if it doesn't involve Clint Weeks, other than he's a
friend of our bureau chief? I'd like to hear what the rest of you say and
your ideas."

"It's possible it's something else." Sam was the first to speak up.

"I agree," Jeff said, picking out more chicken.

"I'd like to take those kids back to Milwaukee," Greg added.

"I agree with Greg. Why not take them back instead of risking them?" Tag said. "Now we have Grace shot at, a dead girl, and Frog's missing. Have you read my computer notes? And what my friend, the doctor, told us about the autopsy?"

"The way she was killed reminded me of X-Girl," Jeff said.

"And remember Frog had never heard of Clint Weeks." Tag turned to Jeff. "Did Frog say anything about the girls?"

"We didn't have much time when she gave me the sketch, but we've seen those girls, a lot. They're young, get yelled at all the time, and look hungry."

Grace sat beside Tag. "Nothing connects Weeks to any of this that we can see except that little girl made up to look older at the lodge. Maybe that's what they're really here for." She left the thought hanging in the air.

The group confirmed what AJ had been stewing over. "The only connection I made with Weeks is his grand opening and all the people that'll be in town. Could he have brought the girls up for that? I've said as much to Maddie. Plus we all know Donna Seesom is just a front woman, managing the motel. If you'd see that house we went through today you'd wonder why they're messing around with the motel in the first place. Sam, pass those papers she gave us around so everyone can see. Look at the price. It's cheap and in perfect condition."

Grace scanned the paperwork and lifted an eyebrow over the price. "I don't believe that," she said, passing the paperwork to Tag. She bent forward and looked at AJ. "Did you see that information I left on your email, AJ?"

"I did, but I'm having a problem with that. Aren't you?"

"What is it?" Tag said and handed the paperwork to Jeff.

AJ took a breath. "It's information about Jay. He's not only on the only board of the only bank in town, but one of his lawyers is Donna Seesom's lawyer. I know you didn't know that or you would have said something."

Tag froze. "You must be kidding. Jay told us he didn't know her. I can't believe he'd lie."

"And that's why I'm having a problem." AJ frowned. "This isn't personal, Tag, and I'm not saying he's involved. I'm only saying it's a problem." She got up and opened windows to let the cool night air inside. A car stopped below, doors slammed, and a woman laughed. It was familiar, but AJ couldn't place it and went back to the table.

Sam was talking about the house when AJ heard voices in the hallway, then a rap on the door.

"Maddie?" AJ said as she walked inside with a very big man following her.

"Omigod, food." Maddie laughed at them. "We haven't eaten since this morning and we're starving."

"What are you doing here?" Sam stood, almost knocking his chair over.

"We'll get to that." Maddie pushed a chair next to Sam and said something under her breath to him that made him laugh. She pointed at the man with her. "Meet Richard Sawyer, my counterpart from Illinois."

Richard was big enough to stand in as a linebacker on a football team. He pushed a chair to the end of the table and took a plate.

Maddie grabbed a chicken leg off a platter and waved it at everyone. "Did you know we were coming and had this dinner ready?"

AJ laughed. "Why are you here?"

"I'll tell you, but first we get food," Maddie said, and dug into the salad.

Richard took a generous helping of potatoes, but AJ had seen his eyes practically x-ray the group and the suite.

"Do you happen to have milk?" Maddie smiled at Grace.

Grace got up and poured a glass from the milk in the refrigerator.

"Your eye looks much better. Also, great work on the computers." Maddie drank at least half of the glass, then zeroed in on Greg and Jeff. "I haven't met you, so let's do that now. I'm Margaret Hershey, the head of the FBI-DHS operation, and my group coordinates your information from Milwaukee. Sam is one of my agents. All of you have done a wonderful job up here." She turned to the big man beside her. "Richard is from the middle of Illinois. He's here because of what happened in Milwaukee yesterday." She took another drink of milk. "Brace yourselves, everyone. We're about to have a real come-to-Jesus moment."

Once again, AJ felt her group take a breath.

Maddie spoke as she loaded her plate. "I was leaving my downtown office yesterday afternoon and walked right into your bureau chief,

Lawrence Kelly. I spent the next hours with him and Clint Weeks at the pathology lab down the street. The morgue."

"Lawrence Kelly is in Milwaukee?" AJ said.

"We officially identified X-Girl yesterday, and it's not good news. She was Clint's daughter, missing since she was twelve."

Surprised into silence again, everyone stared at her. Maddie might as well have shot a gun, AJ thought, scrambling to make sense out of her words.

"But that was years ago. Where's she been?"

"It appears she spent time in Chicago, some of it with the woman from up here, Donna Seesom. That's why Richard is here. His people were tracking the Seesom woman, but they weren't quite ready. Suddenly, Seesom, or whatever her name is, moved up to Milwaukee, and Richard's group followed her. She became a part of John Owens's organization that you worked on last summer. Chief Whiteaker and the new Milwaukee task force are all over this as we speak, but Richard gets first shot at her in Chicago." Maddie gave them time to absorb her information. "We helped Clint ship the body home about midnight."

She dished more vegetables onto her plate. "After we made the identification official, I told the chief I'd notify you, and Lawrence Kelly said he'll be in touch with you tomorrow, AJ." She paused and looked around the table. "Then, just as I thought we were done, your medical examiner called our office. That girl that was murdered here at the motel was the same thing as X-Girl. There was rape and missing hands. They skipped the acid."

"The hospital called your office?" Tag said.

Maddie shook her head. "Not the hospital. The Niagara medical examiner called. We've been at the hospital, viewing the body and talking with him. She was murdered at the motel, nailed to the wall in an empty room. The FBI will handle this. We'll have more people here tomorrow to arrest the two men, and Seesom, and take the girls back to Milwaukee. Your group will assist." Maddie reached for more chicken. "I read the notes on your doctor, Tag. Good woman, that April Stewart."

"You spoke with her?"

"On the phone, and she doesn't know you're involved." Maddie looked across the table at Tag. "Apparently, after she talked with you and Grace, she raised hell with the ME and he found us. You've known her since childhood?"

"Her family has the next farm over from ours." Tag got up for a bottle of water.

"And that's what we have, so far," Maddie said and gestured at the table and food. "So, what's this about?"

"Well, hell, what a night," AJ said and pushed her dish away. "I got us all together to discuss what else besides Clint Weeks to focus on. We all agree. It feels like smoke."

"And?" Maddie said.

"And my CI, Frog, is missing."

Maddie closed her eyes briefly in a grimace. "I'm sorry."

"Sam and I were at Donna Seesom's house this afternoon, posing as buyers. That's probably where we should go first to look for Frog." AJ put her plate on the serving cart. "Take a look at those papers. There's the selling price and everything else on that house."

Maddie picked up the papers and laid her hand on Sam's shoulder. "Can we go with you to the Seesom house? I'll read these on the way. The whole thing's doing a one-eighty, and a little backup might help. Richard, would you bring our bags up when you're done eating? Sam, give him a hand."

AJ walked back to the window, breathing the fresh air. "Greg, you and Jeff finish your food, go back to the motel, and keep an eye on things. If Donna's there, text me." She thought about Frog. The kid was too savvy not to be alive. Then she thought about what Maddie had said about the little dead girl from the motel. Things happened.

The cars pulled into a small clearing about a quarter mile from the dark Seesom house. AJ took the lead as they stood together.

"Grace and I will go in through the deck. Tag and Richard, go in through the attached garage through the kitchen. Maddie and Sam, take the front through the dining room, and everyone meet in the living room. I looked at the locks today. They're easy. You agree, Sam?"

"Standard locks. Apparently, they never had a problem out here."

The full moon brightened the night, and AJ heard the forest rustle around her. Dry leaves and pine saturated the air, and she took a deep breath, going over the layout of the house mentally. Her gut told her the basement was the most likely place.

A deer broke out of the trees ahead and everyone stopped. The doe ran directly at the house, and the whole area was flooded with light.

"Damn," Sam muttered. "My bad. She mentioned sensors. Look. The garage is still open."

"We probably have about fifteen minutes until the lights go off," AJ said. "All we have to worry about is that they're connected to a security company or worse, the police."

It didn't take long on the deck and AJ had the lock undone. Grace stood beside her inside, everyone quiet until the sensors went dark. AJ could see Sam and Maddie against the living room wall and Richard and Tag moving in from the kitchen. She motioned for them to follow her to the basement. The house was so solid she couldn't hear a single footstep. They started down the steps, and AJ stopped. The air carried an odor. "I smell something," she said to Tag behind her.

"I do too," Tag said.

She and Tag took a step at a time, slowly. "It's stronger over here, whatever it is." Tag moved to AJ's right.

"You and I both know what that is." AJ prayed it wasn't Frog. "Turn your flashlight on."

Tag did and they all saw the source of the odor.

Donna Seesom was nailed to the wall, still clothed, but as dead as she ever would be. Blood and feces pooled at her feet.

"Tag, check that game room," AJ said and pointed to her left. "Everyone, stay in place."

Tag moved quiet as a shadow and came back out, shaking her head. "Hit the lights, Maddie." She did and the entire area was exposed. It was another frozen moment. No one moved.

"Jesus," Maddie said, eyes riveted on the body, the head hanging at an odd angle. Tag holstered her weapon, careful where she stepped, and touched the neck.

"Not just stabbed," she said. "Whoever did this really sliced her up." Grace sank down on the bottom step, her hand over her mouth. Tag sat beside her, pulling her close with an arm around her.

Her stomach knotted, AJ looked up the stairs at Maddie. "Do you want the FBI to take this or should we call it in to the locals?"

Maddie leaned against the door, looking tired and sick. "We'll take the lead. Damn, Richard. There goes our connection."

"Cluster fuck," he said. "I'll stay in Milwaukee, Maddie. They'll need my information, even with this."

"Let's go through the rest of the house and then I'll call the police. When we're done, get your group out of here, AJ." Maddie moved down the steps. "Our cover story will be the dead girl at the hospital and the connection to this woman. Sam, get our vests out of the car."

"Grace, you and Tag tackle those computers in the game room." AJ began to move. "Maddie, a warning. The sheriff's office was at the motel for the dead girl, so if you get the Niagara Police be careful of Lithscom, the cop that talked with Grace. He's got family at the sheriff's, Deputy Miller, the man Grace clocked three times. They know her as 'Gabrial' and don't care for Tag."

Maddie stood in front of Donna Seesom's body for a long moment. "It is almost the same as the little girl from the motel, but they left the hands alone. I'd bet there's no sex involved either. I'll call the ME first, then the police, and report back to you after we're done, but this is going to take some time."

"What did you two find on the computers?" AJ said as they drove away from the house.

"Just games, but they're new and played recently. We didn't see anything that indicated Frog had been there." Grace's voice was distant and she stared out the window.

AJ nodded. She'd expected the house to be empty too as they'd found it.

"Where to now?" Grace snapped her seat belt.

"You're the only one beside me that Frog knows, although she figured out Jeff and Greg. She'd never seen Tag or Sam before. Got any ideas?"

"I think she'd go someplace where she knows we'd look." The dash lights played across Grace's face making her eyes almost colorless and her face pale. "She's street smart, but since she knew about my horse, how about the stables?"

"Think I'd recognize her?" Tag said from the back seat. "I've only seen her on video."

"She's about five foot six and slender, athletic body, brown and brown in real time, but I'd bet she knows what you look like, Tag. She's fast on computers, and you're all over our website, the photos from the military," Grace said. "They have a night watchman at the stable, so let me check in. Some of those horses are worth a lot of money."

AJ parked and turned the engine and lights off. Grace was backlit by the office lights when she leaned inside the office and spoke to the man at the desk, then walked toward the stalls.

AJ and Tag took the other side of the building. Nothing stirred but the horses.

"AJ," Grace called out into the darkness. "Over here."

They stood in the middle of the stall, and she pointed at the small chest crammed into the corner. A drawing of a frog was taped to the front with duct tape. AJ went to her knees, studying the small sketch with a sigh of relief. The kid was alive. AJ stood and brushed the dirt off her knees. "Good. She was here, but where now? Any ideas?"

"How about the lighthouse? She'd be looking for cover but not too far." Tag looked out into the arena.

AJ thought about that. "If I know her, she's bedded down somewhere already. She has a huge start on us. I'd bet she left about the same time Donna Seesom went to meet us or even after Greg saw Tattoo Man drive away. Let's go back to the suite so we'll be in a place that she knows about."

"Do I understand tomorrow right?" Grace looked at her. "Maddie has a group coming in and we'll work with them?"

AJ nodded. "That's the way I heard it." She felt the weight of the moment and stopped, looking at Tag and Grace in the moonlight. Grace looked sick. "I'm going to check in with Greg and Jeff. Let's go back to the suite. Tag, you drive and drop me off. I'll hit my room first to see if Frog's been there and then meet you in your suite."

❖

On the way up to her room, AJ considered the lighthouse. It was a possibility. She turned on the lights, half expecting to see Frog, but no one was there. She checked under the bed and in the closet, then the bathroom. There it was, another sketch of a Frog taped to the mirror with duct tape. Good, she was close by, somewhere.

She thought of Donna Seesom as she walked back to the suite. Nothing was as deeply silent as death. The night she'd shot Ariel, the seconds had been hours long. She couldn't help herself. She kept listening for the next breath.

She entered the suite, but neither Tag nor Grace was there. Confused, she looked around the room. The suite was clean again. The resort staff had removed all the dishes and remaining food. They'd even left a fresh bouquet of flowers on the table. She started to walk toward the computers and then heard voices in Grace's bedroom. Tag walked out and sat at the desk with a sigh.

"What's up?" AJ said.

"She got sick, threw up. I forget that she hasn't seen what I've seen...or you."

AJ stared at the desk. She'd forgotten too.

"Should I go talk to her?"

"No." Tag shook her head. "I talked her into taking a shower." She swiveled in her chair. "Did you know she has that poster of me, the one I did for the Dragons, on her wall?"

"No, I didn't."

"And what's that journal of hers, the doctors, their names and telephone numbers?"

AJ frowned. She hadn't known that either. "Grace is private. You'd have to ask her. What is it again?"

"It's a list of doctors' names, all with dates up to fifteen years ago, right beside her bed. Is she sick and no one's told me?"

AJ shook her head. "She's not sick. That I would know. I'm responsible for the health information of my group, and there's nothing there."

Grace emerged from her room in pajama bottoms and a sleep shirt, her face pale. "I'm sorry," she said, opening a can of clear soda. "That was a first."

"We've all done that," Tag said and scooted her chair next to her. "Remember my story about the day I decided to leave the army? My friends, the doctors, off base in Afghanistan? I tossed my cookies that day, right beside a bunch of others."

Grace gave her a thin smile, but her hands shook as she took a drink of her soda.

Maddie walked into the suite right then and fished around in the refrigerator for a bottle of water. She told them it had gone pretty much as she thought it would. She'd sent Sam and Richard off to sleep.

"Nice setup, Grace," Maddie said, pointing at the computers.

"She had this all done in less than twenty-four hours," Tag said. "I think Tattoo Man killed Donna. I just put the timeline together, here, on the computer. He leaves the motel, Sam and AJ see him at Seesom's house as they leave, and we see the other guy yelling at Greg and the girls on video."

Maddie nodded. "The ME put the TOD right in that time period. Hopefully, we'll have some DNA tomorrow. I take it you didn't find your CI?"

AJ handed Maddie the two pieces of paper Frog had left. "Two notes from the kid. One at the stable and one in my room."

"How old is she?"

"Nineteen. Chief Whiteaker and I would like to get her into the academy in Milwaukee and train her."

Maddie looked at the two sketches and handed the papers back to AJ, rubbing her eyes. "This is good, but I need sleep. You were right. The sheriff's department arrived first and you should have seen the ME and your Deputy Miller arguing." Maddie grinned at Grace. "When the Niagara Police arrived with Lithscom, he all but stuffed his little cousin into the garbage."

Grace looked up. "God, I hope he's not mine."

"I'm amazed he can tie his own shoes," Maddie said. She stood and yawned. "Call me when you get up, AJ. We'll have a quick meeting over breakfast and make sure we're on the same page. See you in the morning."

CHAPTER TWENTY-SEVEN

The resort restaurant was busy the next morning. AJ searched the noisy crowd for Maddie. It was mostly families trying to enjoy the last of the great weather before winter came tromping into the north woods. Their enthusiasm felt good, and then Maddie was suddenly beside her.

"I reserved a table," she said, pulling AJ along. Dressed in jeans, a classy, long-sleeved green sweater, and nice mid-calf boots, she led them to a table near the back and got a waiter's attention for coffee. AJ smiled. Maddie's energy was back.

"Bring me up to date," AJ said, sitting across from her.

Maddie held up her finger, took a drink of coffee, closed her eyes, and smiled. "I needed that." She handed AJ a thick envelope. "Here's all the information on X-Girl, including copies of my notes from the very beginning, our progress, Richard's data, and the conclusion. Also, the DNA results and the men involved. Destroy it when you finish. Deal?"

"Deal." AJ nodded and stuffed the envelope into her bag. "Can we talk about Jay Yardly first? I don't want to discuss him in front of Tag."

"No, you don't." Maddie laughed a little. "Here's the story. Jay and Pete have known each other since high school and worked together for the last ten years. It started with a group of white supremacists up here." She drank more coffee. "Who found the connection between Jay's office and Donna Seesom? Tag?"

"It was Grace when she was in Jay's office yesterday, and that's a problem. He told Tag and Grace he didn't know her."

Maddie looked surprised. "Here's what I got from Pete. I don't think he lied. Jay saw the girls at the motel by pure luck. He was on his way out to the house he's building by the lighthouse and called Pete. Put that together with Clint Weeks and see what you have?" She waved at the waiter for more coffee. "He isn't aware of your two men at the motel nor has he seen you, but he knows you're in town. He's never seen Sam either and doesn't know he's here. Also, you should know he and Clint Weeks are a million miles apart, politically. My advice to you is to trust Jay, but none of you should talk to him about anything you've done here. When Tag and Grace join us, let me handle it. I'll talk them through it."

AJ leaned back in her chair. "So what happens next?"

"Our first priority is the girls at the motel. Once they're safe, we'll go after the two men running the show. After breakfast, we'll go up to the suite and I'll show you our information on these two men on the computer. It's unbelievable what they've done, but we've got them nailed. Richard and I need them alive, especially now that Seesom is dead."

"What about the two women, the minders who watch them every day?"

"They were at John Owens's house in Milwaukee with Seesom. In fact, the day you took that house down you almost had one of them, but she got away."

AJ leaned forward. "I remember a woman there. Well, that answers that question, but how will you rescue the girls?"

"We have a unit that specializes in extractions, recovering victims. They're on their way here right now, about eight of our best. They'll go in SWAT style, so your group stays with me this afternoon. Once we have them, we'll transport them to Hannah's House in Milwaukee. Three of my agents are trained nurses and work there, specializing in recovery, and that's where it gets dicey. It's hard to believe, but some of these girls go willingly. They're the ones you have to be careful with, but so far we've been able to handle the ones we've had. All except Sandra and Happy, of course."

"Are you serious?"

"As a heart attack," Maddie said with a deep breath.

"Will you need to talk to my CI, Frog, when we find her? And we will. Or she'll find us."

Maddie nodded. "Yes, and I thought of something last night. We could use her at Hannah's House. I read her file that covered her time there, and we could use someone like her on the streets. I don't want to steal her from you, but she appears smart and flexible. I'd be willing to put her through school and the academy and train her if you'd agree."

AJ nodded. "All I want is for Frog to have a real life." It was the truth, but she felt a little niggle of missing something and shifted in her chair.

"All right, let's run with that. Another thing. I talked to Lawrence Kelly about using your group again. Would you be up to doing this somewhere else in the state or in Milwaukee?"

"Of course, but what did he say?"

"He said to run it by you and he'll call sometime today. I just wanted this out there before you talked with him."

"Thanks for warning me. Sometimes Kelly is…" AJ smiled, unsure she should finish that statement.

"The best part of all of this is solving the X-Girl murder. That really jolted me, and I know it did you too. The other night in the morgue with Clint Weeks was terrible. Standing in the room with him and the body, explaining all the information. Honestly, AJ, I thought he was going to faint. He looked about a thousand years old when I finished. Even Lawrence Kelly had to sit down, and by the way, he apologized to me." Maddie stared out at the busy room. "I don't know. I haven't figured Clint out yet," she said and then smiled.

AJ followed Maddie's gaze and saw Tag and Grace at the door, hyperaware of each other but trying to look casual.

"I see things haven't changed much since you've been up here," she said.

"God." AJ shook her head. "I've had several moments with both of them, but you should know Grace threw up when she got back to the suite last night. I forget she hasn't had the fieldwork we have, but I'm really proud of how she's handled herself here. I know it hasn't been easy, watching those girls every day and someone shooting at her. I'm not sure what you'll ask of our group would be a fit for her, but she's done a terrific job on the computers. Tag doesn't know about Grace's background but is starting to ask questions." She watched them start across the room toward a large booth, Tag's hand on Grace's back as usual. And Grace's dazzling smile. As usual.

"Ah, love," Maddie murmured and they got up to join them.

"Where'd you two come from?" Tag looked up, surprised.

"It's an ambush." AJ grinned, sitting beside Grace. "I'm hungry. Let's eat."

"My God." Grace grabbed AJ's arm, nodding toward the crowded hallway. "Look. It's Frog."

AJ sorted through the crowd. It certainly was Frog, leaning against the wall, looking at them. She'd styled her hair differently. Now it was her normal brown.

Maddie elbowed AJ. "What are you both staring at?"

"It's my CI. That kid has given me more heart attacks than anyone I've ever worked with. Are you sure you want her?"

"What do you mean 'want her'?" Grace frowned at them.

"I'll need Frog's testimony." Maddie spoke before AJ. "The FBI will transport the girls back to Hannah's House, and I asked AJ if I can use Frog. The girls have been with her over a month, and that'll help us get through what's next."

"What *is* next?" Tag leaned toward them. "I've had experience with this, and I'm not seeing any trafficking here. Murder, yes. Trafficking, no. At least not yet."

"Let's talk upstairs after we eat," Maddie said to Tag.

AJ's brain still itched with the feeling that they were missing something as she got up. She walked toward the restrooms but took a quick right into the hallway.

"I found your sketches," she said, standing next to Frog. "Smart move."

"I think I'm safe here. Boy, that hair color really changes your face."

AJ bumped her with her shoulder. "I could say the same to you. Look at *your* hair. Come on, let's eat. Sit in the middle." They walked to the booth, and Frog squeezed in beside Grace while AJ did the introductions.

They ordered their food just as AJ's mind shifted gears. She had it, the thing that had been bothering her. Who were the "cops" that had hired Frog to come up here?

She waited until they'd finished breakfast. Frog teased Grace about her hair and asked Tag about serving overseas. It proved Grace's point that Frog had read the group's website. Maddie asked her lots of questions about her time at Hannah's House.

Finally done with the food, AJ opened the conversation.

"Everyone, be patient with me for a minute. We'll go upstairs for the answers on the video we want to show Frog, but here's the question. First, Maddie, do you remember how all of this started? Why I called you in Milwaukee right at the beginning?"

Maddie frowned at AJ. "Yes. Clint Weeks and Lawrence Kelly."

"No. The reason I took it to Pete was Frog stumbling into trafficking at the house, the one that burned. Then, the two 'cops' that paid her all that cash to come up here. Remember the money? You and I talked about that and my fight with Lawrence Kelly."

Maddie carefully placed her fork on the table, thinking. "I remember. I showed you Clint's email. As the evidence came in, I *assumed* the 'cops' were the motel men here that impersonated the police. They've impersonated everyone else."

"Can't be them. You would have known, Frog, and told Jeff." AJ looked at everyone. "We all did what Maddie did. *Assumed* it was Tattoo Man and his buddy. Frog, you're the only person who's talked to everyone except Clint Weeks. Let's go upstairs and look at our video."

"Who's Clint Weeks?" Frog said. "Jeff mentioned him too. And what house burned?"

They all looked at each other. They'd forgotten the house had burned after Frog left.

❖

"Where have you been?" Tag said to Frog, holding the door open to the suite.

"In the resort's van, the one they use for back and forth to town."

"Grace, notify Jeff and Greg that we have Frog here," AJ said, moving chairs to the big desk and the computers. She brought up video of the gym with John Owens. "Watch this, Frog. Let me know if you recognize anyone."

Frog turned with a disbelieving grin. "That's the cop that contacted me." She pointed at John Owens. "Are you guys playing with me? There's his aide." She touched the screen and Robert Owens. "This looks like a gym. Are they undercover?"

"No," AJ said, reaching for her phone. "That's Grace and me, undercover, trying to bait your so-called cop. He's never been law enforcement. The chief has him under arrest in Milwaukee. I've got to call him." She walked away when the chief answered and gave him Frog's information.

Tag and Grace caught Frog up on what they'd found and what had happened in Milwaukee after she'd left. The two shootings and both fires.

Frog reached into her jeans back pocket when they were done. "You are going to fucking love me. Look what I've got." She handed Maddie a piece of paper with a handwritten list of names and addresses.

Maddie looked stunned, reading the list. "You've got the motel girls' names?"

"I was really close with them. I also helped Donna in the office, and the two women, the minders, even after the men came up from Milwaukee."

AJ took a hard look at Frog. She'd lost weight and looked older, the softness gone from her face. "Whatever you can tell us is important, Frog. It'll make a difference, like that list."

Frog retied her shoelaces. "It was kind of fun when we first got up here and replaced the other group. We had plenty of food, TV when we wanted it, whatever. We were down at the stables once." She looked at Grace. "I spotted Greg and Jeff right away and tried to make myself useful, to learn whatever I could and help those girls. They're not bad, just young and scared." She sat up and took a deep breath. "Everything changed when the two men came from Milwaukee, the ones in the black car. I got really tight with a couple of the younger kids, especially Lizzy. She was my favorite. Tattoo Man took a liking to her too. That bastard would take her into his room almost every night, and then he murdered her. Things got so scary that we all wrote our names and addresses down, just in case." She swallowed hard. "I couldn't believe that son of a bitch murdered her. He made me clean the floor in there after the cops and the ambulance had left. He knew I tried to protect her." Frog wiped her eyes.

"You replaced what other group?" AJ said carefully.

"The kids that were here when we came in. There were some boys in that group, and the minders were a man and a woman."

"Was Donna here, when you came?" Maddie tucked the paper in her pocket.

"Yes. I'm not sure if she actually owned that motel, but she said she did, and a house in the country. We played games at that house and helped her clean the place. She said she and the two women, the minders, were from Tennessee but had lived in Chicago for five years with Tattoo Man, then lived Milwaukee for a while. She'd worked with him for years. Kept track of the money. You'll have to ask her for more than that."

"I can't, Frog. Someone killed her yesterday at that house in the country. That's where we were last night." AJ put her hand on Frog's shoulder.

Frog looked down at her feet and took a deep breath.

"What did the chief say, when you told him about Frog and her cops?" Tag turned to AJ.

"He's doing a happy dance and said Jock will too. Two birds with one big frog." AJ grinned at Frog.

Maddie's phone rang. She answered it and made a face, swearing softly. After she hung up she said, "The team is going to be delayed until tomorrow. Damn. I've got to notify Sam and Richard." She punched a number on her phone. When she finished, she pulled a chair close to Frog, holding the paper in front of her. "This list is genius, thanks. Tell us what you know about the kids you replaced. Anything will help."

"I only saw them that first night, and I think there was about as many as our group, but they were older. A man that Donna called 'the lawyer' drove them north the morning after we got there, but we didn't see them leave. We were still asleep. The other girls might be able to add something."

Maddie inhaled sharply and gave AJ a hard look. Tag looked angry.

"That's what Clint Weeks described when we met with him. Remember the video he claimed he turned in to the police, the one we could never find?" Grace said.

AJ stood. "All right. We've got some extra time. Frog, do you have a bag anywhere? Extra clothes? You could use my room to shower and clean up. Let's go. I'll wrap up some odds and ends while you're cleaning up. We'll come back up here when we're done. If Lawrence Kelly calls, I'll let everyone know."

Maddie went toward the door. "I'll work with Richard and Sam for a while and connect with my office. AJ, stop by our room and introduce Frog to them before you come back here." She looked at Tag and Grace. "Will you girls keep watch on the motel?" She checked her watch. "Two hours. Is that good?"

Chapter Twenty-Eight

The room was quiet after everyone left. Grace took her place in front of the computers. "Where are Jeff and Greg? Their vehicles are gone."

Tag was standing at the window, watching a crow wing its way over the lake. "I heard AJ send them to work at Clint's since we thought the FBI was going to recover the girls today. I'm sure she thought it'd be better if they were out of the way." Tag poured coffee and sat down beside Grace. "I'm confused about Jay. Do you think he's playing us?"

"Honestly? I don't. Of course that was before Frog mentioned 'the lawyer.' Both AJ and Maddie were surprised, and you didn't look too happy either."

"Where did you find the connection between his office and Seesom?"

"On the computers at his office. It's under Clients."

"Damn it. I should have looked." Tag looked at the computer in front of her. "I don't know about you, but I have a hard and fast rule. Never research your friends."

"You've never researched any of us or—"

"Never," Tag said firmly. "It's a point of honor. Only what's publicly available or what I heard from Charles and Lawrence Kelly. Or others."

Grace stared at her. "I don't either. I didn't go any deeper on you until AJ asked me to look at your trafficking ops. That's as far as any of us have gone." She grinned. "That's why I asked you about your parents and how you grew up."

"Because we can, we don't. That's what it is, isn't it?" Tag watched Grace's mouth curve into a smile and thought about how it tasted. "Which reminds me. Where did you get my Dragons poster?"

"A friend of yours that works for the FBI. Ellen DeNeave. She sent it to our office in Milwaukee with some of the papers our group needed to make your transfer. Since I do all of our mail, I snapped it up. I love that poster."

"She's an ex-Dragon." Tag straightened. Ellen was also her contact in the current FBI probe working with Maddie. "Did you write her back?"

Grace looked at her, uncertain. "Is there something wrong?"

"Not at all. I just haven't seen the poster in a long time. I was surprised." Tag tapped her fingers on the desk, wondering if this was a good time to talk about what else she'd seen. "There are things about each other that we don't know. Remember what my therapist said to me? The right time. The right person? I still feel that way, Grace."

They stared at each other silently.

Grace took a deep breath. "This is one of those things that I don't know how to talk about. There are a lot of things you don't know about me."

"When I was looking at the poster I looked at your books. And the addresses, all those doctors you have written down. The phone numbers." Tag held her breath.

"Oh," Grace whispered. "I'll be right back."

Tag watched her graceful body move away. She was named perfectly. *Grace.*

Grace laid the wine-colored leather address book on the desk between them.

"You've probably noticed a lot of my books are about survival? Abuse?" Grace was pale but held Tag's gaze.

"I noticed them in Milwaukee too."

Grace cleared her throat. "My father and his brothers, my uncles..." She finally looked away.

"No," Tag said, fearing what was coming.

Grace nodded. "From the time I was nine. My mother got me to my grandparents when I was eleven. That photo you found? I was leaving our house for my grandparents' that day. About a year later, he killed my mother and went to prison. He's dead now...not that it makes any difference. I miss my mother. Every single day." She took a deep breath. "These people…" She ran her fingers down the list of doctors' names. "They've helped me." She smiled, looking down at the names. "Sometimes I call them."

Heart in her throat, Tag didn't know what to say. She took the book and looked at it. "What are the dates?"

"The day I decided their name should go into this book." Grace inhaled. "Rape is about power, not sex, and this doctor was the first to explain that to me, in a way that I could understand and live with." She leaned back in her chair. "Would you pour me some coffee?"

Tag stood, poured a cup, and handed it to Grace. "I thought you might be doing some sort of online education with all those books."

"But that's what it is, isn't it?" She pointed at two highlighted names. "I'm actually helping these two with books they're writing. It helps me as much as it helps them."

Tag looked into Grace's incredible eyes and remembered AJ saying *it's like there's a step missing*. "Does AJ know?"

Grace gave a little shrug. "That was crazy. Both she and Charles knew, but we never talked until we had to come up here. Maddie brought it up because the FBI was concerned that I might have a problem with trafficking. My records are public if you know where to look. These days up here have opened up a new part of me, and I have to watch myself. Those little girls down there…" Her voice trailed off.

"And Happy and Sandra."

"That too. That day you told me about your therapist and the helicopters? I thought about it. It does feel *right* to talk to you." She placed a finger on the name on the list. "I called this doctor, and she said to talk to you. We know good people, Tag."

Tag searched for words, but failed, and so leaned in and kissed Grace with all the unspoken words in her heart.

"I know you. That's enough," Tag said softly.

"I didn't expect you." Grace's eyes shone with tears.

Someone rapped on the door and Frog and AJ came inside.

"What's happening at the motel?" AJ said.

Grace blinked and turned to the computers. "Nothing," she said but then leaned closer. "Wait. The truck is moved. It's backed up to one of the center rooms."

AJ moved to the desk and picked up Grace's address book. "What's this?"

"It's mine." Grace took it out of AJ's hand and closed it.

"Okay." AJ slid a look at Tag and reached for her phone. "I'll notify Maddie about the truck."

"Look. The girls are taking things into the truck. They're moving them." Frog pulled a chair close to the computers.

Everyone was in the suite in about ten minutes, watching the surveillance. Tattoo Man was outside in the motel parking lot, pointing and talking.

"I should have left one of the boys there," AJ said.

"No, you did the right thing. It left them feeling confident," Richard said. "We'll follow, and let's take Frog. The girls know her." He turned to leave then stopped. "Wait, a better idea. Tag, AJ, and Grace, get out on the road ahead of them. We'll sandwich them between us, and keep in touch on the phone."

"Tag and I bugged that truck. We can follow it anywhere," Sam said.

"Good idea, Richard." AJ picked up her jacket and pulled some bottles of water out of the refrigerator.

Maddie was on her phone to the DHS group in Iron Mountain, and she nodded the okay.

❖

Tag drove because she was familiar with the area and went north toward the Michigan state line. AJ rode shotgun, on the phone with Maddie. Grace was in the back seat tracking the GPS. She kept them miles ahead.

"Look at the sky. We're going to hit rain, maybe a thunderstorm," Grace said.

AJ looked through the Dodge Charger's front window. "You're right. Maybe it'll slow them down."

"What is that?" Tag said, pointing at the steel fence on their right, to the east.

"I'll check it out," Grace said from the back seat. "It's Marine Bio-Tech. Remember what Jay told us that night at the sheriff's when the helicopter flew over?" Tag nodded. "He said it belongs to the state. No. He said the state built it and Clint Weeks is the major investor. I never followed up on that, and I should have."

"Slow down, Tag." AJ was listening to Maddie on the phone. "The truck took a right, went east on that county road we just passed. Let's take the next right and run parallel. Do you know a way to get ahead of them from here?"

Tag slowed and did a right turn at the next county road. "If I remember, there's another county road that does just that. Look it up, Grace."

"You're right. This intersects with the main highway and we can go south. The road they're on will pass in front of that big plant."

Thunder rattled over them, and a few drops of rain hit the windshield as Tag gunned it. They followed the road and made another right turn. "Look. There they are, just topping the hill down the road." She looked to the right. They were about almost to the big gates and guard shack in front of Marine Bio-Tech. "I'm going to do something. Hold on. AJ, you and Grace get into the trees across the road."

Tag did a half one-eighty; the car tires screamed and the wet pavement smoked. AJ and Grace were out of the car and into the woods quickly. Tag took her time and got out of the car, looking underneath as if something was wrong.

The lumbering truck slowed and stopped, its rusty brakes squealing. Tattoo Man was driving and the other man following in the black car. They stopped both vehicles, and the man in the car got out and approached her.

"Damn," Tag said to him and bent down again to look underneath. She stood up, brushing the water off her jeans. Her car completely blocked the road. "I blew a tire, but I've got a spare. I'll have it changed in a minute."

"Want some help?" the man asked and she shook her head. Tag saw Richard's and Maddie's car stop behind them. He started back and spoke to Tattoo Man in the truck's cab. Tag checked the trees. She couldn't see either Grace or AJ. Tattoo Man climbed down from the truck, and she saw Richard pull his car across the road behind the black car as if he was going to turn around.

Tag opened her car's trunk, faking a look for a spare tire. She took her time, moving things around. She saw AJ and Grace leave the tree line and move to the other side of the truck, away from both of the men.

Richard was out of the car, walking toward the truck. She threw up her hands as if stymied and started toward Tattoo Man. He crawled down from the cab and leaned against the truck, trying to light a cigarette in the rain.

"What's going on? Can I help?" Richard said just as AJ came in from the back. She took the other man down, knee in the middle of his back, fist across his head. Tag heard something crack on his body. At the same moment, Richard hit Tattoo Man and had him down. They bound their wrists with plastic ties and stood them up against the truck. Frog scrambled inside the back of the truck and the girls screamed, yelling her name. It was over in what seemed like seconds.

AJ stood, hands on hips, and cocked her head at Tag. "That was too easy," she said and looked toward the plant. She straightened and shouted, "Look out!"

A gun went off, then another, and AJ was down on the pavement in the rain.

Years of training kicked in for all of them. Grace slid left, returning fire, and Tag shot too. One man behind the factory fence toppled sideways and the other ran toward the big factory. Tag's shot hit the running man but he kept going. Richard ran, following Grace, gun drawn.

Maddie was on the pavement beside AJ with her phone and giving instructions to 911.

"Keep the girls inside," Tag yelled at Frog.

Maddie ran back to their car, returning with T-shirts. She held them against AJ's head.

Tag kept her gun on the two men.

Grace was back, breathing hard, down beside AJ. "She's hit, twice. Give me one of those T-shirts and I'll hold it against her shoulder. Richard went after that man you hit, Tag. There's blood on the driveway."

Maddie looked over her shoulder. "Here comes the DHS. Tag, send them inside."

Three vans broke the wooden driveway barriers to the plant and sped to the entrance. Agents spilled out, running inside. Tag turned back to the two men still standing against the truck. Tattoo Man gave her a greasy smile and Tag knew why. She should have seen the shooters.

Chapter Twenty-Nine

The familiar scent made her heart jump. *Katie.*
Eyes closed, AJ tried to inch closer to the warm skin against her, but pain shot through her head and across her shoulder. Her eyes popped open. Katie was asleep, her head resting on AJ's hip, a hand firmly on her arm. What the hell was beeping and why was their bedroom all white?

She looked up. An IV ran down into her arm.

Suddenly, Grace was leaning over her, whispering. "Quiet. It's the first time she's slept since she got up here."

The pain was horrible, and AJ closed her eyes again. "My head."

"You got shot. Twice. Head and shoulder."

"No crutches this time," AJ managed. Her throat hurt.

"You've had surgery, so don't move. Lie still while I get the nurse."

"Katie?" AJ breathed out.

"Maddie flew her up here yesterday with the neurologist. She wouldn't sleep. That's a pile of exhaustion lying on you."

"Everyone else?"

"Fine," Grace said, and spoke to someone.

A tall, dark-haired woman in scrubs stepped inside and adjusted the IV, checking the beeping machines. "How are you doing?" She bent over her.

"Been better," AJ said. "How long?"

"Two days. How's the pain?"

"Terrible."

"Okay, let me give you something for that." She turned away as

Grace moved to the other side of the bed. AJ tried to remember but couldn't get past the pain.

"Catch me up," AJ whispered.

"It was crazy." Grace leaned closer. "The DHS arrived and went into the plant. Then the ambulance and cops were everywhere. Tag and I went inside after they got you into the bus and on your way here. The cops took the two men from the motel."

Grace stopped talking as the nurse fed something into the IV. She looked at Grace. "She's going under again, so talk fast."

"They got Frog and the girls to Milwaukee. Everyone's safe, but you're not going to believe what they found at that plant."

"Damn," AJ mumbled and her mind fell away.

Tag sat at the table in the suite across from Lawrence Kelly. They'd gone over the time up here for what seemed like hours and her brain felt mushy. Her phone beeped with a text from Grace.

"AJ was awake briefly, but they put her back under," she said and kept the rest of it to herself. Grace had added that Katie was still asleep.

Kelly gave her a tired smile and shuffled papers, dropping them into his briefcase. "That's enough, Tag. You need to sleep. We all do." His phone rang and he answered, listening to the message. "My plane's in Green Bay, so I have to go. The helicopter's waiting to take me to the airport." He knotted his tie. His expensive steel gray suit matched his hair and fit his tall frame impeccably. "All of you did a good job. I'll send the plane back to Green Bay for Maddie. Tell her to let me know."

"Sir. One more question. Where's Clint Weeks?" Tag said.

"Milwaukee. Maddie's FBI bureau chief is working with Peter Adams on the charges. I waited in Milwaukee until the DHS brought him down from up here. Jay Yardly was with him." Kelly's voice shook. "Jesus Christ. I've known that guy over twenty years and he had me fooled. Do you know what he said…God, I couldn't believe it. He said he had to get back because of the money. *The money.* I couldn't believe he'd said that, and Jay looked like he'd just been hit. Clint admitted to working with John Owens's family right away. And then he knew the two men, the ones from the motel here, had shot at AJ, twice, and burned the house and the cars. What a mess." He took his wire-rimmed glasses off and rubbed his eyes. "It's this damned election. It's messed everybody up and sideways. I know you're on standby for testimony on that other issue. You'll make a difference."

"You know what I can't figure out? Why Weeks brought that information to Pete at the Milwaukee DOJ in the first place."

"Because, damn it, he's crazy. And the money. I was with his wife at their home, trying to help them with a memorial for their daughter when he disappeared. One of their kids came running in and said he'd driven away. I thought he'd figured out that it was his fault she was dead…that he'd bankrolled the Owens men who killed her and then…" Kelly stopped talking and cleared his throat. "I think he suspected it when he saw those kids up here, in Niagara…I don't know. Anyway, he flew back here to the plant because he knew where those kids were." He pulled in a deep breath. "As we now know—and Clint now knows—that man with the tattoos and his buddy were part of the men who killed X-Girl, his daughter. What we don't know is why Clint killed those two kids at the plant. We'll get some of the answer from the rescued victims at Hannah's House, but I want to hear it from Clint."

"I agree with everything you just said, but it still goes back to why he brought the information to Peter Adams." Tag shifted in her chair.

"What more is there, other than that?" Kelly rolled his shoulders and stared out the window. "I mean…"

Tag watched him. He was getting there. She'd done a lot of debriefing with commanders and saw him begin to sift past all the excuses.

"Ah, shit." He leaned on his elbows. "I see it. He wanted to be on the inside. Keep up with what we knew, didn't he? He knew X-Girl had punched everyone hard and we weren't going to let it go. But he didn't know that girl was his. Yet." He nodded to himself. "Allison Jacob is one on my best agents and fought me all the way on this one, and now…" He took a breath. "This is on me." His hands shook and he jammed his glasses back onto his face and moved toward the door. "Somebody call me when they bring Allison back to Milwaukee. I'll stay in town until she's there." He picked up his briefcase and left without another word.

The silence in the room was unnerving. Tag cleaned the table and the coffee cups to fill the space. She straightened the desk next. None of them had slept last night, and she'd helped Grace with Crow this morning. Maddie had shown up, and all of them had gone over the vacant motel. That had been a moment.

Grace had sent Jeff and Greg to Milwaukee, then left for the hospital to check on AJ and Katie. Tag had stayed at the suite to begin to take down their equipment. Lawrence Kelly had unexpectedly shown up at the hospital, spoken to Grace, and called Tag from there. She'd asked if he could meet her here and he'd agreed.

Her final report to Lawrence Kelly was much like the military. She'd done a ton of them. She stared at the dark computers. It was done. She took the packing boxes out of the closet, but stopped and headed for her shower instead. She'd get some rest first and then start to get ready to leave.

Standing under the water, Tag felt a moment's pity for Lawrence Kelly. The truth was often damned uncomfortable.

She thought of AJ on the pavement and all that blood. *I should have seen the shooters.* She blocked her mind, dried off, and crawled into the bed. She'd get to the hospital after she woke up and finished the packing.

That night they all gathered in AJ's hospital room. Maddie leaned into Sam against the wall. Grace and Tag sat on one side of the bed, Katie on the other. AJ's bed was up so she could see all of them, her right hand threaded with Katie's.

AJ spoke. "They gave me fifteen minutes to talk, so make it fast. Take me from the moment I got shot."

Grace began. "There were two men in the guard shack behind tinted glass. We couldn't see them, and since we didn't know that was where the truck was going, we didn't expect it. That's why Tattoo Man and his buddy didn't resist."

"I still should have seen them," Tag added.

"I should have too," AJ said.

"What *none* of us saw was a very big sign that said the plant was *Temporarily Closed.* After the ambulance, the cops, and the DHS showed up," Grace continued, "Richard, Tag, and I went inside to help the DHS. Maddie stayed with you and rode back here, to the hospital. The DHS put Tattoo Man and the other guy into one of their vans and they're here, in Niagara at the police station. Richard drove the truck back to Milwaukee with Frog and all of the kids last night. They're at Hannah's House being looked after. I sent Greg and Jeff back too. Maddie's bureau chief has Clint Weeks in Milwaukee with Lawrence Kelly. Pete is helping them on the charges against him." She took a drink of water. "Tag did the final report at the resort to Kelly."

AJ looked at them, shocked.

"Kelly was here? And son of a—it was Clint? Damn it. What about Jay?"

Maddie spoke next. "Couldn't have done it without him. He got the chopper that brought Katie and the surgeon up here from Green Bay. He got Lithscom to hold the two motel men here in jail and he rode back to Milwaukee with Clint Weeks."

"Everyone's safe? No one else hurt?"

"There were two dead kids in the plant, but all of that will come later when we have more than this fifteen minutes," Maddie said. "We're staying here until they release you." She looked at Katie before she spoke again. "We'll have you transported back to Milwaukee in an ambulance when you're ready."

AJ took a breath. "Whatever works. I'd rather be home." The Milwaukee doctor had already spoken to her. They'd leave tomorrow.

At that moment, the doctor stepped into the room. "Time's up. Everyone out."

AJ started to argue, but he shook his head. "No. I'm going to run those final tests we talked about. There's a waiting room right down the hall."

Katie leaned over with a kiss, her gray eyes gorgeous and wet. "See you soon, love," she said and was the first to leave.

AJ sighed. "Somebody stay with her while he has me. Thanks. You did great. Damn, I can't believe it was Clint. I'll bet Kelly is furious. I am."

❖

Katie stood at the waiting room window, her curly black hair shining in the low lights. Tag saw her wipe her eyes.

"She's going to be all right." Tag put an arm around her shoulder.

"The doctor said so too when he talked to us earlier." Katie turned to face everyone. "The doctor doesn't want to leave until he's satisfied the internal bleeding's stopped. That's what he's checking now. The shoulder was a through and through and should heal fine, but the brain's another matter." She straightened with a breath. "After he gives us the results of this test, I can leave. I'll sleep in AJ's room at the resort and pack her things. Will one of you give me a ride?"

Grace smiled. "I will. We're doomed to stay together. Last spring and now."

Katie almost pulled off a smile. "I didn't bring anything with me. Chief Whiteaker picked me up at work and took me to the airport. My car's still there. I can have someone take it home, but I need clothes and stuff."

Grace teased her. "If you weren't so short..."

"If you weren't so tall," Katie shot back and turned to Maddie. "About that transport. I'll ride with AJ."

Maddie nodded. "Okay. We've already got a room for her at the hospital where she was last spring, and I've talked to Dr. Light. Ride back to the resort with Tag and Grace. You'll need clothes and I'll see to that. You also need to eat. I called the resort and they'll have it ready when you get there. Sam and I have to arrange for the transport to Milwaukee for Tattoo Man and the other guy right now, so we're leaving. We'll see you at the resort."

"I'll get us some coffee," Grace said and trailed Maddie and Sam to the door.

Katie sat down next to Tag. "AJ hates hospitals, and I have to thank the stars above that there won't be any crutches this time. The doctor said this procedure will take about an hour, and if the tests are positive, we'll go tomorrow." She tried to straighten her wrinkled business suit.

Tag stretched her long legs out in front of her. "We've got things for you at the resort. Of course..."

"I know. You're all trees and I'm a shrub," Katie said and finally laughed.

Chapter Thirty

The wheels hitting the runway at Mitchell International Airport woke Tag with a jolt. Her briefcase fell to the floor and the older man next to her bent to retrieve it.

"It's Milwaukee, Captain," he said, handing her the well-worn leather case.

Still fighting the headache she'd had for hours, Tag rubbed her bleary eyes and looked down at her uniform, her mind catching up fast.

"Thanks. I can't believe I slept the whole flight." The field lights flew by her window in a rainbow of colors, and she straightened in the seat. They'd talked on the plane when she'd first sat down, and he knew she'd been in Washington DC and was out of the service after ten years. He'd not asked why she was back in uniform and in the nation's capital. Thank God.

They'd flown her commander in from the base at Bagram. He and Tag and two others had testified for over seven hours. She felt another "Thank God" that the meetings had been closed. They'd had a late meal and she'd gone directly to bed. She'd gotten up early this morning and taken the first available direct flight to Milwaukee.

She looked out at the rain drenching the airport as the plane taxied up. Home again, she thought. And the first place she'd seen Grace.

A black SUV with red and blue flashers parked next to the plane. A flight attendant smiled at her and stood by her seat as passengers filed out.

"You'll want to come with me, Captain," the attendant said.

Puzzled, Tag gathered her gear and followed, taking the back ramp. A person with an umbrella stood on the cement beside the black SUV, waiting for her. Tag's heart jumped.

Grace hugged her hard and whispered "I missed you" against her ear, and guided her into the SUV. Maddie drove the vehicle around the plane and out across the tarmac.

"Maddie's people called her and said you were on the way home," Grace said, and gestured at her worn jeans, barn boots, and damp sweatshirt. "I was at the stables and she came and got me. Sorry. I smell like Crow."

"I'd rather smell Crow than what I smelled in Washington DC," Tag said, and grinned.

"I've been there," Maddie said from the front. "I couldn't agree more. Was it bad?"

"Yes," Tag said. "Thankfully, it was a closed hearing. The three of us and our commander testified for over seven hours."

"Did you run into any of the press?" Maddie said. She stopped at a red light and looked at Tag in the rearview mirror.

"Yes, a few, but all the questions were about Clint Weeks, not our testimony. And only because I'm from Wisconsin." She took a deep breath. "I need a drink, a shower, and lots of sleep. Anything else happening?"

Maddie laughed, barreling down the interstate toward Grace's apartment. "Where to begin? According to the national news, Milwaukee is now officially the number three center for sex trafficking in the United States. Our FBI task force in northern Wisconsin has been played on local television a thousand times, mostly because of Clint Weeks. They connected Chief William Whiteaker's unit and the poor man has become a media darling."

Tag stared at her. She'd only been gone three days and two nights. "And AJ?"

"Going to be released tomorrow," Grace said and grinned at Tag. "I know she's better because she yelled at us."

"Oh, yeah." Maddie laughed again. "It took me an hour to convince her that it was 'good press' for the FBI task force."

Tag shook her head. "But how is she?"

"Um." Grace frowned. "Dr. Light said the only side effects might be occasional visual impairment or headaches. She and Katie fought over the 'full bed rest' in front of us." She laughed. "Those two are hilarious when they fight."

"They should have a nationally televised sitcom." Maddie laughed too. "Best one-liners I've heard in years. I've never seen love expressed quite that way."

Tag let the window down a little. The air was damp and wet and made her think of how it had smelled at the resort up north, the way air should smell. "How are the kids at Hannah's House?"

"So far, everything's progressing as we hoped. Frog is a great story. I wish I had about five of her." Maddie smiled. "She sounds like a mini AJ most of the time."

They had her inside Grace's apartment in minutes.

"You pack light, soldier," Maddie said, dumping the clothes bag on the kitchen chair.

"Years of training," Tag said and started toward the cupboard. "Grace. Do you have any painkillers? I've got a damned headache."

"Sit down," Grace said. She found aspirin and shook two tablets into Tag's hand, then handed her a glass of water. "Maddie has to go back to work. You'll need the rest. Tomorrow's a mess. We have to meet with the Niagara victims at Hannah's House. Then there's a meeting with the legal team over Clint Weeks. I'll catch you up over dinner. Grab a shower, and I'll start dinner. You need to eat."

Maddie was at the door. "Check in tomorrow, girls. Grace, I'll let the chief know we have Tag back."

Tag sipped wine at the kitchen table and told Grace about being in Washington DC. Then the waiting at the airport and how hard the airline had worked to find her a seat.

Grace started dinner, working at the stove and counter, turning occasionally with that gorgeous smile and those wonderful eyes. Tag finished her wine.

"Time for a shower," she said.

Grace leaned forward, fingers roaming over her neck and face, playing with the Dragon necklace. "We have as much time as you need. I'll put dinner in the oven and shower after you finish. Mind a little music?"

"Not at all. Thanks." Tag gathered her things and headed to her bedroom feeling much better. She examined her uniform. It would need to be cleaned. She tossed it over the chair and began to take the hardware off it, placing everything in the little box on the desk. She picked up the extra Dragon necklace she'd always kept and remembered the first day her unit had put them on. The ones who hadn't made it home had been buried with them.

She stared at it for a minute before she turned for the shower.

Later, as they ate, she fielded Grace's questions. "What is this?" Tag said and took another bite of the delicious casserole.

"A broccoli casserole recipe that I stole from Katie," Grace said and sipped the amber wine. "It's one of the few dishes that AJ can make. Katie's the chef in the house." She finished and pushed her plate away. "Do I get to know what you testified about or will that come out in the news?"

Tag sighed. "I think it's going to make everyone really angry."

"Just so you know, it's rumored to have *treason* laced through it."

"It's possible. The one thing I can tell you is that we weren't looking for it. It involves another country in our election and we stumbled across it tracking something else. It was Josh, Ellen, and me on a late night. It was a mess and we didn't leave until the next morning. I reported it to my commander, went home, and slept for ten hours."

"Does it have anything to do with the election?"

"Yes, but don't ask me for more. The FBI and Congress have it now. I can't touch it and don't want to think about it. You wouldn't either. You used to work in Cyber Crime, so you know what those moments are like." She took a drink of her wine and let her body unwind.

Grace was quiet, looking at her plate. "Maddie's people sent her photos of your group walking out of the testimony. All of you looked tired and sad."

"We were, but all I heard about from the press was Clint Weeks's mess." Tag took another drink of the wine. "What's going on tomorrow? Tell me again."

Grace laughed a little. "The first part's going to make you laugh, and I didn't mention this in front of Maddie." She fluffed her hair. "Look at this. I need to do something."

Tag did look. She hadn't noticed Grace's natural color was

creeping back into her hair. "Have you looked at women's hair these days? They have as many as three or four colors in it."

"So, the first place we're going is to Katie's sister's and get my hair straightened out. Thank God. Wait until you see AJ's hair. Between the surgery and the different color, her hair is a mess." Grace took her plate to the sink, rinsed it, and put it in the dishwasher. "Then we go to Hannah's House for a discussion with the kids. You won't recognize them. Rest, good food, and safety really changed them." Grace reached for Tag's hand. "Milwaukee CPS will be there for the last part of the conversation. Finally, we meet at Peter Adams's office with Clint's legal team. Jay might be there."

"Sounds busy, but that's fine." Tag frowned down at their hands. "I thought a lot about my Dragons while we were in Niagara. We saved all but three of those kids. It kind of helped my head about the Dragons."

Grace squeezed her hand. "Like the world has a balance sometimes?"

"Exactly." She took her plate to the sink. "Let's clean up and go into the living room."

"Good. I want to talk to you."

The music, sweet and low, drifted in from the kitchen as Tag settled on the couch with a relaxing breath. Grace tucked her feet under her and snuggled close.

"What's up?" Tag put her arm around Grace.

"Remember the morning you left for DC? We were getting dressed and your phone started ringing. You said you had to go and I didn't know anything about anything so I just rushed, trying to help you and get you to the airport on time. They were holding the plane, for God's sake. I came back here and it was like I was empty." She looked away. "I wasn't sure you were coming back. Another *first* for me." Grace fiddled with her T-shirt hem, face turned away. "Suddenly, Maddie was here. She explained what she could and I felt like she'd saved my life."

Grace sat up, looking into Tag's eyes. "I keep saying I don't know how to talk to you. I think I finally do. We've been busy since you were gone, but all the time I had this running conversation in the back of my mind."

Tag smiled. She'd done a lot of thinking in Washington too and had missed Grace.

"I decided that when you got home—like right now—I was going to tell you that I want more than just an occasional kiss." She inched closer.

Tag straightened. Did she hear that right? She could see it hadn't come out quite like Grace had planned as a blush lit up her face. They stared at each other for a long moment. "Thank God," she finally said.

Grace looked confused. "I thought…I don't know what I thought. I'm not sure how this works."

Tag just smiled and kissed her warm, soft mouth, then stretched them out on the couch. "If you want to stop, just say it. I'll stop." She ran her hands up under Grace's T-shirt across soft skin and breasts, barely able to breathe.

"Oooh," Grace said over a breath. Tag ran her hands across Grace's stomach, then kissed the soft skin. Grace gave another tiny moan, then struggled out from under her.

"My bed. More room." She pulled Tag down the hall. The bedroom smelled wonderful, and they both pulled their clothes off and, skin to skin, tumbled into the big, comfortable bed. "You'll have to lead," she said, her eyes that incredible color again, "but I'm a good follower."

Tag braced herself over her, kissed her skin all the way down to Grace's belly, then slowly worked her way up to both breasts. She could feel Grace's heart beating wildly and slipped her hands across ribs, down to the hips, then lower. Grace arched up against her.

"Look at me, Grace. See how much I mean this."

Grace opened her eyes, and they widened as Tag slipped her fingers between her legs into the hot and wet center. She took her time until Grace's arms wrapped around her tightly. Grace muttered something, and Tag kissed her, softly and carefully. It didn't take long before Grace pushed hard against her. "God." She shuddered, legs and arms tight around Tag as she rocked under her. Finally, Grace lay back, trembling.

"I love you. This couldn't have happened without love."

"I love you too, Grace. Always remember that."

Suddenly, she was on her back with Grace hovering above her. "I learn fast," she murmured and kissed her, hands busy across Tag's body.

A long time later, after much exploration, they curled up together, quiet, staring at each other. Grace reached out, touched Tag's face, down her neck, and laid her hand across her Dragon necklace and smiled. Her eyes closed and she took a deep breath, pushing close to Tag.

"Wow," she said softly and fell asleep.

Tag put her arm around Grace. Such a beautiful body and that fascinating, gorgeous mind. All the places she'd been, and this would be the moment she'd always remember. She closed her eyes.

CHAPTER THIRTY-ONE

Dr. Light locked the brakes on the wheelchair, handing instructions and medicine to Katie at the back entry of the hospital.

"I don't want to see you here again. That's an order," the doctor said, her eyes holding AJ's gaze. "While you slept this morning, I took an hour with Katie. She's seen your videos and I've explained everything to her. Consider her my mini-me at your house until I say otherwise."

AJ nodded and stood, looking up at the sky. God, it felt good to be free of the hospital, and the air was fresh after yesterday's rain. She placed her good arm over Katie's shoulder as they walked through the leaves to the car. "Look. Here we are again," she said. "How come it's always me? Why doesn't someone else take one for the team?"

Katie snorted a little laugh. "That's not true. You'd do anything to keep your team safe."

AJ pulled her closer. "There's a meeting at Peter Adams's office in a few hours that I need to go to. I have to change clothes," AJ said as Katie helped her into the SUV.

"No." Katie snapped AJ's seat belt under the sling on her arm.

"What do you mean?" AJ frowned at her.

"Have you looked at a mirror lately?"

"Yes. Well, maybe. What's wrong?" AJ snapped the visor down, took a look at the mirror, and let out a muffled scream. "Holy shit." Her hair was in complete disarray and uncombed, the brown lying over the top of her natural blond. She examined the shave track. "You didn't tell me." She jerked in her seat and groaned as her arm sent a sharp pain through her. She pushed into the seat, riding the pain out.

"I look like some kind of wild animal." AJ stared ahead. "Take me to your sister."

"Oh, as if."

"Damn it," AJ said and gestured at her hair.

Katie sighed and tossed her phone at AJ. "You call her. I'm not touching this. Besides, I've got strict orders to keep you in bed."

AJ didn't answer, just dialed the phone. After a terse, somewhat desperate conversation, AJ hung up. Katie turned onto the street, headed for home.

"She'll come over today during her lunch hour," AJ finally said. "Guess who she's working on right now?"

"Not a clue." Katie made a quick, angry turn.

AJ made a face at her. "No. Tag and Grace are there. It appears Grace's roots are showing. Like a lot." She grinned despite herself.

"And she doesn't have a big shave track down the side."

"I can't help that." AJ grumbled and tried a different tack. "Please help," she whined.

Katie blew out a breath. "She'll actually come to the house?"

"Yes."

"And you promise to go to bed? Like the doctor ordered?"

AJ stared straight ahead trying to maneuver her way through the minefield. "Katie, I know you've gone to the wall for me and…"

Katie didn't answer.

"I mean it. Look what I just put you through. Again."

"You don't plan on following doctor's orders at all, do you?" Katie pulled her sunglasses off and parked in their garage.

"We weren't talking about that."

Katie looked at her. "I can't wrestle you to the ground because of the sling on your arm, not to mention the head injury, but if you insist on taking a risk like this, go right ahead." She opened the car door, took the odds and ends from the hospital out of the back, and strode to their kitchen door.

AJ watched her, unhappy with what she'd just seen. Katie looked so tired, angry, and worse, sad. She pushed her door open, undid the seat belt, and swung her feet around. One foot on the ground, the other following, and suddenly, her world went gray. Her good arm held on to the door and she slowly sank to the cold garage floor. She thought she heard Tag.

❖

"Damn." Tag ran into the garage. "Get Katie. Call the doctor." She went to her knees and slid her hand under AJ's head and checked her pulse. It was strong and steady. Katie and Grace went to the cement beside her. Grace dialed the doctor.

"Her pulse is good. I think she just fainted."

Katie had tears in her eyes. "Damn. We were arguing and I shouldn't have left her alone. She's determined to go to some meeting this afternoon. This is my fault."

"No, it's not," Grace said and began talking to Dr. Light on the phone. "Here, Tag, put this towel under her head. Is she bleeding anywhere? The doctor's asking," she said just as AJ opened her eyes.

"What?" she said.

Katie brushed AJ's hair back. "I think you fainted. Tell the doctor no blood, Grace."

"Tag, you made it back," AJ slurred with a sloppy smile. "Your hair looks great, Grace."

"Katie says you're going to a meeting?" Tag studied her.

Just then, Katie's sister walked into the garage. "Are you kidding me? The garage?" She looked down at AJ. "Oh, for God's sake. Your hair. How am I going to fix that?"

"Let's get her inside," Tag said and she and Grace stood AJ up and walked her to the living room couch.

"I saw what you did for Grace," Tag said to Katie's sister. "I'm pretty sure you can work more of your magic here."

"Dr. Light thinks she just fainted," Grace said, ending the phone call. "Not uncommon apparently, but if it happens again we've got to take her back to the hospital. She says to get her in bed." She looked at Katie's sister. "Don't you dare leave or she'll probably faint again."

"I'll feed all of you lunch," Katie said to them. "Actually, I'll pay all of you good money to stay and I'll go away. She'll behave for you."

"Hey. I'm right here. I can hear you," AJ said.

Grace's phone rang. "It's Maddie," she said to everyone, walking back to the kitchen, and then returned. "Saved by the call, AJ. The meeting with the lawyers has been moved to tomorrow. She'll let us know the time. We'll come and get you. Save Katie the agony." She moved to the refrigerator. "Who wants coffee or whatever?"

"I'll cook," Katie said, and moved to the stove. "Stay until she's done and then you're all off the hook. And thanks."

"We've got two hours and then a meeting with Maddie," Tag said. "What can I do?"

"Grace, help me with the laundry," Katie said, starting the coffee. "You know where everything is. Tag, take a look at our bedroom and set the stuff up I brought from the hospital. AJ's bags from the resort are in the smaller bedroom."

"My hair," AJ said from the couch.

"Aw, such a baby, AJ," Katie's sister said and placed a small table beside the couch, then unpacked her bag. Katie laughed at her sister and handed AJ the pill Dr. Light had ordered. "The doctor said she has to take this, now."

"No." AJ started to argue, but Katie's sister held up a pair of scissors. "See these? Take the pill or else I just pack up and leave. Your choice."

"Crap," AJ grumbled but took the pill and drank the water.

Tag watched the three of them in the living room and then carried things into the master bedroom. Grace peeked in and they shared a grin. "Also, Maddie gave me some other breaking news from Niagara," she said. "Guess who shot at me?"

"I thought it was Tattoo Man," Tag said. "Both of those men admitted to shooting AJ and burning the house and the cars."

"Nope. Good old boy Deputy Miller. Maddie said the sheriff relieved him of duty—translated, the kid got fired—and Lithscom won't have him either. Ha."

Tag grinned. "Good news. Now if they can just do same with Lithscom."

"And there's more missing kids, not connected to the Owens boys or Clint Weeks. We have another assignment." She wiggled her finger. "But we get a week off before we start work on that."

"Want to go up and stay with my parents? Have some time with Emma and look at that horse ranch for the kids? We could take Crow."

"You bet." Grace put her arm around Tag.

Tag dug into her pocket. "I have something for you. Maybe you'd wear it? You don't have to, but I'd be honored." She held a Dragon's necklace in her hand. "This is an extra I had made when we first got them."

Grace examined it. "Oh." She stared at Tag. "Oh. My God."

Tag fastened it and stepped back to see how it looked. "It belongs there. We're the new Dragon Unit. Just you and me."

Grace grabbed her and kissed her. "My life is wonderful, as long as you're around."

Katie peeked into the room. "Ready for food…whoops. I didn't mean to interrupt."

"It's fine." Grace stepped away. "Everything's fine."

About the Author

Born and raised in the Midwest, C.P. Rowlands attended college in Iowa and lived in the Southwest and on the West Coast before returning to Wisconsin. She is an artist in addition to having worked in radio, sales, and various other jobs. She has two children, four grandchildren, a partner of decades, and two cats. She has published since 2008 with Bold Strokes Books. *Jacob's Grace* is the sequel to her Lambda Literary Award finalist, *Jacob's War*.

Books Available From Bold Strokes Books

A Fighting Chance by T. L. Hayes. Will Lou be able to come to terms with her past to give love a fighting chance? (978-1-163555-257-7)

Chosen by Brey Willows. When the choice is adapt or die, can love save us all? (978-1-163555-110-5)

Gnarled Hollow by Charlotte Greene. After they are invited to study a secluded nineteenth-century estate, a former English professor and a group of historians discover that they will have to fight against the unknown if they have any hope of staying alive. (978-1-163555-235-5)

Jacob's Grace by C.P. Rowlands. Captain Tag Becket wants to keep her head down and her past behind her, but her feelings for AJ's second-in-command, Grace Fields, makes keeping secrets next to impossible. (978-1-163555-187-7)

On the Fly by PJ Trebelhorn. Hockey player Courtney Abbott is content with her solitary life until visiting concert violinist Lana Caruso makes her second-guess everything she always thought she wanted. (978-1-163555-255-3)

Passionate Rivals by Radclyffe. Professional rivalry and long-simmering passions create a combustible combination when Emmet McCabe and Sydney Stevens are forced to work together, especially when past attractions won't stay buried. (978-1-63555-231-7)

Proxima Five by Missouri Vaun. When geologist Leah Warren crash-lands on a preindustrial planet and is claimed by its tyrant, Tiago, will clan warrior Keegan's love for Leah give her the strength to defeat him? (978-1-163555-122-8)

Racing Hearts by Dena Blake. When you cross a hot-tempered race car mechanic with a reckless cop, the result can only be spontaneous combustion. (978-1-163555-251-5)

Shadowboxer by Jessica L. Webb. Jordan McAddie is prepared to keep her street kids safe from a dangerous underground protest group, but she isn't prepared for her first love to walk back into her life. (978-1-163555-267-6)

The Tattered Lands by Barbara Ann Wright. As Vandra and Lilani strive to make peace, they slowly fall in love. With mistrust and murder surrounding them, only their faith in each other can keep their plan to save the world from falling apart. (978-1-163555-108-2)

Captive by Donna K. Ford. To escape a human trafficking ring, Greyson Cooper and Olivia Danner become players in a game of deceit and violence. Will their love stand a chance? (978-1-63555-215-7)

Crossing the Line by CF Frizzell. The Mob discovers a nemesis within its ranks, and in the ultimate retaliation, draws Stick McLaughlin from anonymity by threatening everything she holds dear. (978-1-63555-161-7)

Love's Verdict by Carsen Taite. Attorneys Landon Holt and Carly Pachett want the exact same thing: the only open partnership spot at their prestigious criminal defense firm. But will they compromise their careers for love? (978-1-63555-042-9)

Precipice of Doubt by Mardi Alexander & Laurie Eichler. Can Cole Jameson resist her attraction to her boss, veterinarian Jodi Bowman, or will she risk a workplace romance and her heart? (978-1-63555-128-0)

Savage Horizons by CJ Birch. Captain Jordan Kellow's feelings for Lt. Ali Ash have her past and future colliding, setting in motion a series of events that strands her crew in an unknown galaxy thousands of light years from home. (978-1-63555-250-8)

Secrets of the Last Castle by A. Rose Mathieu. When Elizabeth Campbell represents a young man accused of murdering an elderly woman, her investigation leads to an abandoned plantation that reveals many dark Southern secrets. (978-1-63555-240-9)

Take Your Time by VK Powell. A neurotic parrot brings police officer Grace Booker and temporary veterinarian Dr. Dani Wingate together in the tiny town of Pine Cone, but their unexpected attraction keeps the sparks flying. (978-1-63555-130-3)

The Last Seduction by Ronica Black. When you allow true love to elude you once and you desperately regret it, are you brave enough to grab it when it comes around again? (978-1-63555-211-9)

The Shape of You by Georgia Beers. Rebecca McCall doesn't play it safe, but when sexy Spencer Thompson joins her workout class, their nonstop sparring forces her to face her ultimate challenge—a chance at love. (978-1-63555-217-1)

Exposed by MJ Williamz. The closet is no place to live if you want to find true love. (978-1-62639-989-1)

Force of Fire: Toujours a Vous by Ali Vali. Immortals Kendal and Piper welcome their new child and celebrate the defeat of an old enemy, but another ancient evil is about to awaken deep in the jungles of Costa Rica. (978-1-63555-047-4)

Landing Zone by Erin Dutton. Can a career veteran finally discover a love stronger than even her pride? (978-1-63555-199-0)

Love at Last Call by M. Ullrich. Is balancing business, friendship, and love more than any willing woman can handle? (978-1-63555-197-6)

Pleasure Cruise by Yolanda Wallace. Spencer Collins and Amy Donovan have few things in common, but a Caribbean cruise offers both women an unexpected chance to face one of their greatest fears: falling in love. (978-1-63555-219-5)

Running Off Radar by MB Austin. Maji's plans to win Rose back are interrupted when work intrudes, and duty calls her to help a SEAL team stop a Russian mobster from harvesting gold from the bottom of Sitka Sound. (978-1-63555-152-5)

Shadow of the Phoenix by Rebecca Harwell. In the final battle for the fate of Storm's Quarry, even Nadya's and Shay's powers may not be enough. (978-1-63555-181-5)

Take a Chance by D. Jackson Leigh. There's hardly a woman within fifty miles of Pine Cone that veterinarian Trip Beaumont can't charm, except for the irritating new cop, Jamie Grant, who keeps leaving parking tickets on her truck. (978-1-63555-118-1)

Death in Time by Robyn Nyx. Working in the past is hell on your future. (978-1-63555-053-5)

The Outcasts by Alexa Black. Spacebus driver Sue Jones is running from her past. When she crash-lands on a faraway world, the Outcast Kara might be her chance for redemption. (978-1-63555-242-3)

Alias by Cari Hunter. A car crash leaves a woman with no memory and no identity. Together with Detective Bronwen Pryce, she fights to uncover a truth that might just kill them both. (978-1-63555-221-8)

Hers to Protect by Nicole Disney. Ex–high school sweethearts Kaia and Adrienne will have to see past their differences and survive the vengeance of a brutal gang if they want to be together. (978-1-63555-229-4)

Perfect Little Worlds by Clifford Mae Henderson. Lucy can't hold the secret any longer. Twenty-six years ago, her sister did the unthinkable. (978-1-63555-164-8)

Room Service by Fiona Riley. Interior designer Olivia likes stability, but when work brings footloose Savannah into her world and into a new city every month, Olivia must decide if what makes her comfortable is what makes her happy. (978-1-63555-120-4)

Sparks Like Ours by Melissa Brayden. Professional surfers Gia Malone and Elle Britton can't deny their chemistry on and off the beach. But only one can win… (978-1-63555-016-0)

Take My Hand by Missouri Vaun. River Hemsworth arrives in Georgia intent on escaping quickly, but when she crashes her Mercedes into the Clip 'n Curl, sexy Clay Cahill ends up rescuing more than her car. (978-1-63555-104-4)

The Last Time I Saw Her by Kathleen Knowles. Lane Hudson only has twelve days to win back Alison's heart. That is, if she can gather the courage to try. (978-1-63555-067-2)

Wayworn Lovers by Gun Brooke. Will agoraphobic composer Giselle Bonnaire and Tierney Edwards, a wandering soul who can't remain in one place for long, trust in the passionate love destiny hands them? (978-1-62639-995-2)

Breakthrough by Kris Bryant. Falling for a sexy ranger is one thing, but is the possibility of love worth giving up the career Kennedy Wells has always dreamed of? (978-1-63555-179-2)

Dark Euphoria by Ronica Black. When a high-profile case drops in Detective Maria Diaz's lap, she forges ahead only to discover this case, and her main suspect, aren't like any other. (978-1-63555-141-9)

Fore Play by Julie Cannon. Executive Leigh Marshall falls hard for Peyton Broader, her golf pro...and an ex-con. Will she risk sabotaging her career for love? (978-1-63555-102-0)

Love Came Calling by C. A. Popovich. Can a romantic looking for a long-term, committed relationship and a jaded cynic too busy for love conquer life's struggles and find their way to what matters most? (978-1-63555-205-8)

Outside the Law by Carsen Taite. Former sweethearts Tanner Cohen and Sydney Braswell must work together on a federal task force to see justice served, but will they choose to embrace their second chance at love? (978-1-63555-039-9)

The Princess Deception by Nell Stark. When journalist Missy Duke realizes Prince Sebastian is really his twin sister Viola in disguise, she plays along, but when sparks flare between them, will the double deception doom their fairy-tale romance? (978-1-62639-979-2)

The Smell of Rain by Cameron MacElvee. Reyha Arslan, a wise and elegant woman with a tragic past, shows Chrys that there's still beauty to embrace and reason to hope despite the world's cruelty. (978-1-63555-166-2)

The Talebearer by Sheri Lewis Wohl. Liz's visions show her the faces of the lost and the killers who took their lives. As one by one, the murdered are found, a stranger works to stop Liz before the serial killer is brought to justice. (978-1-63555-126-6)

White Wings Weeping by Lesley Davis. The world is full of discord and hatred, but how much of it is just human nature when an evil with sinister intent is invading people's hearts? (978-1-63555-191-4)

A Call Away by KC Richardson. Can a businesswoman from a big city find the answers she's looking for, and possibly love, on a small-town farm? (978-1-63555-025-2)

Berlin Hungers by Justine Saracen. Can the love between an RAF woman and the wife of a Luftwaffe pilot, former enemies, survive in besieged Berlin during the aftermath of World War II? (978-1-63555-116-7)

Blend by Georgia Beers. Lindsay and Piper are like night and day. Working together won't be easy, but not falling in love might prove the hardest job of all. (978-1-63555-189-1)

Hunger for You by Jenny Frame. Principe of an ancient vampire clan Byron Debrek must save her one true love from falling into the hands of her enemies and into the middle of a vampire war. (978-1-63555-168-6)

Mercy by Michelle Larkin. FBI Special Agent Mercy Parker and psychic ex-profiler Piper Vasey learn to love again as they race to stop a man with supernatural gifts who's bent on annihilating humankind. (978-1-63555-202-7)

Pride and Porters by Charlotte Greene. Will pride and prejudice prevent these modern-day lovers from living happily ever after? (978-1-63555-158-7)

Rocks and Stars by Sam Ledel. Kyle's struggle to own who she is and what she really wants may end up landing her on the bench and without the woman of her dreams. (978-1-63555-156-3)